Ray rose and looked down at her. Her mouth was set. Her arms were crossed. She didn't look pleased at all.

"I'll tell you what. You relax here for a while and, if you don't mind, I'm going to get that briefcase you tripped over and put it in the car.

"Why?" Bev's interest seemed minimal as she massaged her ankle.

"I noticed the initials on the top. The case belonged to Mitch and I'd like to go through some of the legal papers on it." Ray tried to sound nonchalant.

Bev shrugged. "It's okay. I don't think Dana would mind."

Ray stepped into the hallway and gathered the papers on the floor. He stuffed them into the leather case, closed it and headed downstairs. He would go through Mitch's papers and see if he could find a clue as to what Dana's last words might mean.

When he returned upstairs he found Bev on her feet. It was apparent that she was in pain.

"What are you doing?"

Bev jumped, startled by Ray's unexpected reappearance. She had been determined to be mobile before his return. She didn't want him picking her up again.

"I can walk," she insisted as she tried to limp slowly across the room. She didn't get far before Ray swept her up into his arms a second time.

"Raaaay!" Bev kicked her feet in protest. "Put me down!"

"Noooo," Ray mocked her as he carried her downstairs and toward the door. She had opened her mouth to continue her protest when he covered it with his mouth. Bev tried to resist but the kiss deepened. Her eyelids fluttered shut. The heat intensified and her world began to whirl. Then it all came to a screeching halt. The kiss ended. Ray drew back. Bev's eyes popped open.

"I guess that'll shut you up." Shifting her in his arms, Ray continued walking.

STILL WATERS . . .

CRYSTAL V. RHODES

Genesis Press, Inc.

INDIGO LOVE STORIES

An imprint of Genesis Press, Inc.
Publishing Company

Genesis Press, Inc.
P.O. Box 101
Columbus, MS 39703

ISBN: 13 DIGIT : 978-1-58571-433-9
ISBN: 10 DIGIT : 1-58571-433-x
Manufactured in the United States of America

First Edition

Visit us at www.genesis-press.com
or call at 1-888-Indigo-1-4-0

DEDICATION

This book is dedicated to each of my good friends who helped make this happen, and to my beloved Aunt Flora, who was the Alpha and Omega in our family.

ACKNOWLEDGMENTS

I would like to thank all of you who have read my books and have offered the words of encouragement that have helped me move forward. You don't know how much your support is appreciated.

New to my list of acknowledgements is my friend Shirley who was a big help with this one. Of course, I want to say thank you to Joni for her continuous support and assistance. It has been unwavering, as has that of my friend, Eunice.

Also, thank you Sidney Rickman, for your editing advice.

CHAPTER 1

"What do you mean, Ray is coming here?" Bev Cameron gripped the telephone tightly, uncertain that she had heard her daughter correctly. Everyone in their family knew the strict criteria that had to be followed in order to bring a stranger to her hometown, and Ray Wilson, the man who had been shamelessly flirting with her for years, did *not* fit the criteria. "There must be some mistake. Who told you this?"

"Thad."

Bev knew that there was no doubt about the validity of the information. Her daughter's husband was movie star Thad Stewart and he adored his wife, singing superstar Darnell Cameron. She was the love of his life, his confidante, and his best friend. Thad's word was his bond.

"We were talking and he was excited about playing golf on the new course," Darnell explained. "Then he said that he couldn't wait for Ray to get there. When he thought about what he said he clammed up, but it was too late by then. It's my guess that Ray's coming with Dana."

Bev was shocked. "My sister?"

"Who else could it be? Aunt Dana said that she was coming home, and the two of them are friends."

"That's true, and it does make sense." Bev could tell by Darnell's tone that she was also finding it difficult to believe the scenario.

"What should we do?" the younger woman asked. "Tell the Council to have them stopped at the gate?"

"I'm not sure." Bev considered the alternatives. "I'm just wondering why she's bringing him here, and how she expects to get him into town."

"There's only one way that she can get him in," Darnell affirmed, "and that's with a lie."

Bev knew that she was right. "Why would she do this?" Her heart sank at the idea of the deception her younger sister might be capable of.

"Maybe it's some move to stop Aunt Tessa's family from taking over." Even through the telephone Darnell could feel her mother's pain. The two sisters had been estranged for quite a while and Dana's return home might have provided an opportunity for their reconciliation, except for this new development. Darnell could hardly comprehend what her aunt must feel about their family to do something like this.

"You might be right," Bev's voice was hollow. "She's probably plotting some legal maneuver that could wreak havoc in the family." She gave a shuddering sigh.

"So what's the plan, Mama?" Darnell's voice was filled with sadness.

Bev tried to think. "We'll keep this to ourselves for now. If they get past the gate, let's see what Dana is up to."

Darnell was receptive. "That sounds reasonable. Meanwhile, I'm going to see if I can pump some more information out of Thad. Kiss my little gem for me."

The women disconnected and Bev sat reflecting on their conversation. What *was* Dana up to, and what part did Ray Wilson play in her sister's scheme? She was familiar with her younger sister's escapades, but why had she paired up with that middle-aged playboy and dared to breach the security of their family haven?

A loud yawn interrupted Bev's musing. She looked down into the face of the bundle nestled in her arms, six-month-old Nia Cameron-Stewart. Her granddaughter was awake.

"Hey there, little one." Bev gently caressed the baby's soft cheek and was rewarded with a toothless grin. The dimples inherited from her father winked at her happily. Bev melted. Her granddaughter had to be the most beautiful baby in the world.

"Let's get you something to eat." She rose and headed toward the kitchen with Nia. "Then we're going to wait for your Aunt Dana and your godfather Ray to arrive. When they do, there's going to be some fireworks lighting up this town, and it's not even close to being Independence Day."

"What in the hell do you mean that you told your mother that we're engaged?"

Ray Wilson was as mad as hell. He glared at Dana Mansfield, the woman sitting in the driver's seat, and he wanted to wring her neck. When the cocoa-colored beauty responded to him with a nonchalant shrug, that only fueled his anger.

"Damn it, Dana! Thad and Darnell know that we're not engaged," he spewed, referring to his client and best friend, Thad Stewart, and his wife, Darnell. The relationship between Dana and Darnell was close. Not only were they related by blood, but Dana was the singing star's attorney. "Don't you think that they're going to tell your mother that you're telling a lie?"

Dana looked unconcerned. "I haven't spoken to Darnell about anything but business in a long time. She doesn't know about my personal life."

"Well, Thad knows about mine, and he knows that you're *not* my fiancée."

"I thought about that. All we have to say is that we chose to keep it a secret."

Ray bristled. "*We?* What we? It's *you* who's telling the lie! Why should I keep it going?" An even better question was why was he even here, speeding along this isolated road headed toward some town in the middle of nowhere? He and Dana were good friends, but this was a bit much. He didn't know that she had ulterior motives when she invited him to spend his vacation with her in her hometown.

The two of them had met years ago before their clients, Thad and Darnell, were married. The superstars had been locked in a legal battle with each other, and when the haggling was over a love match had been the result for the actor and singer and a friendship had been formed between their attorneys. Later, Ray had introduced Dana to his golf buddy and fellow attorney, Mitch Clayton. To his surprise, Dana and Mitch became engaged a month later. According to them it was love at first sight. Yet despite a three-year engagement, the relationship hadn't ended in marriage. Mitch had died unexpectedly nine months prior. Ray had helped Dana through the ordeal of his passing. He had done so without ever crossing the line between friendship and lover, and he was proud of the fact. That made the lie that Dana had told her mother even more despicable as far as he was concerned.

"I didn't want to come with you in the first place," he spat.

"I know that." Dana ran her hand over her slicked-back hair. "And it was hard for me to imagine you spending a week in the boondocks."

"You got that right."

He was a city boy, born and raised in Detroit. Most of his adult life had been spent in L.A., enjoying a Hollywood lifestyle that would be the envy of a lot of people. Backwater towns were not his thing. But he had felt sorry for Dana, who had confided in him that she was apprehensive about her return to the family fold after years of having been estranged from them. She hadn't gone into detail about what had caused the rift and he had never pried. Ray had finally agreed to come as a friend offering moral support. Dana had also informed him that Thad would be there with Darnell and the baby, so that was a plus. Of course there was the possibility that there was someone else who might also be visiting Dana's mother who he might want to see, but that was another story. As for now—

"How do you plan on pulling this little fiancé farce off?" Ray asked contemptuously.

Dana shot a glance at his stern profile and then returned her eyes to the road. She flexed her fingers on the steering wheel of the luxury automobile that had been waiting at the airport. She gave a long, drawn-out sigh, but instead of answering his question she asked him one.

"How long do you think it's been since we turned off the main highway?"

"I couldn't care less!" Ray's eyes were ablaze with indignation. "I don't like being used, Dana, so stop the car and let me out! I'm going to hitchhike back to the city."

"That's a long way back." Dana gave a sardonic chuckle. "And would you believe that since we left that highway every acre of land that we've been driving on belongs to my family?" That stopped Ray's oncoming tirade.

"What?" He looked at her, dumbfounded. "I don't believe you!"

He looked out the window at the rolling countryside. They had passed so many trees that for a while he had thought that they were in a national forest. He had seen lakes, waterfalls, grassy plains, herds of cattle, and grazing horses. He was hardly able to comprehend the value of what he had seen.

He returned his attention to Dana. "This land has to be worth a fortune!"

She was matter-of-fact. "Of course it is."

"I've never heard of any African-Americans in this country who own this much land," Ray marveled. "Are you telling another lie?" Was this really possible?

"No, I'm not," Dana huffed.

Ray still wasn't sure that she was telling the truth. "We've known each other for years. Why didn't you tell me that your family was wealthy?"

"You never asked."

"Thanks for the brilliant answer." Ray returned his attention to the passing scenery. "How did they get so much land?"

"That's a long story." Dana's mouth twisted into a crooked smile. Raising a manicured finger, she pointed beyond the steering wheel. "We're almost there."

Ray peered ahead but could see nothing in the distance but a small aircraft flying above them in the cloudless sky. Except for a few cars that passed them some time ago and a sign indicating an exit to a town about an hour back, the plane was the first indication of civilization that Ray had seen for a while. To his surprise, it started to descend.

"Is there an airport around here?" They were in the middle of nowhere. Dana had told him that the population of her hometown was roughly three hundred people when everybody was there. Why would someplace that small have an airport?

"No," Dana answered, "but there is a landing strip outside of the wall."

Ray frowned. "What wall?"

"You'll see."

Abruptly, Dana turned off the paved two-lane road on which they had been driving onto another road and headed in the direction of the spot where the plane had disappeared. In the distance Ray could see the outline of a wall.

"Does that answer your question?" Dana asked dryly. "And it looks like another family member has arrived." The plane that they had been tracking was landing.

Ray wondered how she would know that it contained a member of her family. Just how small was this town? It was hard to believe that a woman like Dana Mansfield would have grown up in such a place. At thirty-nine, she was the embodiment of the modern career woman. Intelligent and sophisticated, she was always impeccably dressed and she never had a hair out of place. Even now after their long flight from the West Coast to the South, her meticulously applied makeup still appeared fresh. Over the years, Ray had begun to notice that, despite her show of independence, Dana was needy, yet he never would have guessed that small-town living had been any part of her background. He wondered how that had helped form her character, but right now he didn't have time to dwell on that. He had to figure a way out of the mess that Dana was trying to drag him into.

"I'm not going along with your lie," he said again.

She gave an impatient sigh. "I'm sorry that I had to trick you, Ray, but there's a lot to all of this. I just want you to see some things and then listen to my reasoning before you make a final decision. As a matter of fact, I was forced to say that you were my fiancé. It was the only way that I could get you into town."

Ray scoffed. "That's a good one."

Undaunted, Dana continued. "I swear that I'll tell you everything after we get settled. I'm just asking you—no, I'm begging you—to go along with me on this. Just trust me."

Ray snorted this time. "You've *got* to be kidding! Trust you? You're getting ready to tell the lie of the century, and I don't even know why!"

"You will soon," Dana assured him. "Right now we're here." She slowed the car down to a crawl.

Ray looked beyond the windshield to find that they were only yards from the mysterious wall. To the left of the stone structure was the landing strip on which the plane had landed. On one side of the paved strip, lined up like tin soldiers, were other small aircraft. They were a colorful contrast to the surrounding landscape, which was noticeably devoid of vegetation.

Ray's curiosity was heightened. "What happened to all the trees?"

"The area had to be cleared a long time ago so that the landing strip could be built."

Ray nodded. "That makes sense, but where is the town?"

Dana nodded toward the wall. "Behind there."

Ray's look of confusion deepened. The massive structure was built of colorful stones and stood at least ten feet tall. It seemed to stretch endlessly and looked more like a fortress than a decorative structure.

"It looks like the Great Wall of China. How far does this thing go?"

"It surrounds the entire town."

"Why?"

"It was originally built for protection." Dana brought the car to a stop. "Welcome to home sweet home."

Her answer had begged for a follow-up question on Ray's part, but they had stopped in front of an intricately carved gate with ironwork that had drawn his attention. It was reminiscent of the style he had seen gracing many of the homes in New Orleans. As tall as the wall, it rose in graceful splendor, demanding that it be admired.

"My great-grandfather made that gate," Dana said as she searched through her overstuffed purse. "He was an artisan and worked with iron."

Ray noted the touch of pride in her voice. She had a right to be. It was a work of art.

"Your family must be very important in this town, owning all of that land and—" Ray stopped short as it dawned on him that there was something strange about the gate. It was closed. How in the world could the gate leading to an entire town be closed? He was about to ask Dana about that when she shrieked in triumph.

"There it is!"

Withdrawing a plastic card from her purse, she opened a metal box standing outside of the wall and punched numbers into its keypad. The gate slowly opened. Putting the card back into her purse, she started the car.

Ray felt a wave of anxiety as his eyes drifted to the words written in script on a plaque attached to the wall. The words announced to all the name of the town that they were entering—Stillwaters.

CHAPTER 2

"She's got nerve, I'll say that for her!" Bev fumed as she watched her mother bustle around the bedroom, getting it ready for Dana. "You mean to tell me that she told you a week ago that she's bringing a fiancé to town and you didn't even tell me?"

"Don't start." Ginny Little's voice was stern as she gave the decorative pillow that she had placed on the king-size bed an extra pound with her fist. Rising to her impressive six-foot height, she turned to her eldest daughter, who stood two inches shorter, and gave her a look that had made Bev wither as a child. It still did.

"I didn't tell you because I didn't want to hear all of the fuss." Ginny was blunt. "I'm sick and tired of this petty jealousy between you and your sister . . ."

"Jealousy?" Bev tried to look insulted.

"Yes, that's what it's always been." Ginny gave a frustrated sigh. "You've been sniping at each other for years, and it's time that it stopped."

Bev's jaws tightened at hearing the truth. Her mother was right. She and Dana were much too old for this feud between them to continue.

"For years your daddy and I blamed ourselves. It never occurred to us that a fourteen-year age difference would put this much distance between you. You're sisters, for goodness sake. You are all . . ."

"That the other one has." Bev finished the sentence that had become her parents' mantra. "I know, Mama, I know." And she did. It seemed that from the time her sister reached adulthood their relationship had grown worse. The reality was that the two of them had lived together as siblings for only four short years and really didn't know each other well.

Bev had been eighteen when she eloped with Colton Cameron. She was nineteen when she was left a widow with a child to raise. Her parents and Dana had moved back to Stillwaters while Bev and Darnell had continued to live in Chicago. It was during this period of time that the distance between the sisters had become more than mere mileage. When Bev went home to visit, she found Dana to be a spoiled, self-absorbed child, and not much had changed in adulthood. As much as she loved her sister, she wasn't sure that she liked her because Dana wanted *what* Dana wanted *when* Dana wanted it. That was the way it was. To keep peace in the family her parents had accepted such behavior, but Bev had not.

Ginny resumed bustling around the room. "I'm glad that she's found happiness. It's been three years since I've seen my child."

"That's two husbands before the last three years," Bev quipped sarcastically, "and two fiancés after."

"Oh, stop it." Ginny refused to hear criticism of her daughter's latest announcement. "And don't you dare bring up those other men to her. They were mistakes.

She's trying to start a new life, so be happy for her and keep your mouth shut."

"Mama, she won't even tell you this latest fiancé's name! Don't you find that strange?" Bev knew who was coming with Dana. She wanted to know what other lies that her sister had told their mother.

Ginny didn't take the bait. Instead of responding, she picked up a pile of towels on the foot of the bed and headed toward the adjoining bathroom. Bev followed her.

"Suppose she accuses us of not liking this fiancé like she did that last one? If that happens I guess she'll pull another tantrum and go into self exile for three more years."

It still made Bev angry to think about how much pain her sister's irrational behavior had caused their mother. Their father had died only a year before Dana brought Mitch Clayton around to meet her family, and Ginny had still been grieving. When her youngest daughter had pulled her little trick it had broken Ginny's heart. Their mother had been through enough.

"You and I were right about that Mitch guy and she didn't like it. He strung her along for years, and if he hadn't died, he never would have married her. She knows it, and so do you."

Ginny didn't react as she placed the fluffy towels in the linen closet and closed the door. After a cursory glance around the room to reassure herself that everything was in place, she moved past her daughter back into the bedroom, but Bev refused to be ignored.

"I called Darnell and we discussed this latest fiancé thing," Bev said cautiously, not wanting to reveal too much about her conversation with her daughter and what they both knew and suspected. "She said that it's the first she's heard about it."

Over the years it was Darnell who had kept her grandmother informed about Dana's welfare. She and her aunt were fairly close in age and that had proven to be a bond between them—an advantage that Bev had never enjoyed. "Dana knows what bringing that man here to Stillwaters means."

Ginny headed toward the bedroom door determined to ignore her eldest, but as she started to exit she changed her mind. Before closing the door behind her, she looked back at the daughter that she loved so dearly and uttered the two words that were meant to stop the flow of negativity coming from Bev about her sister: "Family first."

The iron gate closed behind Dana and Ray, and he felt trapped. The feeling intensified as they encountered a small guardhouse immediately inside the gate. Painted white, it stood in the middle of a small patch of perfectly manicured grass and boasted a window box filled with flowers. A paved parking lot occupied by numerous cars and several golf carts sat across the street from the building. Security cameras were mounted discreetly on light poles. They were aimed at the entrance. Standing at the foot of the brick path leading to the building was a portly guard dressed in sharply creased black slacks and a pristine white shirt. A badge was attached to the pocket of his shirt. Ray was taken aback—first a stone wall and then a security check. What kind of town *was* this?

Dana brought the car to a stop. Walking to the passenger side, the guard peered past Ray to the driver.

"Ms. Mansfield!" He flashed a grin of recognition. "I saw your name on the list, but it's been so long since you've been here that I didn't recognize you at first. How have you been?"

"Fine, Mr. Monroe. How's your wife doing?"

"She's well. Thanks for asking." He glanced down at the clipboard in his hand and began flipping through some papers. He found her name. "Here you are!" He checked her off and then looked at Ray.

"And who is your guest?"

"This is my fiancé, Ray Wilson. Ray, this is Mr. Monroe."

The man gave him a courteous nod, which Ray returned. He noted that Dana hadn't looked at the guard when she told him the big lie.

Ray's name was written down. They both were waved forward. "Okay, Ms. Mansfield, go on through, and congratulations."

As Dana continued their drive, Ray turned to her. "Is this a town or a prison?"

"When I was growing up sometimes it used to feel like both, but there is a reason for all of this."

"Well, it would be nice if you would tell *me* the reason," Ray snapped. All of these precautions made him uneasy.

Dana remained silent and kept driving. They passed a two-story Colonial house on the same side of the road as the guardhouse. Painted white and trimmed in green with matching shutters, it was surrounded by a white picket fence. Weeping willow trees stood on either side of the brick walkway leading to the front door.

"The guard and his family live there." Dana nodded toward the house.

"That's quaint," Ray observed. The setting reminded him of a Norman Rockwell painting, minus the guard, the wall, and the gate. He was beginning to relax a bit, that is until they reached yet another barrier between them and Stillwaters.

It was twin gates this time. They were not as high or as decorative as the one at the first entrance, but they were wider and sat between two stone pillars that melted into thick, well-tended shrubbery. A brass plate was attached to one of the pillars. Etched in regal script were the words FAMILY FIRST.

"What does that mean?" Ray asked.

"Just what it says," Dana answered. "It's our family motto, and we take it seriously."

"Oh yeah?

"Yes. You'll see what I mean. Believe me, Stillwaters is one place that you won't easily forget."

Ray doubted it. "What makes you so sure?"

"Because it holds mysteries that will entice you." Dana punched more numbers into the second keypad.

Ray watched as the gates opened silently. He wondered if the next barrier would be a moat and a fire-breathing dragon.

They continued their slow drive on a road that was much narrower than the one that they had been on previously. Trees with fragrant pink blossoms lined both sides of the road for about a quarter of a mile. Then suddenly the road began to widen. Buildings began to appear. They had finally reached Stillwaters.

The streets of the town were empty of pedestrians and there were no other cars in sight. Ray did a double-take as the first building came into view. It was a small structure, daring in its contemporary design, reminiscent of the work of the renowned African-American architect Armon Casey, whose name in some circles was being whispered with the same reverence as that of the late Frank Lloyd Wright. People waited for years to have him design their homes and buildings. Only the wealthiest of the wealthy could afford his designs. One of his buildings couldn't possibly have been built in this small town. Just as surprising was the business that was located in the Casey knock-off. The sign hanging above the bright red door of the building read Bo Designs.

A frown creased Ray's toasted brown features. The clothes in the display windows looked like the work of Bo Buchannan—known internationally as Bo—but they couldn't be. It was hard to believe that there were people in this town who could afford the designs of one of the icons of fashion. Still, he had to ask.

"Is that an authentic Bo clothing store?"

"Yes, it is," Dana answered matter-of-factly. "And the building is an Armon Casey design."

Before Ray could recover from the shock of that revelation he was in for even more surprises. Across the street from the clothing store was a familiar looking building, built of rustic wood. Bricks had been added to the bottom half of the building to modernize its look. The hand-lettered sign identified it as the Healthy Heart Grocery Store, and next door to that, separated by a small parking lot, was a small, bright red building with a door striped like a candy cane. This was the signature design of another exclusive franchise, the Perfect Concoction Creamery and Bakery. Like the Healthy Heart stores, these sweet shops only occupied the most elite neighborhoods. Where in the hell was he? What kind of place was Stillwaters?

"That's The Cove over there," Dana said and pointed to another building. "It's the town's entertainment center. It was designed by Armon, too."

Ray turned to see the building next to Bo Designs. Long and sleek, it took up the rest of the block. The arcs and angles of the structure were fascinating, but what caught Ray's eye was the marquee listing the multitude of activities being offered inside. There was bowling, roller skating, and pool. In addition, according to the marquee, there was a film being shown in the theatre at various times. Ray recognized the title immediately.

"That's Thad and Darnell's latest movie!" It hadn't been released yet.

"Yes, it is. We get their preview copies here all the time."

"What!" Nobody had told him about this. Even *he* hadn't seen a preview of it yet. "How did that happen?"

"Thad," she said as if he should have known the source.

Ray swallowed the sharp retort that threatened to escape. Thad hadn't told him anything about previewing the film in this hick town. He was Thad's manager, and the least he could have done was extended him that courtesy.

Ray refocused his attention on the passing scenery. They had left the rows of buildings and were continuing down a two-lane road, lined on both sides with graceful weeping willows. As they cleared the trees, the residents of Stillwaters seemed to appear out of nowhere. Everything around them seemed to be bustling with life. Joggers abounded. Bikers sped along marked trails. Tennis courts were filled with players. They passed a baseball field and a basketball court where spirited games were in progress. People were everywhere, and they all had one thing in common.

"So this is a black town." Ray's words were a statement, not a question. Everyone he saw was African-American.

He had heard about such places. After the Civil War emancipated slaves had established quite a few towns throughout the United States. Few still existed, and Ray had read that those that did were in dire financial straits. That didn't seem to be a problem in Stillwater. The buildings that he saw were well maintained, and the streets were immaculate. Golf carts, bicycles, and bicycle-pedaled surreys appeared to be the modes of transportation. They were parked in droves in the parking lots by the sports fields, but one car did emerge from a side street that caught Ray's attention. It was a white Rolls Royce.

"Damn!" Ray followed the car's progress as it passed. The windows were tinted so that its occupants couldn't be seen. He turned to Dana.

"So who's that, the mayor?" He wasn't joking.

Dana smiled, but once again didn't answer. The woman was beginning to grate on his nerves. He was about to tell her about herself when his attention was caught by a group of teenagers emerging from a wooded area. They were dressed in swimsuits and carrying beach bags.

"Where are they coming from?"

Dana followed his line of vision. "Stillwaters Lake is through those trees." She nodded in the direction from which the kids had come. "There's also an eighteen hole golf course near the lake and a swimming pool in The Cove."

Ray raised a brow. Dana knew how much he loved swimming and golf. She probably threw that in to make him want to stay. He had to admit that this place was intriguing.

Dana turned off the road on which they had been driving and rounded a curve. Ray blinked and blinked again. If he hadn't known better he would have believed that they were in Beverly Hills, California. Sitting back from the street amidst manicured lawns and blossoming flowers, the stately homes on this street rivaled those in that iconic enclave.

"We must be on the rich side of town," Ray marveled. "These people are living large."

"This is Stillwaters Road, where most of the elders in my family live. That house to our right belongs to my mother."

The house was huge, with a pillared porch. A man on a riding mower was cutting the manicured lawn in precise lines.

"That's where I'll be staying while we're here," Dana informed him. "We'll come back there later after I show you around."

They continued driving, passing a narrow gravel road that stood between two rows of flowered trees.

"That's Church Road," Dana pointed out. "No cars are allowed down there. At the end of the road there's a church and a cemetery."

Ray nodded absently. "Baptized and buried in the same place."

Only a row of trees separated Church Road and the house next to it. Smaller than the other houses, it was a quaint two-story brick structure, with two chimneys on opposite ends of the house. White window boxes containing flowers decorated three second-story windows. Flowers lined the winding walkway that led to the front entrance.

"That's where my great-grandmother lives. We call her Grandy. She's the matriarch of our family, and this weekend she'll turn one hundred years old. She's one of the reasons that I'm back here. Her birthday is something I couldn't miss."

As they rounded a bend a house appeared that was more majestic than any of those that they had previously passed. It was huge, with screened-in porches on both floors.

"A Come Right Inn," Ray said, identifying yet another successful high-end franchise. This one dominated the bed and breakfast industry.

"Yes, it is," Dana confirmed. "As my fiancé you would normally be staying there, but I know what happens when that occurs. Everybody is all in your business. I don't want that, so I called my Uncle Gerald and asked him if he would let you stay with him. He said it's okay."

Ray was less than thrilled. "Oh, great, I get to stay with one of your relatives instead of in an inn famous for its elegant accommodations and delicious dining. Why am I being punished for your lie?"

Dana laughed. "I get the message, but really, it's for the best. With people getting married left and right, and the town rule being no unmarried couples staying together, we needed a place for guests, so the inn was built."

Ray gawked at her. "The town rule is what?"

"You heard me."

He shook his head in astonishment. "Am I in the *Twilight Zone*? Whoever heard of a town with an old-fashioned rule like that?"

"It's hard to believe, isn't it?" Dana rounded another bend and emerged onto a cul-de-sac. There were only two houses on this section of Stillwaters Road. Both were large, but while the others that they had passed were older structures, both of these homes were contemporary and appeared to have been recently constructed.

"That's Uncle Gerald's house over there." She pointed to a crème-colored stucco that was a designer's dream—

another Casey design. Across the street, a smaller house built from recycled bricks was equally as impressive. "And that's my sister's house."

Ray's heart lurched. He had known that he might see Bev in town, but he'd had no idea that she actually had a house here. A luxury car was parked in the driveway. A woman was leaning into the backseat. Long brown legs that went on forever teased him from a pair of linen shorts. He couldn't see the heart-shaped brown face framed in the stylish cut that she wore sculpted close to her head. Nor could he see the large expressive eyes that usually looked at him with contempt, but he knew that it was Bev. How often had he studied her *assets*—the ample beasts, the shapely hips? He knew every curve of her body.

They cruised past both houses and Dana made a U-turn. "I'll drop you off at my uncle's house after I show you the rest of the town."

Ray nodded absently, preoccupied with the thought that if he did stay in town he would be staying across the street from Bev. The idea bothered and excited him. It was best that he leave ASAP. As they started back down Stillwaters Road, Ray pondered his alternatives, but Dana's next words startled Ray out of his musings

"Every person in this town is a relative of mine, Ray, by blood or by marriage." She paused to let her words have their intended impact. "Armon Casey is my cousin, and so is Bo Buchannan. The Healthy Heart Stores, Perfect Concoctions, and the Come Right Inns are corporations founded by my family members. As we drive through town, you'll recognize faces and names of people who have power and influence in nearly every public, private, or financial enterprise in this country. And they all know how to use it."

As Bev removed the baby from the back seat of her car, she straightened in time to see a car that she didn't recognize moving slowly past her house. It was headed toward town. Curious, she stood in the driveway trying to catch a glimpse of its occupants. Strangers weren't welcome in Stillwaters. That meant that at least one of the vehicle's occupants had to be family. She squinted as the man in the passenger seat turned his head toward her and then quickly looked away. He was too far for her to be positive of his identity, but her brief glimpse had fostered an uneasy feeling of familiarity. She was certain that Ray Wilson had arrived in town.

CHAPTER 3

"The Stillwaters left North Carolina after the Civil War. It seems that the clan was pretty notorious around those parts. As a matter of fact, that's how we got our last name. We were Maroons and . . ."

"Maroons?" Ray had read that word somewhere in the past, but he couldn't recall what it was about. Dana gave a simple explanation.

"Maroons were African captives who rebelled against slavery in the Caribbean, Latin America, and the United States. They escaped and survived in mountains, swamps, and other areas where it was hard to find them. Whole societies were formed in some cases. Before the Civil War ended, there were about one hundred people that made up the band that my great-great-grandfather led.

"His grandfather had been an escaped slave in Cuba and had headed a large Maroon community there, but his teenage son had gotten recaptured when they raided a sugar plantation and he was shipped to the United States to be broken. Usually they disposed of rebel slaves by killing them, but they made a big mistake when they changed tactics with him."

"Let me guess. He escaped." Ray had often wondered where Bev, Darnell, and the woman sitting beside him had gotten their spunk. Dana had just revealed the source.

"Not only that, but he took a dozen others with him. Over the years even more were freed. People used to say that the Maroons living in the mountains would swoop down on the slave owners' plantations and steal everything but their water. My great-great-grandfather on my father's side had a sense of humor, and after the war he decided to have a little fun with that reputation. But the spelling isn't s-t-e-a-l-w-a-t-e-r-s, because there's also another reason for the name as well. The family elders felt that since black people had been emancipated and since being enslaved was no longer a fear for our family that we could finally be as at peace as the waters that had carried our ancestors to these shores." Dana turned to Ray. "So we became the Stillwaters."

Ray was fascinated. "And what was the family name before that?"

"Our family consisted of escaped slaves on both my mother's and father's side. The head of the families refused to use the last names of their ex-slave masters, so those names were never spoken. But on my mother's side of the family they took the last name of Freedom. Grandy's maiden name was Esther Freedom."

"Amazing!" That was the only word that Ray could think of that seemed appropriate. "How long did they live as Maroons?"

"For generations. Freedom or death were the only two options. There was *never* another member of our family in chains again."

Ray could hear the sense of pride in Dana's voice as she told him about her family. This was the second time that she had displayed such emotions. He felt pride simply hearing about it.

"So the Stillwaters clan was sort of like Robin Hood and his band of merry men, huh? You took from the rich to give to the poor."

"You could say that. There was quite a reward for the capture of the men and women who led our clan."

"There were women leaders, too?"

"When necessity called for it, the Stillwaters family members have always risen to the occasion."

After hearing the family history, that wasn't difficult for Ray to believe. By the time that Dana had finished giving him a tour of the town, he had no doubts at all about her statement.

After leaving Stillwaters Road, she had driven him past other well-appointed homes, many of which were built around the tranquil blue water of the huge man-made lake. The homes rivaled those in Malibu, California. Each house that she pointed to belonged to someone prominent— doctors, attorneys, judges, educators, entrepreneurs, the list went on and on. Nearly every name that was mentioned was one that Ray recognized. These were people who had been heralded in newspapers, magazines, and on television. It seemed that the little town of Stillwaters was a cornucopia of the best and brightest that America had to offer, and they were all members of the same family.

"So Stillwaters is really a family compound, not a town?" Ray couldn't keep the astonishment out of his voice.

Dana shook her head. "No, it was incorporated as a town a long time ago, but the only people who can live inside its walls are family members, not outsiders." She added pointedly, "Future family members can visit. As a matter of fact, it's strongly encouraged."

Ray got the message. "That's why you had to say that I'm your fiancé."

"You wouldn't have been welcome here if I hadn't."

For some reason the thought of deliberate exclusion rubbed Ray the wrong way. "What about Thad? You're telling me that he wasn't welcome here until he was engaged to Darnell? He's a superstar."

Dana shrugged. "Everybody in our family is a superstar in some way, shape, or form."

She was right. The family members that she had mentioned had been recipients of some of the most prestigious honors America had to bestow on its citizens. It turned out that Dana's father had been among them.

She had rarely spoken to him about her parents, although she had mentioned once that her mother was a noted heart surgeon. As they drove around, she revealed to him that her late father had been a biophysicist who had been nominated for the Nobel Peace Prize. The information reinforced for Ray just how little he really knew about Dana's life. In addition, it had never dawned on him that there was something that he didn't know about Thad or his wife until Dana pointed to a luxurious beach home of wood and stone, visible through an array of flowering trees.

"That house belongs to Thad and Darnell."

Ray was speechless. The Stewarts owned a home in Stillwaters! At this point he was shocked that anything else could surprise him. If he hadn't seen this town for himself and recognized the faces of the renowned, he would never have believed that a place such as this existed.

"Who doesn't live here?" Ray was being sarcastic, but it was a legitimate question. "What about the gardeners and the other workers I've seen around here, where do they live?"

"Some of the workers live in the town whose sign we passed before arriving here, and there's another town about twenty miles past Stillwaters. Other workers live there. Like I said, the main guard lives in the house I pointed out to you, but as you'll recall, we did go through two gates to get here, so the guard doesn't actually live inside the community."

Ray shook his head at the ingenuity of it all. "Is working in Stillwaters the major industry around here?"

Dana gave a sardonic chuckle. "No, working *for* Stillwaters is the major industry around here. In the town north of us there's a wind farm and a microchip factory that the family owns. Our farm, ranch, dairy, and horse breeding businesses support the town south of us. There's also a variety of other smaller enterprises around here that we own. There's not much locally that the Stillwaters family doesn't have its hand in, and that's also nationally and internationally.

"Here in town a lot of the employees that you see are family members. The kids in our family are submerged in entrepreneurship almost as soon as they can walk. The businesses that you see here are more for training than for profit. Kids in our family who live in Stillwaters or come here on vacation must take a job or create their own business. This is ground zero for any member of the Stillwaters family who wants to learn how to add to our wealth and power. All are expected to do so. We also have a family foundation that supports humanitarian and nonprofit endeavors worldwide, and it's also mandatory for each of us to support that in some way."

Ray massaged his temples. "This is mindboggling; I didn't know that there was a black family on earth with all of this." He indicated the enormity of it with a sweep of his hand.

"People who live around here know about it, so do others with power in this country who matter. You aren't supposed to know about it unless you have Stillwaters blood pumping through your veins, or unless you're married to one."

"Then why did you tell me?"

"Because I need you to know what you're up against when I tell you why I brought you here."

Ray's eyes narrowed. She was back to talking in circles. "And why is that?"

"Justice."

"What does that mean?"

"Just be patient. I'll let you know." Dana pulled into the driveway of the house that belonged to the Stewarts. "Let's see if the lovebirds are in town yet. I want to test their reaction to our *engagement*." She turned the ignition off and looked at Ray. "That is, if you're willing to go along with this."

"I already told you that I wasn't, but I am curious as to how you think you can pull this off." What he didn't say was that he didn't know whether to strangle Dana or to kiss her for bringing him here. Since passing through the gates of Stillwaters his curiosity wasn't simply piqued, it was in overdrive. He wanted to know everything there was to know about this place, but not at the expense of being labeled a liar.

He slid out of the passenger side door and offered her a surprise of his own. "I did tell you that I told Thad that I was coming here with you, didn't I?"

Dana leaped from the car. "No, you didn't! It was supposed to be a surprise. I asked you not to say anything to him." Her tone was sharp.

"I know that you don't have the nerve to be indignant. I don't feel guilty. I didn't know that I was coming here under false pretenses."

"You're not going to tell him we're not engaged, are you?" Dana looked alarmed.

Ray rounded the car to face her, knowing that he held the power at this point. "I don't think that you can do this without my cooperation, especially in there." He nodded toward the house. "Besides, they're not going to believe it anyway."

"We'll see." Dana didn't look too happy, but it was obvious that she planned to go forward with her charade. She snapped her fingers. "Oh! I forgot."

Slipping back into the car, she opened the glove compartment and withdrew a velvet ring box. She opened it to reveal a diamond engagement ring which she slipped on the third finger of her left hand. Tossing the box aside, she exited the car and extended her hand.

"What do you think?"

"That you're crazy." Ray inspected the marquis diamond. It was a nice size. "But at least you're not cheap."

"Neither is my friend's husband. A couple of months after their engagement, he bought her a larger ring, with matching earrings. She loaned me her old ring."

"That's a good friend. Now if she had only loaned you some common sense you'd be set." He shook his head at her actions. "I don't like this, Dana."

She grinned up at him reassuringly. "Don't worry. I'll do all of the talking. You don't have to say a thing." She gave him a quick kiss on the lips, hoping against hope that she hadn't made a mistake by bringing Ray along. Taking his hand, she started up the driveway toward the house.

"I don't believe this!" Darnell Cameron Stewart reported to her husband as she peered from behind the vertical blinds covering the window. The sound of car doors slamming had alerted her to the presence of visitors.

"What, babe?" Thad asked, preoccupied with the script that he was reading.

"Aunt Dana just got out of the car with what is supposed to be her new fiancé."

"Yeah? How's he looking?" Thad mumbled.

"Like Ray."

Thad snapped to attention. "Ray? Ray who?"

"Your Ray!" Darnell sputtered. "Our Ray! Ray Wilson."

Thad looked at her in confusion. "He's not engaged to Dana. They're just friends."

"That's not what Dana told Grandma," Darnell said triumphantly. She hadn't told him about his friend's deception. Let Ray explain it to Thad.

"He couldn't be Dana's fiancé. He said that he was coming to town with her, but . . ." Thad's voice faltered.

"But what?" Darnell glared at him. "You know the family rule about people who pass through the gates of Stillwaters. How did you think that he was going to get in here?" She returned her attention to the approaching couple. "Oh, my God!" Darnell squealed.

"What?" Thad dropped the script.

"She kissed him!"

It took everything he had not to get up and join his wife at the window, but pride kept him seated. "They're going to see you spying on them if you don't come away from the window."

"Let them." There was venom in Darnell's voice. "Here they come up the driveway, holding hands like teenagers. Oh, I've got something to say to them."

The door chime rang. Darnell stalked to the door like a woman on a mission. "First he flirts with my mother and now he messes with her sister? I'm getting to the bottom of this."

Thad winced. He hoped that Ray had a good explanation for what was going on because he was about to step into the lion's den. It took exactly ten minutes for Darnell to circle her prey and determine the strength and weaknesses of their story before she attacked.

"You two must think that I'm a fool." She glowered at Ray and Dana. "I don't know about Thad, but I don't believe for one second that you're engaged."

"Well, here's the ring." Dana wiggled her fingers. "Isn't it beautiful?"

Darnell wasn't impressed. "Anybody can buy an engagement ring."

"They wish," Dana gushed, seemingly unaffected by her niece's skepticism. She played her part to the hilt as she smiled at Ray with adoring eyes.

Ray didn't know how she could lie so easily. He was racked with guilt. His integrity as a man had always been something of which he had been proud, and here he was in his best friend's house going along with a lie. Worst of all, he wasn't sure of the reason for the deception. He couldn't blame Darnell for her growing hostility toward him. He shouldn't be showing up on the couple's doorstep with Darnell's aunt as his bogus fiancée, especially when he was enamored with Darnell's mother.

When he first met Bev Cameron he hadn't been coy about his interest in her, and she hadn't been shy about rejecting his attention. He was a younger man and she wasn't interested. Over the years, as he and Bev were forced to see each other in social settings, he had become more discreet about his feelings. He tried hard to suppress them, but he knew that they were still there and he was troubled about what Bev would think about all of this. As for her daughter, he liked her a lot. He respected her intelligence and talent and liked the way that she loved and treated his friend. As he sat there and endured Darnell's assessment as Dana's intended, Ray was beginning to regret that he hadn't turned around and left town at the guard's gate.

He chanced a glance at Thad, who seemed amused by the present scenario. His friend hadn't said much since their arrival, not that Darnell had given him a chance to express his opinion; she had plenty to say.

"You need to come up with a better lie," she told her aunt pointedly. She sat back and crossed her arms tightly to emphasize her point. With every second that ticked by, her aunt was putting their good relationship in jeopardy. "None of this makes sense, Dana. You had a three year relationship with Mitch. It's been nine months since he died . . ."

"Which was of no concern to anyone in this family," Dana countered. "Everyone hated him."

Ray had heard Dana say that her family didn't like Mitch, but this was the first time the word *hate* had been used. Once again he glanced at Thad, who gave him a roll of the eyes, indicating that there was more to the story. Ray refocused on the unfolding drama.

"Nobody hated him," Darnell shot back. "Mama, Grandma, and I just didn't like him; nobody else got to meet him. But the point is if you were so madly in love with the man, then why would you be so open to finding a new one so soon, *and* to keeping that a secret?"

Her hostile glare turned on Ray. "I don't know why you're going along with this. I, personally, don't appreciate it." She turned back to her aunt, and said, "And if it's a joke I don't think that it's funny."

Dana didn't falter. "I've got the right to be loved, Darnell, and I don't need your permission or anybody's approval. We're engaged, and that's that."

Rising, she headed toward the door. "Come on, Ray." It was a command, not a request.

Ray followed. "I'll see you later, man," he tossed over his shoulder at Thad.

Darnell was undaunted as she stalked her aunt to the door. "Does Ray's being here have anything to do with the power struggle everybody thinks that Aunt Tessa's family is going to wage? Is that why you brought another attorney here? You're trying to pull some sort of legal maneuver, aren't you?"

Having reached the door, Dana looked back at her niece contemptuously, "Oh, please! I don't give a damn about that bunch of breeders. If they want to outvote the rest of us about who will head this family, then let them." She snatched the door open and headed toward the car with Ray on her heels.

Darnell had a parting shot for them both. "It's a lie and you know it, Dana! And I'm disappointed in you, Ray." The front door slammed behind them.

Outside, Dana and Ray sat in the car in silence for a moment and then he quipped, "That went well."

Dana chuckled. "You think?" She started the car and pulled out of the driveway.

Ray's next comment held no humor. "I sat there in silence and let you lie to my best friend. His wife hates me, and I'm in danger of being tarred and feathered by your family and run out of town on a rail when they find out that I don't belong here. So I think that now is the time for you to tell me why we're here."

Dana gave a deep sigh. "You're right."

She turned off the paved road on which they had been riding and onto a gravel one that faced the lake. They parked. The crystal clear water was tranquil, but it was apparent that Dana was in turmoil. She turned toward Ray.

"I brought you here to help me investigate a murder."

Ray started. "A murder in this town? Who?"

Dana's face hardened. "There's a criminal living in Stillwaters. Somebody in my family murdered Mitch Clayton, and I want you to help me find out who did it."

CHAPTER 4

It was hard for Bev to believe that Dana and Ray were engaged. The whole idea of the two of them together was ridiculous. She couldn't think of a more unlikely pair. Ray was a player, and, as smart as her baby sister might be, the reality was that the woman was a flake, especially when it came to men.

Dana's first husband had been a piece of work, as was her second husband, whose name she still carried. Both had been cheats and liars. As for Mitch Clayton, the less said about him the better. Besides, from what she'd been able to discern about Ray Wilson, Dana wasn't his type. He apparently liked women with artificial boobs, and Dana's slim physique certainly didn't fit that criterion. Who could forget the ingénue actress with the silicone implants that Ray had brought to Darnell and Thad's wedding reception? Bev certainly hadn't.

At the time her opinion of him had not been high, but she had to admit that after watching him over the years her opinion had changed. Sure, his choices in women were pedestrian, but she had also noticed another side of him. She had seen him engage in acts of kindness and generosity with his friends. She had discovered that he had started a mentoring program for inner city youth interested in entertainment law as a career. He also volunteered his services to a poverty law center in Los Angeles. Knowing those things about him had increased his credibility with her.

Thad and Darnell thought the world of him. He was like an older brother to Thad, and when their daughter Nia was born, Darnell and Thad did not hesitate to ask Ray to be Nia's godfather. That Thad had wanted to give him such an honor came as no surprise, but for Darnell to have agreed to it meant that she trusted him as much as her husband, and that was nearly miraculous. Darnell rarely trusted anyone outside of the family. Of course after today's encounter with Dana and Ray, those feelings might be in question. Mother and daughter were in agreement that something was definitely fishy regarding that pair. After they left her house, Darnell had called Bev and reviewed the "happy couple's" visit.

"It's bad enough that Aunt Dana turned her back on this family just because of that Mitch guy, but now she's going to bring Ray here under false pretenses to stir up trouble!" Darnell was seething. "This is too much."

If Darnell was right about Dana's reason for being here, the Stillwaters clan might be headed for turmoil that could have been avoided, and that was an issue of concern. Bev prayed that the animosity that her sister held toward her immediate family wouldn't spill over into the affairs of their extended kin just because of one man.

Weeks before the rift that had left Dana estranged from her mother and sister, Mitch Clayton had been introduced to the immediate family at an intimate dinner in Bev's Chicago home. Darnell had not been present, but she had met Mitch before and had informed her mother that she didn't like him. However, Bev and Ginny were determined to form their own opinions.

They met a man who was intelligent and affable, but closer to Bev's age than Dana's. He wore expensive suits, bragged about being a connoisseur of fine wines, and exhibited a charm that to some might have been captivating, but neither woman was impressed. Their instincts told them that he wasn't the man for Dana, but neither of them had been prepared for the bombshell that she had dropped that evening when she announced that they were engaged. She had known the man for one month. After meeting him both Ginny and Bev had informed Dana that Mitch wouldn't be welcome in Stillwaters. It was that declaration that had ignited the storm that had weakened their family ties. If her sister had brought Ray Wilson here under clandestine circumstances in an attempt to sabotage the entire family because of some need for revenge, Bev was prepared to intervene—but not quite yet.

"Let's sit back and see what she's up to with this fiancé thing," she advised her only child. "Mama is astute; she knows Dana and her track record with men, and so does Grandy. If either one of them challenges her about him, that's on Dana. Right now Mama is on cloud nine because her daughter has come home, and I don't want to spoil that for her. Time will tell what Dana is trying to pull."

Darnell hadn't been so sure. "I hope you're right, because the family has enough going on without Dana sticking her nose into it. Bringing Ray in here to help her could wreak havoc."

Bev tried to soothe her daughter's concern. "I think that you're giving Ray more credit than he deserves. After all, he's an entertainment attorney . . ."

"And a skilled negotiator."

Bev couldn't dispute that. "Yes, but I think that he has more common sense than she has. Taking that into consideration, maybe she won't let whatever is happening go too far."

It was agreed that Darnell and she would take a wait-and-see position regarding this supposed engagement. So as the introductions to her mother were being made, Bev watched the interaction between Dana and Ray carefully.

Ray tried to appear composed as Bev securitized him. He knew that the farce that Dana had created wasn't going to work. Darnell hadn't believed it for a minute, and if he thought that she was tough when they met with her and Thad, he had no illusion that facing Dana's mother would be easier. He was right. It was worse, but not because of Ginny; because of Bev. From her stance, it was obvious to him that she had spoken to Darnell. The icy stare that she was giving him while he was being introduced to her mother could not be denied. He had butterflies in his stomach. That usually happened whenever he was near Bev.

Ray returned his attention to Dana's mother, whom he'd had the pleasure of meeting at Thad and Darnell's wedding. The meeting had been brief, but the lady had been as gracious then as she was now as she greeted him warmly.

"It's so nice to see you again, Mr. Wilson." She flashed him a smile that was so much like Bev's that his stomach fluttered.

Bev favored her mother. She had inherited her large, dark eyes and her height. In her seventies, Ginny Little's mocha-brown face defied her age. The silver mane that framed her face was cut into a modern, symmetrical style that gave her a chic, sophisticated appearance. Like her daughter, she was a very attractive woman.

"I'll be honest with you, Mr. Wilson . . ."

"Please call me Ray."

"All right, Ray, then I'll tell you the truth. I only vaguely remember meeting you." She turned to her youngest daughter and caressed her cheek. "But if you're the one responsible for bringing my girl back into the family, then you've got my vote for future son-in-law."

Dana slyly dismissed her mother's words. "Oh, Mama." Hugging the older woman to her, she didn't want to feel guilty about her deception. She also didn't want to admit to herself that she was glad to be home. She had missed her mother. If something had happened to Ginny before the breech between them had been mended, she never would have forgiven herself. Yet she still couldn't deny the anger that she harbored regarding Mitch, or the resentment that she felt toward the other woman who occupied the room. She turned to her sister.

"Hello, Bev."

"Dana."

The chill in their mutual greeting spoke volumes about the relationship between the two sisters. The gulf between them was wide, and it looked as though it would take more than the prodigal daughter's return home to close it.

Later, as they headed to her uncle's house where Ray would be staying, Ray questioned Dana about the tension that he had observed. "What's this thing between you and Bev? Are you still mad at her because of Mitch?"

"That's part of it, but we didn't get along even before that."

Ray sensed that there was subtext in her statement and it made him ask, "What exactly was it about Mitch that Bev didn't like?" He had known Mitch on a professional basis for about six years, but on a personal level less than that.

He and Mitch had shared a love for women, sports, and the law, in that order. Mitch had been a gregarious man who tended to be a braggart, but he was a good golfer and Ray and he had gotten along well. Mitch never talked about himself much, and Ray really hadn't known that much about him. He assumed that he told him what he wanted him to know.

"Bev is just a busybody, that's all," Dana sniffed. "She never learned to keep her nose out of my business. She's always taken the overprotective big sister role a little too seriously."

"Seriously enough to kill Mitch?"

Dana physically recoiled at his words. "No, my sister may be a lot of things, but I don't think that she's the killer."

Ray agreed. He didn't think for a moment that Bev had harmed anyone. As a matter of fact, he wasn't sure that a crime had been committed. He had told Dana that earlier when the subject had been broached.

"As hard as it might be to accept, Mitch committed suicide, Dana . . ."

She had been defensive. "No, he didn't!"

"It was a self-inflicted wound to the head that ended his life."

Dana had been adamant. "I'm telling you that you're wrong!"

After leaving the Stewarts' house, they had parked the car and taken a stroll down to the lake. Dana had turned away from him in her anguish, as resistant now to the reality of the situation as she had been when it first happened. Gently, he turned her to face him and looked into her eyes.

"I know that he didn't leave a suicide note, but he did have cancer and he couldn't face what lay ahead. You've simply got to face the facts."

"I won't face a lie, Ray." She had jerked away from him.

Ray had looked at her with pity. After all of these months she was still grasping at straws, trying to escape the reality of Mitch's death. How desperate could a person be that they would accuse a member of their own family of murder? Had the shock of her fiancé's death pushed Dana over the edge?

In making her accusation, she had offered no proof to him that Mitch's death hadn't been a suicide. Her entire theory was based on intuition rather than facts. That contradicted their legal training.

Dana had said, "Mitch had too much to live for to kill himself. He had his career and he had me. He wouldn't have given up so easily just because he was ill." She was insistent. "I'm telling you, someone else had a hand in his death."

"Just because your family didn't like him?"

Dana nodded. "Isn't that enough?"

Her resolve regarding Mitch's demise seemed absolute, and Ray wasn't sure that he could change her mind. Bringing him to Stillwaters to assist her in finding this so-called murderer had been an irrational act. Dana needed help, all right, but not the kind that he could give her. He was thinking about talking to Thad and Darnell about what could be done about her when Dana seemed to read his mind.

"I'm not crazy, Ray. I wouldn't sit here and accuse my sister of murder just because I don't get along with her."

"I hope not." Ray's words were said disparagingly, but he quickly softened his tone. "I know that Mitch's death was devastating . . ."

"You don't know anything," Dana hissed, "except what you *think* that you know. I brought you here to show you power that you and most of this country would never believe existed. Money is power, and we Stillwaters have plenty of money. If you hadn't seen this place for yourself, you never would have believed it existed. That being true, then there's little that such power can't do, and that includes covering up a murder. "

After thinking about it, Ray had to admit that she had a point.

From the upstairs window of her mother's house, Bev had watched as Dana and Ray drove away.

"What kind of man is he, baby?"

Bev turned to the elderly woman who was seated across the room on a damask-covered lounge chair. An open book rested on her lap. With questioning eyes, Esther Freedom Stillwaters, the grand matriarch of the gathered clan, looked up at her granddaughter.

"I think that he's a good man," Bev answered quietly as she turned back to look out at the empty driveway.

There was something in the tone of Bev's voice that caught Esther's attention. She studied the tenseness in her grandchild's posture as she stood gazing out of the window at nothing. Her arms were wrapped around her body as if she were protecting herself from something unknown. But what?

"How long have you known this man?"

"About four years." Bev didn't turn around. "I met him when Darnell and Thad first got together."

"I see." Esther paused thoughtfully before continuing. "And you say that he's a good man?"

Bev nodded. "Yes."

"But he's not the man for her."

It wasn't a question, and Bev didn't answer. She didn't want her grandmother to know her suspicions and doubts about Ray, and particularly about the conflict that she was feeling regarding his having come here with Dana. But, as usual, the wisdom of age, partnered with acute observation, overshadowed that reasoning as Esther gave her favored grandchild a wily smile.

"But I'm guessing that he just might be the man for someone in this family."

Bev whirled to face her. "What do you mean by that? You haven't even met him yet!"

"I will in time." Esther's smile deepened. "And then we'll see."

Bev frowned. She didn't like the sound of that.

As Ray and Dana sat in the driveway of her uncle's house, Ray evaluated what Dana had told him about her family. According to her when a member of the Stillwaters family wanted to marry, the prospective in-law was taken to the family's town for "interrogation and inspection."

"It all appears to be pretty innocent," she had informed him, "but believe me, it's dead serious. When we add a member to our family it means expanding a dynasty that's worth more money than you can even imagine. You see, nobody fails in the Stillwaters family. It's not an option, and we don't marry losers. If our family doesn't approve of someone one of us wants to marry, you won't believe the pressure that's exerted."

Ray read between the lines. "And they put pressure on you about Mitch. But that doesn't mean that somebody murdered him."

"You don't know the Stillwaters family." Dana didn't hide her bitterness. "After my mother and sister put the word out about how much they disliked him, family members started swarming on me like locusts. I think that Mama or Bev might have had him investigated."

That surprised Ray. "Why would they do that?"

"Because they can." Dana turned to him. "As I said, money is power, and with the Stillwaters clan family is first."

Considering the reason that Dana had brought him here, that motto rang hollow. He pondered what she had told him so far.

"You know, all of this is well and good, but you still haven't given me any evidence that a murder has been committed."

She gave a heavy sigh. "Let me tell you about my Aunt Marva, Nedra's mother."

Ray had met Nedra Davis-Reasoner and her husband Sinclair through Darnell and Thad. Darnell and her cousin Nedra appeared to be close. Dana continued.

"Aunt Marva fell in love with her husband when they were in high school, so instead of going to college—which is a Stillwaters *must*—she married him right out of high school. She defied the family and left the family fold to avoid the drama. The night she gave birth to Nedra, my aunt's husband was killed by a hit-and-run driver. They had been married for only two years."

"And?" Ray didn't get the point.

"After his death, the family found Aunt Marva, who by that time was steeped in religion. They rallied around her, paid for her education, and she's now the pastor of one of the largest and wealthiest churches in Kansas City, Missouri."

"And that's a crime?"

"No, it's an example of how our family members prosper when they go along with the program, obey the creed. Because she's the oldest child, it's Aunt Marva's mother who everyone assumes will head the Stillwaters family when Grandy passes. That would make Aunt Marva next in line after her."

Ray was frustrated by her story. He still didn't get the connection, but he was glad that she wasn't involving Bev in her conspiracy theory. She could have easily done so, considering their strained relationship. He was feeling good about that until Dana said—

"Bev did the same thing as Aunt Marva."

"What do you mean?"

"She ran off and married a man that our parents didn't like. I was little, but I remember how upset they were."

"What happened?" Ray asked.

"Bev was the same age as Aunt Nedra when she ran away and married her husband. She had scholarship offers from all over the country and was set to go to Spellman in Atlanta. I don't know if her husband even had a high school diploma. She broke away from the family, and when she was pregnant with Darnell her husband died."

"I know, in some kind of automobile accident."

"The family found her, rallied around her, and paid for her education, straight through grad school. Bev became a CPA, founded her financial consulting firm, and prospered."

Ray sighed. "I still don't understand what you're getting at, Dana."

"The authorities could never verify exactly what caused the accident that killed Colton Cameron. They thought that perhaps what happened might have been some sort of hit and run, just like with Aunt Marva's husband." She paused dramatically. "The members of our family may appear to be as gentle as lambs, but we're lambs with the bite of lions." Dana looked into Ray's eyes. "That's how we are raised, and lions destroy their prey."

She spoke the last words slowly and distinctly. This time Ray got the point.

CHAPTER 5

"The women in the Stillwaters family don't play," Gerald Stillwaters informed Ray as the two men sat on the porch of the Come Right Inn, rocking contentedly in the oversized rockers that dotted the wraparound porch. "When someone does them wrong, there is a price to pay." He took a moment to glance over at Ray, who sat sipping a beer.

Ray knew that the words had been spoken for his benefit. This was part of the process that he had been going through since his arrival in town with Dana yesterday. He had been introduced to the first layer of the Stillwaters family this morning by Dana's Uncle Gerald, and the elders had welcomed, studied, and subtly interrogated him.

None of it came as a surprise. If he had been a real fiancé he would have expected as much from Dana's family. What he hadn't expected was how much he was enjoying the people who were putting him under the microscope. The ones whom he had met so far were warm, friendly, and a wealth of information about things that they assumed Ray already knew about Dana. In the short time that he had been here he had found out more about his friend then she had revealed since he had known her. Much of it came as quite a surprise.

Yesterday, after Dana had informed him of her suspicions regarding a killer in the family, they had vowed to discuss the matter in more detail later, after they were refreshed from their journey. She had taken him inside the impressive home of her Uncle Gerald and introduced him to the man who, she had informed Ray, was her mother's twin brother.

"Actually, they were a set of triplets," Dana had clarified, "but their brother, Gardner, died at birth."

Gerald Stillwaters was a large, vivacious man who stood at least six feet, six inches to Ray's six feet. Dana had said that he was in his seventies, but his fit appearance defied that. There wasn't an ounce of fat on the man. He was quite handsome—mocha-brown like his sister, with a head full of gray and white hair and a well-trimmed mustache. His smile was wide, revealing sparkling white teeth. His eyes were large and expressive. That appeared to be a Stillwaters trait. Ray liked him immediately.

He and Uncle Gerald didn't get the opportunity to talk at length at their initial meeting. Ray had been dead on his feet. His plan had been to ask the older man how he could get transportation out of town, but the housekeeper had shown him to his room where he showered and lay on the bed for a short nap. When he awakened it was the next day, and nearly noon. Ray washed, dressed, and then made his appearance downstairs. He found Uncle Gerald alone in the house, sitting in the nook of the ultra-modern kitchen.

"Well, here he is!" The older man's booming voice had resonated throughout the room. "Mrs. Owens, my housekeeper, made some gumbo and hot water cornbread that will make you slap your mama. Come join me."

Ray had done just that. In the conversation that followed, he found out that Uncle Gerald was a widower who had retired from the world of finance several years ago. In answer to Ray's inquiry regarding his position in finance, he had casually replied that he had founded Williams Financial. Ray's spoonful of gumbo had nearly slipped from his hand.

"Williams Financial was one of the first investment firms founded by an African-American in this country," he stuttered, unable to keep the awe out of his voice. He had read about the accomplishments of that institution with pride when he was a young man in college. One of the required books for his business course had been authored by this man. Ray could hardly believe that he was sitting across from him eating lunch. The man had made a small fortune for himself and many others until he retired. He was a financial genius.

Gerald nodded, confirming that he was indeed the same man. Then he overlooked the idol worship and went on to ask Ray some questions. "How did you and Dana meet? How long have you known each other?"

Ray was able to field those questions honestly. It was when Gerald asked him how he felt about becoming Dana's third husband that he faltered. *Third husband?* He knew about one of them, but had no idea that there had been another one. It took all of the skills he had acquired as an attorney not to react to that news. He had shrugged indifferently and then stuffed a piece of mouthwatering cornbread into his mouth with the hope that Gerald wouldn't ask any more questions. He was lucky. All he received was a slightly raised brow and then the subject was changed to that of the town of Stillwaters.

"I'm the city manager," he told him. "It's my job to keep everything around here in tip-top shape."

"From what I see you do a great job." Ray meant the compliment. The town was beautiful.

"Thank you. I try, and everybody here does their part. After breakfast I'll show you around and introduce you to some more family. "

Ray decided to wait before raising the question of his departure. He was curious about the others in this unusual family, so he let Gerald Stillwaters drive him around in a bicycle-pedaled surrey, which, along with golf carts, appeared to be a favored form of transportation for residents of the town. Most of what he showed Ray he had seen already with Dana, with a few exceptions. After the tour they had ended up on the front porch of the Come Right Inn. It seemed that Ray's earlier cavalier dismissal regarding his acquaintance with Dana meant that Uncle Gerald had some additional questioning to do. It all appeared to be innocent enough, but Ray knew better.

They talked about Ray's job and about his family before Gerald returned his attention to the Stillwaters clan. It was while he reminisced about family members that the subject of Dana's first husband came up. Both Dana and he had been college students, and it seemed that her family had a specific reason to harbor animosity toward him.

"She did tell you that he beat her?" Gerald asked Ray, as if he was certain that he already knew.

Ray told him the truth. "No, I didn't know." He was beginning to wonder if he knew anything about Dana.

"Well, he did," Uncle Gerald added solemnly. "And Stillwaters family members don't take that from anyone. We are to be respected." His brown eyes bore into Ray's much as Dana's had done yesterday. "Anyone who disrespects us suffers the consequences."

It was a clear warning. *Lambs with the bite of lions.* Perhaps this was the underside that Dana had been trying to tell him about regarding her family.

"What happened to him?" Ray had to know.

Uncle Gerald didn't spare any words. "Let's just say that he's no longer with us."

It sounded ominous to Ray, and he was about to ask for an explanation when their conversation was interrupted by Bev Cameron pulling up to the front porch in a golf cart. Acknowledging her uncle with a nod, it was Ray she addressed.

"I've been sent to get you. It's time to meet Grandy."

"So, Mr. Walker, you want to marry Dana?" Esther Stillwaters got straight to the point.

Ray wasn't surprised. The grand matriarch of the Stillwaters family had turned out to be nothing like he expected. Instead of a bent old woman with a tremulous voice, she looked like a queen on her throne as she sat straight and tall on the wicker chair placed on the screened-in back porch overlooking a magnificent flower garden. Time had treated her well. The age lines were not as prominent as he'd thought they would be at her age, and the brown face, accented by a snow white afro, still held the beauty that must have broken the hearts of many men in her youth. There was no doubt that Esther Stillwaters was formidable. The smile that she had bestowed on Ray when they were introduced had been open, but he sensed no pretense in her. This was a woman who did not tolerate fools.

Ray didn't want to lie to this lady. Instead, in answer to her question, he gave her a noncommittal smile, leaving her to interpret it any way that she wanted. This was Dana's lie. Let her claim it and explain.

Grandy studied the man sitting across from her intently. Seconds ticked by and neither of them spoke. Ray held her eyes steadily, but it wasn't easy. She had some of the most beautiful eyes that he had ever seen, but her gaze was unnerving. Darnell's cousin, Nedra, had those eyes, and so did one other person in the Stillwaters family, his own goddaughter and Grandy's great-great grandchild, Nia. Ray knew from experience that looking into those honey-colored orbs could be hypnotic. It was as if they could see right through him. Considering the position that he found himself in at the present, he didn't want that to happen. Right now he didn't feel too good about himself.

It was just the two of them sitting on the back porch of Grandy's house. Dana, Bev, and their mother had been dismissed. Ray had been invited to enjoy a slice of home-made pound cake and lemonade with the older woman. Both were delicious. If their meeting had been under different circumstances he might have thoroughly enjoyed the visit. But Dana had put him in a difficult position, and he was not comfortable with it. He was glad when Grandy broke the silence, until he heard the next question that she asked.

"What is it about Dana that you like so much, Mr. Wilson?"

"Please call me Ray," he insisted, stalling for time, because at this moment he couldn't think of one good thing to say about his traitorous friend. He hoped that she was inside sweating bullets as hard as he was.

"And you may continue to call me Mrs. Stillwaters," Esther said smoothly. "Once again, what is it about Dana that you like?"

Her smile never wavered. This was one tough lady. Ray was glad that she didn't have him on the witness stand. Or did she?

"Let me see." He paused in thought. "She's smart and she's funny."

At least he'd told the truth about that, but he hated this. He sounded like an owner describing his pet. He didn't like lying. It wasn't his thing. His mother had taught him that a good man was an honest man. Was he no longer a good man?

It looked as though Mrs. Stillwaters was wondering the same thing as she slipped into silence once again and studied him. She seemed to be turning his answer over in her head. They continued to stare each other down, neither one of them backing down. At this point, Ray was too ashamed to look away. He liked this lady and he wanted her to like him.

Much to his relief, the older woman finally broke eye contact as she turned to speak into the intercom on the wall.

"Dana, come out here, please." Her words were not a request.

It didn't take long for Dana to answer her summons. "Yes, Grandy?" She didn't look at Ray, a sure sign of a guilty conscience as far as he was concerned.

Her grandmother motioned for her to sit in the wicker chair next to Ray. Dana sat down, clasping her hands together tightly in her lap. She looked nervous. Good! Now it was her turn to sweat.

Esther resumed her silent act as she gave the couple a thorough perusal. Ray could see from the determined look on Dana's face that she was ready to play out the scenario that she had created to its dramatic conclusion. Ray knew from the legal maneuverings that he had witnessed her make in the past that Dana could be ruthless. But, until now, he had never realized that she would allow such actions to permeate her personal life. Esther broke his train of thought.

"Dana, what do you like about Ray?"

It was the same deceptively simple question that she had asked him. Dana should have kept her answer simple, but she didn't. She started to go on and on about Ray so effusively that he didn't know if she was talking about him or the second coming. It was overkill, and it was embarrassing. By the time that she finished Ray had decided that he would just apologize to Mrs. Stillwaters for his part in this debacle and ask one of the relatives to fly him out of there.

As soon as Dana finished, he braced himself for the denouncement he was sure that Mrs. Stillwaters would be delivering. Instead, with the same ingratiating smile, the woman dismissed Dana and asked her to send Bev out to the porch. The request brought frowns of confusion on the faces of both Dana and Ray, but neither of them asked any questions and Dana did as she was told. The only conclusion that Ray could draw was that perhaps Bev was going to be given the pleasure of escorting Dana and him out of the compound. He was sure that she would be delighted to do so.

After Bev had picked him up at the Inn to transport him to her grandmother's home, he had tried unsuccessfully to make small talk. She was as cold as she always had been toward him, if not worse.

The look on Bev's face when she stepped onto the porch verified that she was as surprised by having been called outside as Dana had been. Esther motioned for her to sit in the chair her sister had occupied. She did so, sitting stiffly erect and not acknowledging Ray's presence.

He tossed her a cursory glance and then returned his attention to Esther as he waited for the axe to fall. He would be glad when it did; then this farce would be at an end and he could go home. But her next words were more startling than her previous ones had been.

"Bev, what is it that you don't like about Ray?"

He chuckled. Esther Stillwaters was his kind of woman. After all of these years of Bev treating him like a leper, he was going to find out why. He turned to her with his brows raised.

"Yes, Bev, what *is* it?"

Bev wanted to slap that smug look off his face. Why would Grandy put *her* on the spot? Hadn't she suspected by now that Ray was here under false pretenses? She had hoped that her grandmother would see right through whatever game Dana was playing and expose her and her so-called fiancé. Her mother had advised her to keep any negativity about her sister and Ray to herself and not to burden Grandy. She had agreed, but she had never expected anything like this.

"Why would you ask me something like that, Grandy?" she asked anxiously.

"Because I'm sort of confused. Yesterday I asked you what kind of man he was, and you said that he was a good man."

Ray's eyebrows shot up. He hadn't thought that Bev would have anything positive to say about him. He was delighted to see her embarrassment and discomfort. Both confirmed for him that what Mrs. Stillwaters said was true. He wanted to hear more.

"What you said at the time made me think that there were things that you admired about Ray, but I can see by your body language that you have some reservations about him. I'd like to know what they are."

Bev knew that this was the perfect opportunity to expose and denounce Dana and Ray, but she had to remember her promise to her mother. She didn't want to get Grandy involved. Whatever drama that Dana had brought to this town would be handled within their immediate family. So she took a deep breath and answered.

"I really do think that he's a good man, Grandy. The two of us have had some issues in the past and I haven't quite let them go . . ."

"Which you should," Grandy urged her.

Bev nodded. "Yes, you're right. He *is* Nia's godfather, and my son-in-law's best friend, which means that he's going to be around for a while." She hoped that sounded conciliatory enough, because that was all the props Ray was getting from her.

Grandy studied Bev again before speaking. "So you're telling me that there's nothing that you don't like about him? He'll make your sister a good husband and you a great brother-in- law?"

Bev couldn't help but bristle. Her acting skills only went so far. "I didn't say all of that. Anyway, why am I being questioned? This is Dana's thing. I've been out here longer than she was." Her resentment about that was clear.

Grandy shrugged. "All right, go on back inside."

Bev did so, obviously happy to comply. Ray was amused.

The porch grew quiet again as Mrs. Stillwaters looked past Ray and out into the yard. She appeared to be deep in thought: Ray didn't disturb her. He was still reeling from the conversation between the elderly woman and Bev. The chances of Bev and he getting together romantically might be nil, but the possibility that they might at least become friends could become a reality.

"Walk with me, Ray." Mrs. Stillwaters held her hand out to him for assistance.

He helped her up from the chair. Hooking her arm through his, they left the porch. As they walked deeper into the yard, Ray began to realize just how beautiful it was. Flowers, plants, and trees abounded. They had been strategically placed to trail the brick walkways that led in several directions. There were fountains, butterflies, and exotic birds flying about. It looked and felt like paradise.

The path that they took led them to the edge of a brook with water so clear that the fish in it could be seen swimming upstream. Esther stopped and rested on a stone bench placed between two trees while Ray stood looking down into the water. Neither had said a word on their leisurely stroll, but Ray knew that there was something on the woman's mind. He waited patiently for her to speak. He didn't have to wait long.

"My late husband William and I used to walk down here together all of the time. It was our favorite spot." She turned to look at Ray. "I don't know why, but you remind me of him. There's something about you that I can't put my finger on." She paused and gave him another one of her securitizing looks, then turned back to gaze out across the water. Ray remained silent, sensing that this was a moment of solitude for them both.

"My William is buried in the cemetery next to the church that's just beyond those trees over there." She nodded in the direction. "I buried my baby son Gardner next to him." She gave a shuddering sigh, and then turned her attention back to Ray. "I want you to go back to the house and tell Bev that I said to take you to the family cemetery and tell you our story. Then will you please tell Dana that I want to see her out here again?"

"Yes, ma'am."

She stuck her hand out. "It was a pleasure meeting you, Ray. We'll talk again."

"Thank you." Ray shook her hand. He had been dismissed. Turning, he headed back toward the house.

CHAPTER 6

Ray followed Bev as she moved from headstone to headstone relating the story of each family member. The remains of both sides of her family rested in the Stillwaters Cemetery.

"Grandy's parents and grandparents are buried in that section over there." Bev nodded toward the north side of the cemetery. "As I've told you, my great-granddaddy's people take up the other spaces. Generations of the Stillwaters and Freedom families rest here, and so will generations more. This is a sacred place, and we honor it as such."

"And well you should." Ray was impressed. "There aren't many African-American families that can trace their heritage as far as you can, let alone come to one place to honor their ancestors."

Bev nodded in agreement. "That's true, and that makes it all the more special."

"What's the entire Stillwaters story?" Ray knew that there was one, and he was curious. "How did this town get here?"

Bev turned to him with questioning eyes. "You mean Dana hasn't told you?" There was condemnation, not curiosity, in her tone.

"No, she hasn't."

Bev studied him just as her grandmother had less than an hour ago. Ray held her eyes. He didn't like what he saw in them—distrust. Still, he was persistent.

"And since she hasn't told me, why don't you?"

"You're supposed to be Dana's fiancé, not mine. Let her tell you, but I will say this. In spite of unbelievable obstacles, everyone resting here has a story of success. If Stillwaters blood runs through your veins, failure is not an option."

When speaking of her family, Bev showed the same sense of pride that Dana had exhibited. That's what made it so difficult to believe that she really thought that a Stillwaters family member might be a murderer.

"Since perfection is a Stillwaters family requirement, I take it that divorce is considered as failure." Ray was teasing about the perfection crack, but he did wonder what her opinion was on the subject of divorce.

"We may not be perfect, but members of the Stillwaters family usually marry well," Bev replied. "There have been very few divorces in our family."

"Except for Dana," he countered. She must have known that he was steering her in that direction. "From what I've heard she's been divorced twice."

Bev lifted a brow. "From what you've heard? You mean you didn't know? Dana didn't tell you? It appears as though you and your *fiancée* don't talk very much."

Ray let his silence answer her question as they continued their stroll. It was peaceful here, and at the moment he needed that peace. He didn't like the turmoil that Dana was creating, and he wanted no part of it. It was time to end this, but not here on hallowed ground.

Bev could sense that he had something on his mind, and it wasn't difficult to guess what it was. She didn't know him that well, but she knew Dana. She was quite familiar with her tactics; whatever truth there was to be told, it wasn't going to come from her. Without a word, she led him from her family's resting place. Getting into the golf cart, they drove away. Bev came to a stop in the middle of the road leading away from the church and cemetery and turned to Ray expectantly. He looked at her. Now was the time to speak.

"I found out that I was engaged to Dana just before we reached Stillwaters. You're going to have to ask her about what's going on."

"You're saying that you don't know the reason she did this?" Bev was still suspicious of him.

Ray wasn't budging. "Like I said, ask Dana."

"And you weren't in on this from the beginning?"

"I'm not repeating myself, Bev. Either you believe me or you don't. I just need a ride out of here so that I can go home." He looked and sounded exhausted.

"All right." Feeling suddenly energized, Bev gave up the questioning. "I can help you with that."

Ray noticed that she seemed to be as relieved as he was that this farce was over. That made him feel better. There was just one more thing.

"I want to say that I'm sorry that I didn't say anything when I first got here. It was never my intention to let this lie continue."

Bev didn't answer. Instead she gave him a sad smile. Ray hadn't seen a smile on her face since—

"Hey, I can't remember the last time I saw that happen." He grinned at her.

Bev ignored him. She wasn't interested in lighthearted conversation with this man. She was just glad that he had come clean, although about what still wasn't clear. Dana held the answer to that, and once again it was time for her to confront her sister.

"I should have known that you would talk Ray into telling you!" Dana's angry eyes flashed.

"Oh, don't be silly!" She couldn't believe this woman. "The man simply didn't want to get caught up in your drama." She and her sister had been arguing for about half an hour and nothing had been resolved. "Dana, you've been playing your silly games since you were a child. Whenever something didn't go your way you'd concoct your little schemes to manipulate things until they pleased you. But you're a grown woman now, and it's time to act like it.

"I know that you're still angry at us about Mitch, but don't start a family feud because of it. Our mother has a chance to head this family after Grandy leaves us. Don't deny her that honor."

Dana gave her sister a disgusted grunt. "I've already told you that I couldn't care less about that. Believe it or not, the world does not revolve around the Stillwaters family." Tired of the discussion, Dana headed toward the bedroom door. Bev was on her heels.

"So if you didn't bring Ray to town to interfere with the family's selection of Grandy's successor, then I'm asking you again, why did you bring him?"

Dana stopped and turned toward her. "You mean Ray didn't tell you? I'm shocked! You got everything else you wanted to know out of him. Not that I should be surprised. I knew that he was weak when it comes to you."

She started to walk out of the door, but Bev moved to block her exit. "What do you mean by that?"

Dana felt a sense of satisfaction at the disquieted look on her sister's face. It wasn't often that she got the upper hand on Bev.

"You're no fool. You know exactly how to play him to get what you want."

"Oh, please. If you thought that, why in the world would you bring him here, especially as your fiancé?" Bev scoffed.

Dana gave a wicked smile. "Don't worry about it. I have my reasons."

The look on Dana's face was malicious, verification of how wide the gulf between the two sisters had become. Saddened by that reality, Bev turned and left the room. This time it was Dana who did the following. She smelled blood as she stalked her sister down the stairway.

"I've suspected for years that Ray had a thing for you. I've noticed his reaction whenever the two of you are in the same room, but I never said anything." They reached the end of the stairs and stood face-to-face. "As a friend I thought that he would show me some loyalty. But I guess that lust trumps friendship. "

Bev was incensed. "And in our case, family."

"Uh-uh. Play stupid all you want, but I came here for some answers and I mean to get them."

"Answers to what, Dana?" Bev was just about through with this foolishness.

"I'll let you know when I get them." She turned and walked through the front door. Ginny appeared in the living room entranceway.

"Are you two at it again?" She looked anxious.

Bev wanted to spare her mother the pain of her sister's deceit. Dana had caused her enough problems. Bev and Ray had agreed that urgent business would be used as the excuse for his leaving town early, and Dana had agreed to go along with their decision. She didn't want to look bad in her mother's eyes. At the moment, Bev just wanted to soothe her mother's concern.

"Don't worry. It's nothing. It's just Dana being Dana."

Those four words should be explanation enough.

"Man, how did you get caught up in this?" Thad Stewart shook his head in disbelief as Ray finished telling him the story of Dana's deceit in getting him into Stillwaters. Ray had called him an hour earlier and asked to be picked up so that they could go somewhere private and talk. They had ended up walking along the bank of

Stillwaters Lake. "And what is it that Dana came home for that's so important that she had to lie to bring you here?"

"I'd rather not say." As he had with Bev, Ray had told Thad everything but Dana's motive. That was her revelation, not his.

"I know one thing. I ought to find the woman and strangle her. Darnell's been sweating the hell out of me trying to find out what you two are up to. She didn't believe for a moment that you two were engaged."

"Who did?" Ray gave a sarcastic laugh. Sweeping his hand over his close-cropped hair in frustration, he flopped down on a nearby picnic table. "Yesterday when I left California I was a happy man . . ."

"And today you've been fronted off in front of Bev." Thad gave a knowing chuckle. "That's what this is about, isn't it?"

"Aw, man, I've been through enough today. Dana's mad at me, Darnell's mad at me and Bev's mad at me, too. She and Dana are probably battling it out somewhere right now. I didn't want to be in the middle of that, so I called you. I just want out of here. Can you help me?"

Thad looked at the pained expression on his friend's face and chuckled. "Yeah, I guess you have been through the wringer. I'll . . ."

The ring of Thad's cell phone interrupted him. He answered it while Ray studied a small fishing boat bobbing on the crystal-clear water while its occupants cast their fishing lines. Thad's voice interrupted Ray's contemplation.

"My man, lady luck is on your side. That was Darnell. Dana told Grandy that you had to leave, and she offered to have someone drive you out of here so that you could catch a plane back to L.A. But you won't be leaving until tomorrow."

"Tomorrow? I want out of here today! What if I pay one of those plane owners to fly me out? There are at least a half dozen airplanes parked out near that strip."

Thad shook his head. "I can tell you right now, I doubt if anybody is flying out of here until they head for home. People came here to relax and have fun. Besides, there's a lot of political maneuvering going on right now in the family and I doubt if you can find anybody who wants to leave. Anyway, buddy, you're in Shangri-La. Nobody in Stillwaters needs your money."

Ray couldn't disagree with that. "And how did Shangri-La get here? How did all of this happen? Why didn't you tell me about this place and about this family? "

Thad raised a brow. "Think about it, Ray. How many old money families welcome the public spotlight?"

Thad was right. Old money was discreet. It was the new rich who craved the spotlight so that everyone would know that they had arrived, especially in Hollywood. Ray saw it all the time.

"Besides, if I had told you that a place like this existed, would you have believed me?"

"Probably not." As Dana had informed him, those people who needed to know did know.

"Brother man, I'm here to tell you that what you're seeing here is another whole level of wealth." Thad took a seat on top of the picnic table, using the bench as a footstool. "I'm not about to blow the benefits I've enjoyed by marrying into the Stillwaters clan, so I keep my mouth shut, and I'm not alone."

Ray could understand that, too. If Darnell was even a small example of the moneymaking expertise of this family, then the possibilities were limitless. Thad had already been a major player in the movie industry as an actor before he married Darnell, but after the two of them combined forces, his star power had soared into the stratosphere. The last two movies that he and Darnell had produced and starred in together had made major money, and that was just the beginning.

Thad had always possessed a great singing voice, but he had never showcased it. Being the consummate musical artist that she was, Darnell had recognized his potential. She had talked him into recording a duet with her, and it had soared to the top of the charts. Overnight he had started an additional career. His already substantial fortune had increased dramatically, and together the couple was one of the wealthiest in the entertainment industry. Thad and Darnell were the "it" couple in Hollywood. Money was pouring in. It appeared that they could do no wrong.

"This place produces winners." Thad lifted his hands to include the whole environment. "Darnell is a product of that. You have noticed that she and I have no problem getting capital for our movie projects?"

"Of course, the two of you are gold-plated. Investors are standing in line."

Thad looked at him steadily. "The major ones don't have to."

Ray's mind raced as he recalled the names of some of the people and entities who had invested in the production company that Darnell and Thad had formed. He didn't recall the name Stillwaters on the list, *but* there was one consistent financial investor—

"The S and F Consortium!" Ray remembered looking the name up online, but there was scant information.

"Family First." Thad remained expressionless.

"No wonder your movies get previewed here," Ray muttered.

"Of course," Thad said. "My wife and I come here for a variety of reasons, but the major one is for our peace of mind. I don't want that spoiled with a lot of publicity. Neither does anybody else here, so discretion is paramount."

Ray pondered his words for a moment. "So you're asking me to keep my mouth shut about this town and what I've seen here."

"That would be the prudent thing to do."

Both men were quiet for a moment, and then Ray asked, "How did all of this start? How did these people accumulate all of this?"

Thad looked at him curiously. "Didn't Dana tell you anything about Stillwaters?"

"Not much."

Thad scratched his head. "So much for communication between friends, but given that you're really not going to become part of the family it makes sense that she would be guarded."

"Oh, so now I can't be privy to any further information about the Stillwaters family unless I marry one of them?" Ray made the statement in jest, but the thought annoyed him.

Thad was amused at Ray's irritation. "Man, there's power and influence in this family that you could not imagine, and I'm not about to challenge it if I don't have to. But I'll tell you this, the Stillwaters family is absolutely fascinating and it's ruled by a remarkable woman."

"Esther Stillwaters."

Thad nodded. "One and the same. From what I've been told Grandy and her husband were kids when they got married. She was only fourteen and William was sixteen. They started having children right away, and, as you probably know by now, they had seven in all.

"Darnell told me that her great-grandfather, William, owned a lumber mill. You see, the members of the Stillwaters family don't work for anybody but themselves or one another."

"How well I know." Ray had found that out when the prenuptial agreement between Thad and Darnell was being negotiated. He had opted out of writing it, since that was not his area of expertise. He had suggested to Darnell that Dana as her attorney might want to do the same. Darnell had told him that she couldn't consider anyone else to do the job other than one of the other attorneys in her family. He had thought nothing of it at the time, but now . . . He listened closely as Thad continued.

"William's father had a successful hauling business. He gave his only son the money to build the mill, and it thrived. He bought this plot of land and built a house for his family."

"The one that Mrs. Stillwaters lives in?" Ray had observed that Esther's house was older than the other ones in town.

"No, that one was built later." Thad's voice faded. His eyes strayed across the lake.

Ray frowned. "So, all of this land, this wealth and power, came as the result of a lumber mill?"

"Something like that." Thad returned his attention to his friend. "Actually, I think you had better ask Dana about the rest of it. This is her family's story. All you need to know right now is that the members of the Stillwaters family are strong, smart, and shrewd, and that their women don't play."

"All of them except Dana," Ray sniffed. "She's playing a little too much for me."

"Stop worrying about it. You'll be out of here tomorrow. Let's get back to the house."

"So that's it? You're really not going to tell me any more about the family?"

"Nope," Thad climbed to the ground and swiped at his clothes. "That's all that you're going to get from me." He drew an imaginary zipper across his mouth.

"That's cold, man." Ray was genuinely disappointed.

Thad threw an arm around his shoulder. "Just chill out and enjoy. There's a dance tonight. Go and have some fun."

As the two of them started back up the trail toward the car, Ray knew that his friend was right. He would be leaving Stillwaters tomorrow, so why worry about Dana and her drama? That he wanted to forget, but when he left town Ray doubted that this place could be as easily dismissed.

CHAPTER 7

Bev watched Dana and Ray boldly as she sat in the banquet room of The Cove Community Center, where the dance that evening was being held. These family conclaves were held yearly, and the social committee for this gathering had planned weeks of activities that would keep everyone entertained. They were meant to help keep the family bonded, but this one was special because of Grandy's centennial birthday celebration. Everyone's spirits were high, except for Bev's. Dana's escapades had her depressed, but she planned to put on a good face for this evening's festivities.

The cover story that had been circulated regarding Ray's coming departure hadn't been questioned by anyone. Every adult in Stillwaters had occupations laden with pressures. They understood business emergencies when they occurred. Until his departure, he was welcomed into the fold and greeted graciously. That's what hurt Bev most about her sister's dishonesty. Family was supposed to trust one another. None of their extended family had doubted Dana, and she had betrayed their trust. It was Bev's hope that no one other than Darnell and she would ever find out that Dana had lied about Ray.

Bev shifted her attention to her sister. She was continuing to play the happy fiancée role, and she wasn't a bad actress. Throughout the evening she stayed by Ray's side, smiling at him and occasionally whispering in his ear. Bev could only imagine what she was saying. Knowing her sister, she suspected that Dana was cursing him out. Despite it all, Ray was playing it cool. Although she really didn't want to admit it, he did look good this evening.

He was dressed casually in a knit shirt that she couldn't help noticing emphasized his biceps, and the finely creased jeans that he wore fit him well. She knew that he worked out. He had done so with Thad. She had never denied that Ray was a nice-looking man. He wasn't the make-your-head-turn handsome like her cousin Nedra's husband Sinclair or the really-cute-with-dimples handsome like Bev's son-in-law. With his dark brown coloring and square-jawed features, she would describe Ray as ruggedly good looking. He had even managed to elicit some flirtatious giggles from a few of her teenage cousins, which he acknowledged politely and dismissed. Despite Dana being upset with him, he appeared to be enjoying himself, and the Stillwaters clan seemed to like him.

Ray's eyes caught Bev's and she quickly looked away. They had been playing this cat and mouse game all evening. He chuckled to himself. This was one evening that he would remember. Simultaneously, he was getting attention from Bev and experiencing the Stillwaters family full force. It was a bit overwhelming.

The grand matriarch of the family wasn't at the dance, but hundreds of her descendents were. Those in attendance ranged in age from their eighties to their teens, and the Stillwaters family proved to be one that partied hard.

Ray's host, Uncle Gerald, was the deejay. Sporting a Kango hat perched backward on his thick shock of hair, he kept the place jumping with a steady mixture of old school soul and hip hop. He was really good at what he was doing and kept everyone fired up. Thad and Darnell pumped the crowd up further when they appeared midway during the festivities and sang their award-winning duets, and then Darnell took the stage alone and sang. As expected, the crowd went wild.

People danced with and without partners and the line dances were endless. Two of the family members that Ray already knew, Nedra Davis-Reasoner and her husband Sinclair, won the salsa contest with moves that put the younger couples to shame. The place was jumping all evening and Ray was enjoying it all, despite Dana's attitude.

She had branded Ray as a "traitor" but she kept up appearances, danced with him occasionally and introduced him to so many esteemed family members that he lost count. There were doctors, lawyers, scientists, artists, and entrepreneurs of every kind. He had read the names of many of those in attendance in some of the most prestigious newspapers and magazines in the nation, unaware that they were related. Each family unit was distinguished by the accomplishments of its members, and as the evening progressed Dana would whisper tidbits of information about each. There was one branch of the family that had ten children. Dana referred to them as

"The Breeders." According to her, nearly half of those in attendance at the dance came from that branch of the family.

One of the highlights of Ray's evening was meeting the architect Armon Casey, who, much to his surprise, turned out to be the brother of fashion kingpin Bo Buchannan.

"Neither one of them use their real names in their businesses," Dana explained. "You'll find a lot of professional names being used among us Stillwaters folks."

She introduced him to other family members. There were more aunts, uncles, and cousins than Ray could count.

Later Dana offered Ray a glimpse into some of the family's political maneuvering that he had heard hinted at when he first arrived.

"My oldest aunt is first in line to head the family after Grandy," Dana told him later. "That would have made her only daughter next, but neither of them wants to do it so some members of our family think that we ought to have a vote on the successor, and of course The Breeders would probably have the largest voting bloc."

"Why can't one of your aunt's sons take over?" Ray wondered.

"Ours is a matriarchal family," Dana replied. "Whoever replaces Grandy will be female."

"Oh, really?" Ray wasn't sure that he liked that idea, but of course his opinion didn't count. "What do the men in this family say about this 'woman must rule' thing?"

Dana looked at him pointedly. “I never asked, but it’s been my recent experience that some men can’t be trusted.”

“Ouch!” Ray said, grabbing his chest in mock pain.

She wasn’t amused. Throwing her napkin down, Dana got up from the table. “Forget you, Ray. I’m going to the ladies’ room.” She stalked across the dance floor, leaving him alone at the table snickering at her retreat.

Bev watched her sister’s exit with interest, noting that she was clearly agitated. She guessed that the strain of keeping up the farce was beginning to get to her. Too bad, but it was Dana’s own fault. She’d get no sympathy from her.

Deciding to call it an evening, Bev was about to leave when her favorite cousin, Gerry, suddenly appeared at her table. Thrilled, she greeted him happily with a kiss and a hug.

Dana’s absence had allowed Ray to resume his eye dodging with Bev. He looked across the room and found her talking with some man. It was clear that their conversation was an intimate one as they laughed and jostled one another fondly. From the look on Bev’s face, this was someone special. For a split second Ray felt a tinge of jealousy, but the feeling was fleeting as he reminded himself that every man, woman, and child in the room was related to one another in some way; except for him, of course. Besides, he had no right to any feelings where Bev was concerned. She wasn’t his woman, and she had made it clear that she did not want to be.

From the day that they had met, Bev had used the fact that she was ten years older as a bridge that was never to be crossed. Now, as he sat watching her, he wondered what she would do if he ventured across that barrier this evening and asked her to dance. After all, this might be his only chance. If she refused, his ego couldn't be any more bruised than it had been in the past, so what the hell! Getting up from the table, he started across the room.

Bev was ecstatic. Gerry was Uncle Gerald's only child. Close in age, she and her cousin had been raised together and loved each other dearly. Business had delayed his being in town any earlier, but he was here now. As they caught up on the news about each other and their loved ones, she noticed movement out of the corner of her eye. Someone was maneuvering through the dancers on the floor. Thinking nothing of it, she continued talking to Gerry until the figure drew closer and stopped in front of her. She looked up. It was Ray.

"Would you like to dance?"

Bev was taken aback. In the years since they'd known each other and the many events that they both had attended, separately, they had barely said ten words to each other. She and Ray didn't dance. They avoided each other. That's what they did! What was wrong with him wanting to dance with her, and why now? Why here?

Ray wanted to laugh out loud at the look on Bev's face. If he had proposed marriage she couldn't have looked more shocked.

The man standing beside her looked from one to the other, wondering what was going on. Ray was grinning as though he were the cat who had swallowed the proverbial canary. Bev looked as though she *was* that canary. The man thrust his hand out toward Ray.

"Hi, I'm Gerald Stillwaters, Jr. They call me Gerry. I know everybody else in this place, so you must be the houseguest my father told me about."

"One and the same. I'm Ray Wilson." He and Gerry shook hands. "And your father is great, and a cool disc jockey, too."

Gerry flashed a grin that looked just like his father's. "That's him, all right. He's one hell of a guy."

An awkward silence followed as the three of them stood looking at each other expectantly. Ray took control.

"Excuse us. I'd like to dance with your cousin." He turned to Bev.

"Go for it," Gerry urged.

Bev stuttered, "Uh, no, no . . ."

Ray grabbed Bev firmly by the hand. She resisted.

"I . . . I was about to go home." She gave Gerry a look that silently pleaded for his intervention. He only shrugged.

Ray kept walking, all but dragging her behind him as he ignored her protest. When he swung around to face her, Bev was standing as stiff as a board.

"I . . . I don't think this is a good idea," she told him above the pulsating music.

"What?" Ray feigned deafness as he took her into his arms and prepared to move to the beat. Bev was still resistant.

"I can't dance with you." She tried to pull away.

Ray wouldn't allow it. "What?" He cupped his free hand behind his ear as if he couldn't hear her. "Did you say that you can't dance?"

"No, I said . . ."

"Is that because you never learned or that you're too old?"

Bev's eyes grew as large as saucers and her face turned as hard as granite. "What? I bet that I can dance you off the floor!"

She proceeded to be as good as her word as the long version of Marvin Gaye's "Give It Up" took its toll on dancers young and old. By the song's end, Ray and Bev were one of a half dozen couples left standing, and Ray was sweating as though he had run a marathon. Bev was exhausted, but she didn't want him to know it. Thank goodness, the music finally stopped.

"I'm ready for another go at this," she crowed as a haggard Ray started to leave the dance floor.

"Oh really?" He didn't believe her for a minute, but he was ready to call her bluff.

"Yeah, really," Bev replied with bravado, silently praying that the turntable would break. No such luck, but it was a slow song. Aretha Franklin's "Call Me" filled the room.

Bev groaned. She regretted having opened her big mouth as Ray took her into his arms. He kept a respectful distance between them, but to her he was still too close. His cologne tickled her nostrils. He smelled good, and dancing with him felt a little too good. She began to feel embarrassed and wasn't sure if it was because of the warmth that was spreading though her body or her perception that everybody was watching them. Over Ray's shoulder, Bev shot a glance at Dana, who had returned to the table. She sat staring daggers at them while Bev tried to retain her self control.

Ray could sense her uneasiness. He could also feel her body heat. He was trying to control his own body. The smell and feel of her was turning him on. He didn't want to embarrass either one of them, especially in front of her family, who—from his observation—could not have cared less about what was happening with them on the dance floor. But it was obvious that Bev was concerned because she was back to her board-stiff posture. That was a sure sign that she didn't want to enjoy the dance with him.

The song was a short one. For different reasons both Ray and Bev were grateful. He thanked her politely. She responded courteously and they retreated to separate corners of the room. The dance was over, or so they thought.

A car came for Ray at seven o'clock the next morning. It was the white Rolls-Royce that he had seen the day that he arrived in town. The young man driving introduced himself as William Stillwaters IV. Ray said his goodbyes to Uncle Gerald and to his son and started to climb into the front seat of the car. The young man opened the back door and directed him there instead.

Ray obeyed and was surprised to come face to face with Esther Stillwaters.

"Good morning, Ray." Her manner was pleasant as she watched him settle into the plush seat next to her. "Don't be alarmed. I'm not leaving town with you. My great-grandson will be dropping me off at The Cove. But I wanted to see you before you left and tell you how much I enjoyed meeting you."

"The same here, ma'am," he said, and he meant it. "You are a fascinating lady with an amazing family."

"Thank you. We're not perfect, but we are loving and respectful toward one another. That's something that I insist on. It's my greatest wish that this will continue after I'm gone."

"Which won't be for a long time, I hope." Ray took her hand in his and squeezed it fondly.

She chuckled. "I'm ninety-nine, Ray. Only God knows how long I have, but I plan on enjoying every second that he gives me. Meanwhile, I'm sorry that you won't be here for my birthday bash. I hope that the business that's taking you away from us will be settled satisfactorily—*all* of your business."

Esther looked at him pointedly, just as she had yesterday, and once again Ray had the feeling that she knew what had happened with Dana, even though Bev and her sister had informed him that neither she nor their mother had been told.

They arrived at The Cove. The driver jumped out of the car and opened the back door. Esther turned to Ray.

"Goodbye, son." Her smile was effervescent.

"Goodbye, Mrs. Stillwaters." He returned the smile. "And thank you for your kindness."

Her great-grandson helped her exit the car. The door was closed behind her, but as Esther started toward The Cove, she turned back and tapped on the car window. Ray lowered it.

"I just wanted to tell you that Bev's bark is worse than her bite. Don't let her scare you off." She winked at him. "And I'll see you when you come back." She turned and walked away, tossing over her shoulder, "And I'm sure that you *will* be back." She disappeared inside.

Ray was still sitting in a stunned stupor when the driver returned to take him through the gates and out of the town of Stillwaters.

The evening of Grandy's birthday party, Bev parked her golf cart in The Cove's parking lot and was getting out of the vehicle when Dana pulled up in her rental car. The two women had tried to avoid each other since their spat days ago. That hadn't been possible. Only yesterday they had engaged in yet another heated discussion at their mother's house. Thankfully, Ginny had not been home that time, but a lot of truth had been revealed.

"Nothing that I do is ever good enough for this family!" Dana had barked as they stood toe-to-toe in the living room. "I've always had to come second to you. I graduated from college cum laude. You graduated magna cum laude, despite being a widow with a young child to raise. In your teens you marry the love of your life, and then you become the tragic young widow and get sympathy ever after. I get married and divorced, then married and divorced *again* and I get criticized and the shaft!"

Bev hadn't been surprised by her words. Even their mother knew that the root of Dana's problems was jealousy of her older sister, no matter how misplaced. All of her life Dana had been living in her shadow and trying to play catch-up. Bev couldn't say for certain that she wouldn't feel the same if their places had been reversed. Yet the depths of her sister's feelings were disturbing and detrimental. She wanted reconciliation and had tried to offer some advice.

"You have to live your own life, Dana, and be satisfied."

Although her words had fallen on deaf ears, Bev thought about them as she stood waiting to speak to her sister. It was hurting their mother to see them continuously at odds with each other. It had to stop.

Bev noticed Dana hesitate when she saw her waiting, but she couldn't sit in her car forever. Bev wasn't about to move. Finally, Dana exited the car, but she tried to ignore Bev and walk past her and toward the building. Bev fell in step beside her.

"Have you heard from Ray since he left?" It might have been the wrong question to ask, but at the moment Bev could think of nothing else to say.

"Since you seem to be his confidante, I'm surprised he hasn't called you." Dana kept walking, and so did Bev.

"I know that we've said a lot of unpleasant things to each other while we've been here, but I'd like bygones to be bygones. We're sisters, Dana. Mama and Daddy always told us that we're all that each other has."

Dana opened one of the double glass doors to The Cove before turning to face Bev.

"You're wrong. You have the Stillwaters family, and you love it and all that it stands for. As for me, I find it hard to be part of a perfect family, especially since *I'm* not perfect." Brushing her sister aside, she entered the building.

With a sigh of resignation, Bev followed her. Dana was so stubborn. Unfortunately, it was a character trait that ran in the family. It seemed to come with the territory.

Grandy's hundredth birthday bash turned out to be a rousing success. Generations of the Stillwaters family filled The Cove gymnasium, which had been turned into party central. The decorations were beautiful, the food was delicious, and the tributes were unending. Love for the great lady herself flowed freely. Esther Freedom Stillwaters was queen for the day. There were tears and laughter as the history of the rambunctious Freedom and Stillwaters families was recounted by the senior members of the family, but, in the end, it was Grandy who ruled the evening.

As savvy at one century old as she had been as a young woman when she first laid the foundation for her family's economic ascension, she eliminated any possibility of infighting by using the celebratory gathering to name her daughter, Ginny, as her successor as the head of the family. There would be no democratic vote. The matriarch had spoken.

Bev's cheeks were wet with tears of pride for her mother. The family's greatest honor had been bestowed on Ginny, and there was no dissension regarding it. Family unity prevailed.

As Bev stood beside her mother on the podium, reveling in the standing ovation that Ginny was receiving, she thanked God that her sister was here to share this moment. A glance at Dana revealed that, despite her sister's attempt to remain stoic, her pride in Ginny's accomplishment appeared to be as immense as her own.

Grandy raised her hand for silence and the audience grew still. She looked out over the generations that she had helped spawn and invited them to join her in a toast.

The elderly woman's voice was strong and clear. "It took blood, sweat, and tears to get us this far. Faith, love, and determination will keep us here." She raised her glass high, and every member of the Stillwaters clan followed suit as she said the words that would continue to take them forward: "Family First." Her words were echoed throughout the room.

As Bev sipped from her glass, it was her hope that those words would one day hold special meaning for Dana and her. Only time would tell.

CHAPTER 8

Ray had been back in L.A. for a week. Since he was supposed to be on vacation, he avoided going to his office and had gone to his house in Tiburon. He had bought the property from Thad after he and his wife had decided to reside on the Peninsula. Ray had always liked the place and enjoyed spending time there. However, when he arrived at the house where he expected to spend the rest of his vacation, he discovered that he had termites. A tent had to be placed over the house, and he found himself back in his house in L.A. Determined to enjoy his dwindling days of freedom, he drove to Santa Barbara for a few days of relaxation and spent a day on Catalina Island and the rest of his time on the golf course, all the while thinking about the time that he had spent in Stillwaters.

It was a fascinating place filled with fascinating people, especially Esther Stillwaters. She was an extraordinary woman, so full of wisdom, but he questioned what she had said to him about Bev. There was a ten year chasm between them that she was afraid to breach, and he still wasn't sure that she had forgiven him for coming to Stillwaters. As for Dana, he wasn't sure whether they were still friends. Her childish antics were not to his liking. The woman was delusional if she thought that someone from her illustrious family would jeopardize all that they had acquired for—what? The answer still wasn't clear. He hoped that she would drop her witch hunt and eventually accept Mitch's death as a suicide.

It was the day before Ray was to return to work that Dana called him. He was loading his golf clubs into the trunk of his car when his cell phone rang. He guessed that this call from her meant that he was forgiven.

"Well, hello there." There was a smile in his voice. Despite her quirks, he did care about Dana and was glad to hear from her.

"Hello." Dana's tone was brisk. "I'm back from Stillwaters."

"And?" Ray was amused. From the tone of her voice he guessed that he *wasn't* forgiven. "And I've found something." Dana's voice rose with excitement.

The smile went out of Ray's voice. "You're kidding!"

"No, I'm not. I want to show it to you and see what you think about it."

Ray didn't like the sound of that. "You're scaring me, Dana. This isn't another one of your lies, is it?" Their already precarious friendship was in serious jeopardy if it was.

"No, Ray. I swear to you that this is no lie. What I've found is very serious, and right now you're the only one that I can turn to. You're the only one that I can trust."

Ray thought that he heard a hint of fear in her voice. "Do you want me to drive to the Valley?" Dana owned a condo in the San Fernando Valley.

"No, I'll come to you. Expect me around six this evening." She disconnected.

Ray stood beside his car with the cell phone still in his hand. What was happening? What could Dana have possibly uncovered that would have frightened her? Was there really a murderer in her family?

Putting his cell phone away, he started the car and headed toward home, anxious about his upcoming visit with Dana and what it would bring. However, it was a visit that was not to be.

It was five thirty-five in the evening when the telephone in his home rang. He had been dozing and it awakened him. Groggily, he groped for the receiver, expecting it to be Dana informing him that she might be late. She usually was.

"Hello."

"Yeah, is this Ray Wilson?" The voice on the other end was male and hoarse from years of smoking.

"Yes, it is." Who was this? He didn't recognize the voice.

"This is Officer Alexander from the San Fernando Valley Police Department. Mr. Wilson, do you know Dana Mansfield? We found your telephone number in her cell phone as the last number called."

Ray was fully awake now. "Yes, she's a friend of mine. What's wrong?"

"I'm sorry to have to tell you this, Mr. Wilson, but Mrs. Mansfield has been in a serious accident. She's been taken to Cedars-Sinai hospital in LA."

Bev tried to appear calm as she hurried down the hospital corridor to her sister's room. Darnell had called her earlier this morning about Dana. It was Bev who broke the news to her mother. Eight hours later they were in L.A. Instead of going home to Chicago, Bev had remained in Stillwaters after Grandy's birthday celebration. After all of the excitement of the previous week she found that she needed the down time in the quiet hamlet to unwind. Dana had left town without the issues between them having been resolved, but Bev had vowed that she would not give up on her effort to get closer to her sister. The telephone call that she had received from her daughter could mean that she might never get a chance.

Darnell had been in tears when she called. Ray had given the authorities her telephone number. According to what she had been told by the police, Dana had fallen down the stairs in her home and hit her head. Her housekeeper had found her unconscious.

Uncle Gerald was a licensed pilot, and he had flown Bev and Ginny to L.A. in the family's private plane. Ginny was on the telephone from the moment that she was told about Dana to the minute that they landed in Los Angeles. There were doctors from a variety of disciplines in the family and she called them all, gathering all of the information that she could to see that her daughter got the best of care.

When they arrived at the hospital, Dana was in critical condition and in a coma. While her mother conversed with the doctor, Bev stood at her sister's bedside regretting all that had recently occurred between them.

That seemed to be how it was in life. Regrets move to the forefront when disaster strikes. As she looked at her sister lying there, she prayed that God would give her another chance to remedy the mistakes that they both had made in their relationship with each other.

As the tears flowed, Bev felt her mother's comforting arms around her.

"The doctor said that she has a lesion close to her brain, and they'll have to operate," she said softly.

"When?" Bev's heart sank like a stone. She didn't like what she was hearing.

"Later this evening, and as a professional courtesy I've asked to be an observer."

"Do you think that's a good idea?" She was concerned about the toll that being in the operating room might have on her mother. Yet in spite of that, she felt relieved that she would be there.

"Yes, I think that it's the best idea. The operation is delicate, but I've got confidence in Dr. Owens. I know his reputation and he's one of the best, but my child will be in that operating room and I will be trusting him with her life. I plan on being in there to remind him of that."

Bev nodded, but as a mother she knew the conflict of emotions that her mother had to be feeling. She hugged her tightly, offering her love, solidarity, and support.

Ray had just pushed the down button on the elevator when an urgent request from the hospital corridor drifted through the closing doors asking that he hold the elevator. He reacted, pushing the open button in time for the voice to appear and step smoothly into the elevator. It was Bev Cameron. For a second they both reeled in surprise from the sudden encounter.

"Thank you." Bev's words were polite but curt. Turning her back to Ray, she started to push the button to the floor that she wanted. It was already lit. The doors closed. The two of them were the only occupants in the elevator. Leaning back against its interior, Ray waited to see what she would do.

He had been aware that Bev and Ginny would be arriving today and he had tried to wait for them on Dana's floor, but having spent most of the night at the hospital, he had decided to take a break and was heading for the cafeteria. How he had missed their arrival he wasn't sure, but he did know that Bev wouldn't continue to ignore him. No matter how awkward their last parting might have been, Bev was gracious. He was right. She turned to face him.

"I want to thank you for being kind enough to call my daughter about Dana."

Ray accepted her gratitude with a nod, but said nothing. There was an awkward silence.

Bev cleared her throat. "Uh, Darnell said that she and Thad might be flying down." Once again, her words were met with silence. "Nia has the sniffles and she wants to make sure that she's okay before they travel."

Ray nodded again. Bev glanced up at the elevator lights to see how far they had descended. It wasn't very far and there had been no stops. How she wished for just one. This elevator ride was becoming uncomfortable, and Ray wasn't helping.

Bev jabbed the down button harder. What was wrong with the thing? Nothing could be this slow. Once again, she tried to fill the silence.

"Did the doctor tell you that Dana has a lesion close to her brain?"

Ray uttered one word. "No."

"The doctor will be operating this evening."

"I hope that she'll be okay."

"Thank you." She was grateful for his consideration and that he had finally spoken more than one word.

The tension that Bev was feeling confined in this small space with Ray was unbearable, but he didn't appear bothered at all as he leaned casually against the elevator's back wall. She didn't like the feeling of unease that she was experiencing. It made her feel out of control. It had always been much easier dealing with him as someone that she disliked. She felt justified, rationalizing that he had given her reason. He had helped Thad with the legal fight against her daughter and then he'd had the gall to openly flirt with her. That had been the only excuse that she needed, and over the years she had been comfortable giving him the cold shoulder, but now that seemed trivial. Ray had displayed integrity when he was in Stillwaters. That had made an impression on her, and she wasn't the only one. Grandy had been nearly effusive in her praise of him. She had encouraged Bev to get to know him better . . . for Dana's sake, of course.

Bev hadn't made any promises. At the time she didn't know when she would see Ray again. But here he was, big as life, and all she wanted was to escape him.

Much to her relief, the elevator doors opened. She stepped out. Ray was right behind her. She whirled on him.

"Are you following me?"

"Relax," he countered smoothly. "I'm going to the cafeteria." He nodded in that direction.

Bev felt about two feet tall. "So am I." Too embarrassed to say more, she continued walking.

Ray decided to save the day. Stepping up his pace, he fell in beside her. "Then we can eat together."

Bev searched for an excuse to decline. "I've got to order a sandwich and drink for my mother and take it up to her."

Ray shrugged. "No problem. Get what she likes and have it sent upstairs to her."

Bev sighed. Unable to come up with another excuse, she relented. "Okay."

It turned out that dining with him was a good decision. Ray was pleasant company. He kept up a steady stream of conversation as he told her about his Detroit childhood as the only child of a widowed mother who worked as a nurse.

"I was always in trouble at school," Ray recalled. "I had a big mouth and didn't know when to shut up. My mother practically lived at the school, and I stayed on punishment. But when I was in fifth grade she finally got fed up. She did a drive-by."

"A drive-by?" Bev looked perplexed. "Was she in a gang?"

Ray had a hearty laugh. "No, I mean that she came by the school unexpectedly one day. She stood outside the door and peeked into the classroom through the glass to see what I was up to. That day I was acting a complete fool."

"What did she do?" Bev leaned forward, her dark eyes shining in anticipation.

"The door opened. She stepped into the classroom and quietly asked the teacher if she could see me for a minute."

"Were you surprised?"

"Yes, but her manner was so mild that I didn't think that I was in trouble. So, I bounce up to follow her outside and when we get in the hallway she snatches me up by the collar and jams me against the wall."

"Whoa!" Bev could visualize the entire scene.

"I'm telling you that the woman swept me off my feet in one swoop." He demonstrated with a brush of his hand. "Then this magic shoe appears. I call it that because I swear it came off her foot so fast that I didn't see it. All I know is that she proceeded to give me the worse spanking that I ever had in my life. That woman spanked me up and down that hallway like I had stolen something. She told me that if I ran she would kill me."

"I bet you took her threat seriously."

"You bet I did. I was the entertainment for the whole second floor that day. I was whooping and hollering, begging and pleading, promising and swearing to her that I wouldn't ever be bad again. People were coming out of their classrooms wondering what was happening."

"What did the teachers do while all of this was happening?"

"They were cheering her on. Of course the kids thought it was hilarious. I had raised hell in that school since kindergarten and everybody figured that I was getting what I deserved. Mr. Carter, the gym teacher, even offered my mother his shoe. He said that the one she had wasn't big enough."

Bev scoffed. "Nobody called the police?"

"Are you kidding? If parents had been jailed for spanking their kids in those days half of Detroit would have been in jail. I'm just glad that she only used a shoe as her weapon of choice."

Bev wiped tears of mirth from her eyes. "I know that I shouldn't enjoy that, but it was funny. What happened after that?"

"You're looking at a reformed man. It only took one drive-by for me to straighten up. After that I became a model student. I went from C's and D's on my report card to A's. I graduated at the top of my high school class and earned a scholarship to college. From there I went on to law school, where I put my gift for gab to work."

"Is your mother still in Detroit?"

Ray shook his head. "No, she retired last year when she turned sixty-two and moved to Arizona. No more snowy winters for her."

"Hmmm." Bev looked thoughtful. "Your mother is only ten years older than me."

Ray understood what her words implied. "And she's twenty years older than me. That seems to be a decent interval between mother and child. It's not likely that a ten-year-old could be my mother."

Bev understood what he was implying, too. She looked him in the eye.

"Nothing is impossible."

Bracing his arms on the table, Ray leaned forward. "You're right about that."

They held each other's gaze, each daring the other to retreat first. Neither one did. Ray decided to change the tone of the conversation.

"What about you?" He sat back in his chair, still holding her eyes. "I heard that you were quite a rebel when you were young."

"What do you mean?" She looked at him over the cup of tea she was drinking. "I was a model student all through high school."

"According to Dana, it was right after high school that you rebelled—ran away and got married. She said that had been done in your family only once before."

Bev broke eye contact then. Draining her cup, she sat it down on the table before answering. She didn't appreciate her sister talking about her personal business.

"It seems that Dana had a lot to say." She didn't try to disguise her displeasure.

Ray kept it simple. "Yes, she did."

He knew some of the story about Bev and Colton Cameron, and he was willing to listen to anything else she might want to share. He watched as her hand went to a gold chain around her neck and absently played with it.

"Some things need to remain private." Bev looked at him hard. "Don't you think?"

Ray agreed with an almost undetectable nod, but by saying little she had told him what he suspected. Bev Cameron was a woman who loved hard, and that was how she had loved her husband. He had died young and was still perfect in her memory. So was the love that they shared. The question that he needed answered was whether she was willing to open herself up to the possibilities of what she could have with someone else.

His cell phone vibrated. Withdrawing it from his pocket, he checked the screen.

"It's your son-in-law." He answered the call.

"We're in L.A.," Thad told him. "I'm having the limo driver take us to your place. Where are you?"

"I'm still at the hospital. Bev is sitting here with me. Her mother is with Dana."

Ray and Thad talked about the possibility of Darnell and him coming to the hospital.

Ray had already made arrangements with the administrative staff to have the superstar couple snuck into the facility through a back entrance. A private waiting room had been reserved for them and for Dana's other relatives. Darnell wanted to speak with her mother. Ray handed Bev his cell phone. Pleasantries and information were exchanged. They disconnected and Bev handed the phone back to Ray.

"I'd better go upstairs and see how Dana is doing." Bev got up from the table.

Ray followed suit. "I'll go with you."

As they made their way to the bank of elevators, Bev slowed his stride with a touch on his arm.

"Darnell told me how you made all of those arrangements for our family's privacy, and I want to tell you how much it's appreciated."

"Thank you." Ray was pleased by the compliment. Progress was being made.

When they reached the elevators it was clear that this time they wouldn't be going upstairs alone. A group of people was waiting to ride. Yet it didn't matter to either of them as they squeezed inside the crowded cubicle and stood side by side. It was a different trip this time.

CHAPTER 9

Other members of the Stillwaters family had arrived at Cedars-Sinai hospital. Joining Bev in the private waiting room as they awaited the results of Dana's surgery were Thad, Darnell, Uncle Gerald, and his son, Gerry. Ginny and one of her nephews, who was a respected neurosurgeon, were observing the operation. Grandy and a host of other relatives were checking in by telephone and text message. At times the waiting room looked like Grand Central Station with people coming and going. Due to their celebrity status, Thad and Darnell were confined to the room, but there was plenty of communication between them and their cousin Nedra. Their baby daughter was still recovering from the sniffles, and they had left her with the Reasoner family.

Bev thanked God this and every other day for her family and their support. She didn't know what she would do without them. She prayed hard that Dana would pull through this experience and that the two of them would be given a second chance to bond. She also sent up another prayer of thanks for someone else whose presence was proving to be invaluable—Ray Wilson.

She watched him as he sat talking to Thad. He appeared to be as comfortable among the Stillwaters family as if he were one of them. It was clear that everyone in the room liked him, and why not? He was affable, considerate, and kind. Not only had he acquired the room for the benefit of Thad and Darnell and arranged transportation to the hospital for everyone there, but he had ordered a sumptuous buffet that had been set up for their convenience. Earlier, before Dana's operation began, he had greeted Ginny and offered her comfort. Ginny and Ray had huddled together for some time talking like old friends, but Bev was not included in their conversation.

Her cousin Gerry had taken an instant liking to Ray, just as his father had done. They made plans at some point to meet at Pebble Beach Golf Course for a few rounds of golf. Bev had to admit that the more that she was around Ray the more she found to like about him. It was becoming difficult to recall the negatives that she had amassed against him over the years.

It was eleven o'clock in the evening when the doctor came to the family with the results of Dana's operation. What they were told turned out to be encouraging. It had gone well. Dana was in recovery. As requested, Ginny was being allowed to stay at the hospital with her daughter. Everyone else was advised to leave.

Gerry had business in San Diego, and his father was flying him down there. Bev wanted to stay with Ginny, but her mother insisted that she leave, get some rest, and come back tomorrow. Bev didn't argue and was preparing to leave when she realized that she had made no arrangements for a place to stay. Thad and Darnell no longer owned a home in L.A. She turned to her cousins.

"Where are you two staying?"

"With me." Ray stepped forward. "I don't live far from here."

"Oh." Bev's brow furrowed. "Okay, so I'll call one of the Come Right Inns and have them send a car for me."

"For what?" Ginny interrupted the conversation. "Isn't she staying with you?" Looking baffled, Ginny turned to Ray.

"That was the plan," he answered.

The furrows between Bev's eyes deepened. "What plan?"

"Ours," Ginny and Ray spoke simultaneously.

"Ray invited us to stay at his place," Ginny continued, unaffected by the look of shock on Bev's face.

"I've got four bedrooms," Ray added a little too quickly.

Bev wasn't happy. How dare they determine where she was going to sleep tonight, and without even consulting her! The rest of the conversation was a blur as alarm bells began ringing in her head. Every instinct that she possessed told her not to accept Ray's invitation. Yet how could she do so without looking foolish, especially when her own mother had contributed to the *planning?*

Everyone was tired, including her. If she insisted on staying at her family's establishment she would have to wait for transportation, and she knew that someone in the family would insist on waiting with her or take the time and effort to drive her there. It was simpler to accept his hospitality.

Ray drove ahead to his home to ready it for his guests. Bev rode with Darnell and Thad. By the time they arrived at Ray's beautiful glass home high above Los Angeles, Bev was exhausted. She vaguely remembered being shown to her room, taking a shower, and slipping into bed. The last thing that she did recall thinking was that the bed into which she had so gratefully crawled belonged to Ray.

Bev was still battling the remnants of exhaustion when she awakened the next morning. Between the flight to L.A. and Dana's operation, yesterday had been among the longest days in her life. As she snuggled between the soft, cotton sheets she was reluctant to leave her cozy bed. She peeked at the clock on the nightstand. It was ten o'clock. How she wished that she were back in Stillwaters, where peace and tranquility had reigned. Here in L.A., not only did she have to deal with Dana being ill, but she also knew that she would have to deal with the feelings that she was aware that Ray still held for her. That was a dilemma that she would rather not face.

For over thirty years she had been content with the memory of having loved only one man—Colton Cameron. Their love affair had been a young girl's dream come true. After his death, she had poured all of the love that she'd felt for him into their daughter and held onto her dream of the past. Over the years there had been other men in her life, but none that she took seriously.

They had failed to awaken that special something within her heart that her husband had aroused, but she had begun to realize that with Ray she was beginning to feel a stirring of something familiar. That's why she kept her distance. It bothered her. It frightened her.

Bev sat up in the bed. Her heart escalated at the very thought of how her world would change if her dream was threatened. She couldn't let that happen. If she took a chance and opened her heart to any possibility with Ray, then—

Her mind went blank. Then what? Would her insulated world come to an end? Not likely. She would survive. That was a tempting thought, and one that might be worth exploring.

Ray was standing in the kitchen at the burner in the center island when Bev breezed in with her cell phone pressed to her ear. She nodded an acknowledgement as Ray mouthed a "good morning."

He watched her surreptitiously as she continued talking. As usual, she looked good. Dressed in stylish designer jeans that hugged the curves of her shapely body and a starched white shirt accented with several strands of gold chains, she wore soft leather sandals on her feet. Ray noticed that her toenails were polished a deep, wine red that matched the polish on her manicured nails. He liked that. As he moved around the kitchen he caught snatches of her telephone conversation.

"Mama, I doubt if Dana will need a nightgown for a while so . . ." She looked frustrated as she paced the length of the kitchen. "But . . . but . . ."

As Ray scooped the fluffy eggs that he had scrambled into a dish, he noticed Bev deflate. Whatever Ginny was saying on the other end, her daughter had relented.

"All right, I'll see if Darnell knows where it is. If so, then I'll go." She disconnected and slipped the phone into her pocket.

Ray picked up on her distress. "Is everything okay?" He moved to the kitchen nook and put the dish of eggs on the table.

"Yes." Bev wandered to the table and took a seat. "It's just that my mother can be so difficult at times." She ran her hand across her short hair. "Is Darnell still here?"

Ray walked to the refrigerator to retrieve a pitcher of freshly squeezed orange juice. "No, she and Thad ate earlier and left. They're going to her music studio and then on to the hospital."

"Oh." Bev sounded disappointed as she pressed speed dial on her cell phone. There was a pause as she waited for her daughter to answer. "Hi, baby. Are you somewhere that you can talk?"

As Ray moved the other breakfast foods to the table, he heard her ask Darnell if she knew where she could get a key to Dana's house. The answer must have been in the affirmative as Bev explained the reason for the inquiry.

"Mama wants me to go there and get her nightgown, robe, and slippers."

Darnell must have made some comment, because whatever was said Bev heartily agreed. They said their farewells and Bev slouched in her chair. She looked resigned.

"Are you ready to eat?" Ray placed the last bowl on the table and took a seat opposite her.

She looked up at him as if noting his presence for the first time. Her eyes shifted to the food spread out before her. "What's this?"

Ray indicated the bounty. "It's breakfast. I was waiting until you came down." He began to fill his plate. "Eat."

She obeyed, spearing a fork into a slice of bacon on the platter and putting it on her plate. "Where's your housekeeper? I'd like to thank her for cooking all of this."

"I don't have one. A cleaning service and a gardener are the only help I have around here. You're looking at the chief cook and bottle washer."

Bev looked taken aback. "My, aren't you full of surprises."

Ray grinned. "I try to be, but actually my mother taught me to take care of myself." With a comical wiggle of his brows he popped a spoonful of eggs into his mouth. "Hmmm, good, just like Mama used to make."

Bev shook her head at his antics. "Nut." She dug into her food with relish.

Ray couldn't deny the pleasure he felt at her being here in his home. In his wildest dreams he'd never thought that this would happen, and she seemed so comfortable. She had barely reacted when she was told that they were here alone, and he wanted to please her.

"I heard you talking to Darnell about going to Dana's house to get some things for her."

"Yes." Bev cut into her bacon daintily. "She told me that Dana hides a key outside of her house and that will get me in. What's the name of the car service you use? I've got to call and have one sent to take me there."

"I'll take you." Ray kept eating.

"No, you don't have to do that." She was touched by his thoughtfulness. "You've done enough—the phone call, the waiting room, the limos to the hospital, even opening your own house to us. I can't let you do one more thing. I'll call a service . . ."

"I said that I'll take you."

Bev knew by the finality in his voice that further resistance was not an option. She didn't argue.

"All right, but I'll pay for the gas."

The look that he gave her said that wasn't going to happen. He resumed eating.

From across the table, Bev studied Ray. She hadn't been wrong when she described him to Grandy as a good man. The more she got to know him the warmer her feelings toward him grew. He had gone out of his way to accommodate everyone in her family and for that she was grateful, but, like old habits, old suspicions die hard.

"Why are you doing all of this for us?" She grabbed a slice of toast and began buttering it. "I know that you and Dana were out of sorts when you left town. Do you feel guilty about what happened in Stillwaters? Is that why you're doing so much? Or is it because of your relationship with Thad and Darnell?"

"It's pretty simple. I'm just a nice guy." Reaching across the table he took Bev's empty dishes, stacked them on top of his, and got up from the table. Then he looked down at her. "And I want to impress you." He walked away.

Bev took a bite of her toast. If she hadn't asked he wouldn't have answered. She bet that she would keep her mouth shut from now on.

CHAPTER 10

The drive to Dana's condo was a quiet one. Bev didn't want to hear another one of Ray's declarations. She hadn't decided how to handle the last one. What was so unnerving was how unaffected he seemed to be about it. Ray had simply continued doing what he was doing. He cleaned up the kitchen, grabbed his car keys, and they headed for the Valley. Bev didn't quite know how she wanted to handle the situation, and there was an air of anticipation in the car. It was clear that each of them expected the other to say something, but when Bev did break the silence she was sure that what she said wasn't exactly what he had expected to hear.

"After you left town, some of the family told me that Dana was going around asking people about the last times they were in L.A. They thought that she was trying to see if anybody came to town and didn't contact her."

"Oh, really?" Ray was noncommittal. He was glad that she had broken the impasse between them, but he had an idea where the conversation was heading.

"I thought that it was kind of strange." Bev slid a sideward glance his way, but Ray kept his eyes on the road. She continued, "I asked her what was going on and she told me that when she found out I'd be the first to know." She paused and looked out the window. "That was the last thing that she said to me."

Ray heard the question that lay beneath the surface of Bev's words. He wasn't one for subtleties.

"Don't beat around the bush with me, Bev. You still want to know why Dana came home, and like I said to you before, that was for her to tell you, not me."

Bev wasn't offended by his straightforwardness. She liked it. He wasn't a man to play games.

"You're right, and what I'm hearing you say indirectly is that it won't benefit me to know. Correct?"

Ray shook his head. "I don't think it will."

Bev understood. Her sister was fighting for her life. It was the present that mattered, not the past. She let the matter drop, for now.

Dana's two story condo was located on a cul-de-sac in a complex of one hundred stucco buildings which all looked alike—painted yellow with red tile roofs. Shrubbery was planted on either side of every entrance. The only thing distinguishing each structure was the address. Ray pulled into the driveway of 4468 Lion Road. He got out of the car and opened Bev's door. Exiting, she looked around the deserted streets cautiously before bending down next to the shrubbery and digging in the dirt. A second later she rose with a key in her hand.

Ray followed her up the stairs and she let them inside. The interior of Dana's house was dark and cool. The air conditioner was running and the vertical blinds at the floor-to-ceiling windows in the living room were drawn. Bev pulled them open and sunshine flooded the room, revealing expensive furnishing placed carefully by someone with an eye for decorating.

As Bev went up the stairway to her sister's bedroom, Ray waited in the living room with her on his mind. He sure hoped that her comfort level with him continued because he was really into this graceful, intelligent woman. Bev was very special. He respected her and he wanted—no, he needed—a woman like that in his life.

Ray started to walk to the window to look out when a glint from something on the floor caught his eye. He bent to retrieve the item. It was a diamond earring, heart shaped and very expensive. Dana had certainly been careless. He wondered if she had even missed it.

He turned to head upstairs to give the earring to Bev so that she could put it with Dana's other jewelry when an agonizing yelp from above had him taking the stairs two at a time. There at the top he found Bev sprawled on the floor, an open briefcase at her feet. Papers from its interior were scattered about.

"Are you all right?" He bent to examine the sandal-clad foot that she was holding.

"No, it hurts," Bev confessed from between clenched teeth. "That briefcase was sitting at the top of the stairs and I tripped over it. No wonder Dana fell down the . . . Heeey!"

Bev squealed as Ray swept her up into his arms. "What are you doing?" She was mortified. "Put me down!"

Ray ignored her. "Where's the bedroom?"

"The bedroom?" Bev croaked. "What do you want the bedroom for?" At the moment she could think of only one reason. Thankfully Ray's mind wasn't in the same place.

"I need to put you on something softer than the floor so that I can get a closer look at that foot."

A few steps took him into Dana's bedroom. Bev was stiff as a board. She wasn't comfortable, and neither was he. The fragrance she wore was different from the one she'd worn the night that they danced together, but it was just as lethal. He felt a sense of relief when he deposited her on the bed. So did Bev.

Being in Ray's arms made her aware of the chemistry between them. She was happy to be released.

Ray exhaled sharply in order to gather himself as he gently took Bev's sandal off. He began to feel her foot for broken bones and examine it for bruises.

"It feels much better now," Bev lied as his probing intensified the heat spreading throughout her body.

"Really?" Ray pressed on the area near her ankle. She winced. He looked at her. "Uh-uh."

"I didn't break anything," she retorted, wishing that he would just leave her alone. "I'm okay."

Ray rose and looked down at her. Her mouth was set. Her arms were crossed. She didn't look pleased at all.

"I'll tell you what. You relax here for a while, and if you don't mind I'm going to get that briefcase you tripped over and put it in the car."

"Why?" Bev's interest seemed minimal as she massaged her ankle.

"I noticed the initials on the top. The case belonged to Mitch, and I'd like to go through some of the legal papers in it." Ray tried to sound nonchalant.

Bev shrugged. "It's okay, I don't think Dana would mind."

Ray stepped into the hallway and gathered the papers on the floor. He stuffed them into the leather case, closed it, and headed downstairs. He would go through Mitch's papers and see if he could find a clue as to what Dana's last words to him might mean.

When he returned upstairs he found Bev on her feet. It was apparent that she was in pain.

"What are you doing?"

Bev jumped, startled by Ray's unexpected reappearance. She had been determined to be mobile before his return. She didn't want him picking her up again.

"I can walk," she insisted as she tried to limp slowly across the room. She didn't get far before Ray swept her up into his arms a second time.

"Raaaay!" Bev kicked her feet in protest. "Put me down!"

"Noooo," Ray mocked her as he carried her downstairs and toward the door. She had opened her mouth to continue her protest when he covered it with his mouth. Bev tried to resist, but the kiss deepened. Her eyelids fluttered shut. The heat within intensified and her world began to whirl. Then it all came to a screeching halt. The kiss ended. Ray drew back. Bev's eyes popped open.

"I guess that'll shut you up." Shifting her in his arms, Ray continued walking.

Bev sat in the chair beside her sister's bed, having taken her mother's place keeping vigil. Dana's condition hadn't changed. By the time Ray and she had reached the hospital her foot felt much better and she was able to walk with the slightest hint of a limp. On the way, she and Ray hadn't discussed the kiss. He seemed to sense that she didn't want to do so, and he was right. Bev rarely acted impulsively. She liked to think things through. Ray impressed her as a man who did the same, because there had been nothing impetuous about the kiss between them. It had been slow and deliberate, and it told her in no uncertain terms that he cared.

Ray was good people. There was no doubt about that. Her family members couldn't say enough good things about him, but her daughter still confessed to having reservations about his complicity in coming to Stillwaters with Dana. However, she had admitted to Bev that she was glad that he had finally come clean.

"Mama."

Bev looked up to see her daughter entering the room. Thad was beside her.

"We're about to head out now. The limo is here to take us to the airport."

Bev rose from her chair and gave her a kiss and a hug. Darnell and Thad were off to Virginia, where they were to begin production on a new film.

"What about Nia?" Bev had wanted to keep her granddaughter while they were on location, but Dana's accident had changed her plan.

"Nedra and Sin are bringing her to us on their way to New York City. That way we won't have to go and get her," Darnell informed her.

"I wish that we could delay filming," Thad said, sounding regretful, "but . . ."

"No, no." Bev kissed him on the cheek. "You two go on. I'll keep you updated on Dana's condition."

With a final farewell to both Bev and Dana, the couple started out of the room. Darnell stopped suddenly and, digging into her purse, returned to her mother.

"I forgot. Dana had a cell phone in her jacket when the police found her at the house . . ."

"The police?" That was the first that Bev had heard about the authorities being involved. "I thought that her cleaning lady found her."

"She did, but when I talked to her she said that she had called the police first because Dana's front door was cracked open . . ."

"I didn't know that." Bev sat up, interested in this new information. "Why would her door be open?"

"That's what the cleaning lady wondered. She said that she knocked, but when Dana didn't answer she thought that the place was being robbed. That's why she called the police. After they arrived she went in and identified Dana."

"Maybe she was on her way out, forgot something, and went back upstairs."

"Who knows? Anyway, the hospital gave Grandma the cell phone, along with her other possessions, and she gave it to me to hold."

She withdrew it from her purse and handed it to Bev. "Dana's secretary came by this morning. She said that Dana's clients and friends have been calling the office for her. She needs to know what to tell people. I told her to keep telling everyone that she's unavailable and leave it at that."

"That sounds good." Bev pocketed the phone.

"Come on, babe," Thad urged his wife from the open doorway. "We've got a plane to catch."

Darnell looked at her mother guiltily. "I'm sorry that I won't be here to help you through this."

Bev waved her away. "You're a phone call away. When you get there don't forget to call me."

Darnell and Thad closed the door behind them, leaving Bev alone with Dana. Getting up, she went to her sister's bedside. If it hadn't been for the array of tubes and beeping gadgets, Dana would look as though she were sleeping peacefully. Bev caressed her sister's hair.

"Ray Wilson kissed me."

It was the first time that she had said the words out loud. Sadly, it was a confidence that she doubted she would have shared with Dana if she had been conscious. Yet who else could she have told? It seemed to be such a little thing compared to what Dana was facing, and she wasn't about to worry her mother with something so trivial. Darnell had business to attend to and was still suspicious of Ray. When they were growing up she had always shared her crushes with her cousin Gerry. He had been the one to spot the losers, and sometimes he chased them away. For some reason he hadn't liked Colton. They had argued about it, and when she eloped he had been devastated. She and Gerry hadn't reconciled until after her husband's death.

Over the years she had been sparing in sharing information about her love life with anyone, including Gerry, but she had a feeling that the family members who knew Ray would be delighted to hear about his kiss. Or would they? After all, he had supposedly been engaged to her sister.

"I don't know what I'm going to do about my attraction to him" she told Dana. "But that man does know how to kiss."

"That's nice, you're talking to her."

Bev jumped, having been unaware that someone else was present in the room. She smiled weakly at the nurse, wondering how much she had overheard. As the woman bustled around the room attending to Dana, she cheerfully informed Bev of the benefits of communicating with comatose patients.

"You would be surprised how much they seem to hear," she said before leaving the room.

Bev wasn't sure if she wanted Dana to remember any of her breathless confession.

Settling back in the chair, she prepared to enjoy the quiet that had returned after the chattering nurse's departure. Opening her purse to retrieve her glasses so that she could read a magazine, she discovered the two books that she had slipped inside when Ray and she had gone to Dana's condo. In the excitement over her bruised foot and Ray's kiss, she had forgotten that she had the address book that had been lying on top of Dana's nightstand. She had found the journal in her underwear drawer. It had been Bev's plan to use the address book to contact Dana's friends just in case—

Dismissing that negative thought, she opened the journal. As invasive as it might be to her sister, she wanted to get to know Dana as she'd never known her before. Right or wrong, she was going to read her journal. Whatever happened, she didn't want her little sister to be a stranger to her ever again.

CHAPTER 11

Ray had taken Ginny home to get some rest and had drifted off to sleep himself. He was sleeping peacefully when his cell phone rang. Groping for it on the nightstand, he answered groggily. A strident voice startled him fully awake.

"How dare you be a part of this?" The voice on the other end was hoarse with rage. He recognized the caller as Bev.

"What are you talking about?" He dragged himself to a sitting position in his bed.

"I'm talking about you knowing that Dana thought that somebody in our family killed Mitch, that's what!"

Ray's mind grasped what she was saying. "Is Dana awake?" He didn't want to confirm or deny Bev's words until he found out how she knew.

"No, she's not." Bev was pacing on the sidewalk outside the hospital. The anger she felt was consuming her. She couldn't stand still. Her cousin had taken her place in Dana's room while she went outside and called Ray. "I found her journal when we were at her house and I brought it with me to the hospital. It's all in here." She shook the journal she was holding toward the sky as if she wanted God to strike it from her hand. "Including the fact that she told you. Are you telling me that you didn't know?"

"You said that it's all in there, why would I deny it?" Ray was glad that she knew. He felt a sense of relief.

"You could have told me." Bev's tone expressed her disappointment.

"I told you that was your sister's place," Ray said firmly.

Bev started to protest, but she knew that he was right. If she had known, she would have confronted Dana and the breach between the two of them would have widened. He had recognized that.

The journal had spelled out how Dana had duped him into accompanying her home, hoping that he would play detective along with her. It also railed against his refusal to cooperate once he discovered what she was up to. Ray came out smelling like a rose, and here she was angry at him because he'd done the right thing. She knew that wasn't the real reason for her call, and he challenged her on it.

"Why did you call me, Bev?"

The wind left her sails. Finding an empty bench, Bev sought refuge on its metal surface.

"How could she think that, Ray?" There were unshed tears in her voice. "How in the world could she even form a thought like that about anybody in her own family?"

Ray heard her pain and confusion. "Mitch committed suicide, and she won't accept that. I think that it's as simple as that."

"If you say so." Bev felt defeated. She was too tired to argue and too hurt to talk any longer. "I'll talk to you later."

She disconnected and slumped on the bench. That was where Ray found her a short while later when he arrived at the hospital. If she was surprised to see him it didn't show. She looked up at him with sad, swollen red eyes.

Without a word, he sat down on the bench next to her, put his arm around her shoulders and drew her to him. Bev didn't resist. She needed comfort. Her soul was in distress. She laid her head on his shoulder.

"How she must hate us." Bev's voice was raw with emotion. "How little she must think of us."

"Actually, I think that she's proud of being a member of your family," Ray whispered into her hair.

"She's got a strange way of showing it!" Bev pulled back and looked at him. "Do you know who we are? What we've achieved? Nobody in our family is a killer! We're about building up, not tearing down. It was the hatred of others who were hell-bent on destruction that led to the death of Grandpa William."

"What do you mean?"

Bev released herself from the comfort of his arms and got to her feet. She resumed pacing. The story of her grandparents was a Stillwaters family legend. It was part of the foundation upon which their family had survived and thrived.

"I don't think that you've ever seen a picture of my Grandpa William, have you?"

"No, I haven't."

"Grandy keeps a picture of him on the nightstand beside her bed. If you ever got the opportunity to see that picture, you couldn't help noticing that my grandfather was very fair. My great-great-grandmother was fathered by her master. Grandpa William looked like her. He was light enough to pass for white. Anyway, Grandpa William's father gave him the money to open a business . . ."

"I know," Ray interrupted. "Grandy told me that her husband owned a mill, and that he was quite successful. She said that he bought a plot of land where Stillwaters is now and built a house for his family."

Bev observed him with raised eyebrows. It seemed that Grandy had told him a lot. That came as a surprise. Her grandmother was rarely open with people she didn't know.

"Yes, that's right. Grandpa lived in the town south of Stillwaters for nearly a year building his business, and the townspeople thought that he was white."

"I assume that he didn't tell them any different."

"No. We have always been a family that lets people think what they want. He had the house built for his family on the land that our family's town is on now, and Grandy and their kids moved there. They didn't socialize or have anything to do with people in the area. They lived quietly and kept to themselves, and they lived far enough from town that they could do that peacefully, for a while. That is, until the folks in town found out that Grandpa was *colored.* That's what people called black folks back then."

Bev sat back down on the bench next to Ray. She didn't like recalling this part of the family history, but it was essential. "By that time Grandpa was making money left and right. Ironically, a lot of the men who participated in what eventually happened, worked for him in the mill. But that didn't matter. Hatred and jealousy have no boundaries.

"A group of them caught Grandpa William coming home from work one evening. They beat him so badly that he couldn't even crawl, and they dumped his bloody body outside of Grandy's house and stood there laughing, waiting for her to come out and get him. I guess she was supposed to be scared. But the blood of Maroons flowed through her veins and she had a surprise for them. Grandy didn't come out of that front door empty-handed."

Ray chuckled. He had no doubt that Esther Stillwaters took care of business. She was a formidable woman, but as Bev continued he discovered just how strong she was.

"The shotgun Grandy was carrying was long, and it was loaded, and she was mad. Her belly was swollen with *three* babies, but she stood there and told those . . . those *dogs* to get off their property or she would kill them. She took dead aim at the leader of that mob and blew the hat off of his head to make her point."

"Did they get the message?"

Bev nodded. "They got it, but Grandy knew that they would be coming back and that they had better get out of town before they did. But Grandpa wasn't in any shape to be moved. So there Grandy was, pregnant, and she had four stair-step babies and an injured husband depending on her. She had to make some difficult decisions. She couldn't move Grandpa by herself, so she made the choice to stay and fight if she was forced to."

"Stay?" That surprised Ray, although he could understand Esther's dilemma.

"Grandy stood guard all night with that gun in her hand while she nursed Grandpa and took care of Uncle William, who was a baby. She put Aunt Sarah, who was six years old then, and her younger sisters on a bareback horse and sent them alone to ride the twenty miles through the night to get to the Stillwaters and the Freedoms so that they could come help her."

"And the girls made it."

"But not before the mob burned the mill to the ground, and then came for Grandy and Grandpa."

Ray was on the edge of his seat. "How did they escape?"

"If it hadn't been for some black people who worked at the mill, they never would have gotten away. The mob came to the house and burned it down. Meanwhile, Grandy and Grandpa had to be snuck out of town, hiding in the false bottom of a wagon like the slaves our people had never been. Grandpa William had to be drugged so that he wouldn't cry out. The journey proved too much for Grandpa's broken body. By the time they reached their people Grandpa was dead."

Bev stopped to gather her emotions. Her grandparents' story always affected her.

"That's heartbreaking." Ray took her hand and squeezed it in empathy.

"Oh, there's more. The stress of what she had been through caused Grandy to go into premature labor. She gave birth to her three babies the day after Grandpa died, but they were tiny and had to struggle to survive. Only two made it. Uncle Gardner died. So Grandy buried her husband and child, then she swore on each of their graves that no matter what it took, she would take them back to the land that my Grandpa had bought for his family and place them where they belonged. She did just that."

Bev finished the story with a satisfied sigh. "These are the people we came from. There are no murders among us, and I'm going to prove it."

"And how are you planning on doing that?" Ray was almost reluctant to ask.

"By proving to Dana that Mitch committed suicide."

"That's already in black and white in the coroner's report," Ray assured her. "I don't know if you knew this, but Mitch had prostate cancer."

"No, I didn't." Bev hadn't been privy to his medical condition. "But what I'll do is get his autopsy report and go over it with a fine-toothed comb, gathering all of the information that I can to verify the original ruling." Bev straightened up rejuvenated. "Did Mitch leave a suicide note?"

"No, but even if he had Dana was so obsessed that she wouldn't have believed it anyway."

"She will when I get through." Bev's melancholy had disappeared. She got up from the bench. "I've got to get back upstairs. Gerry took my place in Dana's room and I've been gone much longer than I told him that I would be. He and Uncle Gerald said that they'll sit with her tomorrow so that Mama can get some more rest.

Meanwhile, I'm going to call the car service and have it take me back to Dana's house to see if I can find some more of her journals."

Ray stood up and faced her. "I don't think that she's going to like you invading her privacy."

Bev was dismissive. "So she can sue me. If she can disgrace our branch of the family with her scandalous accusations, then I can invade her privacy."

Ray was still resistant, especially as he recalled his last conversation with Dana. "What if she found evidence that it wasn't a suicide, but that it really was a homicide?"

Bev looked incredulous. "How could she? The proof is on record, and I'm going to make sure that she knows it."

Ray sighed in resignation. "You don't have to get the service to take you to her house. I'll drive you."

"You've done enough." Bev smiled up at him. "Besides, don't you have to go back to work?"

"I'm like the Stillwaters family," Ray said and stood up. "I own my own. I can do anything that I want. What time do you want me to pick you up tomorrow?"

"Ten should be fine."

"Okay, I'll be here. First, I'll take you back to my place to get some rest . . ."

"But . . . ," Bev started to protest. Ray pressed a silencing finger to her lips.

"I'll take you to Dana's place *after* you get some sleep."

Bev took a soldier's stance and saluted. "Yes, sir!"

Ray laughed. "So you're a comedienne now?"

Bev walked up to him until their bodies were flush. She took his chin in her hand and gave him a kiss that was long and slow. She broke it, then backed away.

"No, I'm the woman who wants to thank you for coming to be with her," she whispered.

Stunned, Ray could only look at her. Long after she had disappeared through the hospital doors, he still stood rooted, unable to move.

CHAPTER 12

The early morning sun awakened Bev from her slumber. Sleeping in the chair wasn't the most comfortable place she could think of, but if her mother could do it, so could she. Stretching the kinks out of her body she glanced over at Dana and was greeted with only the beeps of the hospital equipment. There was no movement in the bed. She would never verbalize it, and she felt guilty even thinking it, but Bev was glad. Last night she was so angry at her sister that she'd wanted to harm her. That feeling had vanished as the evening passed. At this moment she felt only sadness and disappointment.

She and Dana had been raised by their parents to have pride in themselves and in their family. Yet it seemed that Dana's love for a man superseded everything else in her life, even reality. Bev had loved a man like that. The members of the Stillwaters family did love hard, and she knew that love could make you do foolish things, but in Dana's case what she was claiming was pure insanity.

Getting to her feet, she started across the room to check the hallway for a nurse, but the ring of a telephone surprised her. She glanced at the silent phone by Dana's bed. A second ring helped her trace the source of the sound. It was coming from her jacket pocket.

She withdrew the cell phone, remembering that it belonged to her sister. She had used it last night to call Ray.

"Hello?" she spoke softly.

"Dana?" The voice was small and uncertain.

"No, this is her sister, Bev. Who's calling?"

"Uh, this is Renee Ingram, I'm a friend of hers . . ."

"Let me call you back, Miss Ingram. I can't talk now." Bev disconnected without explanation and pocketed the cell phone just as the nurse came into the room.

After getting an update on Dana's condition, she asked her cousin Gerry to take her place and went outside to return Renee's call.

"Hello, Miss Ingram . . ."

"Mrs. Ingram." The woman was firm about the correction.

"Sorry, Mrs. Ingram, this is Beverly Cameron, Dana's sister. I just spoke to you."

"Yes, I've called and left messages for Dana at her house, her office, and on her cell, but I haven't heard from her. Is something wrong?"

"There's been an accident." Bev sat down on the same bench she had occupied last night. "My sister is in the hospital."

"Oh, no! Is she all right?"

"I'm afraid that her condition is serious. She's in a coma."

"Is she expected to recover?"

Bev felt the weight of that question on her heart. "We pray that she will."

She looked up and saw her mother walking toward her. Ray followed.

"Which hospital is she in?" asked Mrs. Ingram. "I'd like to send some flowers."

Bev told her and said a hurried goodbye just as Ginny and Ray reached her.

"How is she this morning?" Ginny asked, greeting her daughter with a hug.

Bev looked at her mother. Her face was drawn and the sparkle that she was used to seeing in her eyes was not there. "She's about the same, but look at you. Why didn't you get more rest? We've got it covered here. Gerry is with her now. Uncle Gerald said that the two of them would sit with her today."

"I tried to tell her that," Ray interjected. His concern was evident.

"Thank you, Ray, but as I told you, that's my child in that hospital bed, and if God hears my prayers I plan on being beside her when she wakes up." Ginny addressed Bev. "What would you do if it was Darnell?"

Bev didn't answer. She didn't have to.

Ginny kissed her on the cheek. "I'll talk to you later." She waved goodbye to them both and headed into the hospital.

Ray joined her on the bench. "I'm beginning to think of this as our meeting place."

Bev gave him the smallest hint of a smile. He could see the signs of fatigue around her eyes. "Let's get you back to the house so that you can rest. You can't convince

Ginny to do something that you won't do." Standing, he held out his hand to her.

Taking Ray's hand, Bev walked with him to his car. She fell into the passenger seat listlessly. She was tired and she was depressed. The brief ride to Ray's house was a quiet one.

Bev was glad. She didn't feel like talking. Relaxing on the headrest, she closed her eyes, appreciating Ray's understanding her need for solitude. He was quite a man. That was her last thought as she drifted off to sleep.

Bev awakened to the shadows of the early evening creeping between the closed vertical blinds of the bedroom suite that she occupied in Ray's house. Turning, she peered at the clock. It was late. The illuminated numbers read 5:00 p.m.

She rolled on her back, trying to remember how she'd gotten into bed. But it wasn't a difficult question to answer. Ray. He had taken her shoes and most of her jewelry off. The chains that she wore had been carefully placed on the table next to the bed, except for one—the one holding the ring. It was still around her neck.

Bev gave a contented sigh. She had known Ray for all of these years and truly regretted having wasted them not really getting to know him. Her perception had been based solely on her speculation of the kind of person that she thought him to be. When she first met him, he had been pushy and bold about his attraction to her, and his boldness had been her excuse to reject him, that and his age. Now she was running out of excuses. They no longer had the potency they once had, especially the age factor. Ray was no youngster, and time after time he kept proving how much of a man he was.

Of course she really didn't have time for a man in her life right now. There were family obligations to consider. The last gathering had all but assured her of becoming the leader of the Stillwaters clan one day. She was Ginny's eldest daughter. That made the line of succession in her favor. Until that time, Bev would be assisting her mother whenever she needed her. She had even considered giving up Freedom Financial Services, her investment consulting business in Chicago, and moving to Stillwaters as a permanent resident. There was nothing to stop her.

She was a self-employed businesswoman who had invested her money wisely, profited from those investments, and was now wealthy enough to wield power that few women in America enjoyed. If she wanted, she could retire early and live as she pleased for the rest of her life, which if her family was any indication, would be a long, long time. That was what she was considering when she'd had a house built in Stillwaters. Ray was a product of large cities. He wouldn't want to live in a small town.

Bev sat straight up, jolted by that thought. Where had that come from? What was she thinking? She'd gone from rejecting the man to thinking about living with him? They had shared two kisses, the meaning of which neither of them had discussed. That certainly didn't lay the foundation for a relationship. She and Ray were simply developing a friendship, nothing more.

Flipping the covers back, Bev bounced out of the bed, grabbed some clothing from her suitcase, and headed for the shower. It was time to get back to real life.

In his downstairs office Ray went through the papers in Mitch's briefcase. There was nothing unusual that he could find. Settling back in his swivel chair, he pushed the case aside on his desk. He had been hoping that something in it would give him a clue as to what Dana was referring to when he last spoke to her.

Just how much had Dana loved that man? Was it enough for her to be delusional about his death and its cause? Had it affected her mentally? Hell! Did love drive you crazy? The thought wasn't all that outrageous. He remembered when he was in college and had fallen in love with the woman who was now his ex-wife. He had been twenty and she nineteen, and they'd thought that they couldn't live without each other. They married too soon and fell out of love quickly. It had been a mistake from the beginning, but they were crazy in love and hadn't known that love could be destructive until it was too late. Yet over the years Ray had observed relationships that looked as though they would last a lifetime. The marriage between Thad and Darnell was one of those.

When his best friend fell in love with the talented songbird and got married, all of the wild nights and wilder women that Thad and he had enjoyed together had fallen by the wayside. The relationship between the two men had undergone a change. His friend had found the love of his life in Darnell Cameron. She had become his life. Every thought he had was about her, every plan he made revolved around her. His boy was completely gone. There wasn't much that Darnell asked of Thad that he would deny her, and she was as much in love with him as he was with her. Yeah, theirs was a crazy love, but it wasn't insane. He was beginning to think that the latter might have been the case when it came to Dana and Mitch.

The two of them hadn't even known each other that long before they were planning to get married, and if he was counting correctly, they would have had six spouses between them if they had tied the knot. Even though their engagement had lasted for years, Ray's guess was that the marriage wouldn't have lasted six months. He really wished that Dana hadn't dragged him into this. If it wasn't for Bev he would forget the whole thing.

Bev. Putting his hands behind his head, he leaned back and visualized her lovely face—the chiseled cheekbones that gave her such an exotic appearance, and those flashing, dark eyes that were so expressive. If there was a woman who could entice the crazy love out of him, she would be the one. He hadn't felt like this about a woman since—he thought hard and couldn't think of anyone who had ever made him feel this way. The signs that she was warming up to him were plentiful. All he needed was to be patient.

As if he had willed it, Bev appeared at his office door. Dressed in an ankle-length sundress, she looked casually chic. Everything about her was perfect, from the dangling gold earrings to her painted toenails. Her vibrant smile brightened his day.

"I didn't know that you wore those." Leaning against the door frame she nodded at the stylish eye glasses perched on his face.

Ray removed them. "They're for reading."

"So are mine." Bev pushed away from the door frame and entered. "You didn't have to take them off. You look sort of distinguished."

"Do you mean older?" It was time to lay all of his cards on the table.

"I take it that you bringing that up means that we've got something to talk about."

Bev took a seat on a leather sofa opposite his desk.

Moving across the room, Ray sat down next to her. "Yes, I think that there is a little something that we might discuss."

Bev shifted her body to face him. "Like when you kissed me?"

Ray hadn't meant to discuss that yet. "No, like when you kissed *me.*"

"Did you like it?" Bev wiggled her eyebrows.

Her reply surprised him. "So the sophisticated Mrs. Cameron has jokes. Now tell me something else about yourself that I don't know."

Bev's tone turned serious. "I've loved one man as long as I can remember and I don't think that I'll ever love another one as much as I did him."

Ray didn't like the sound of that. "Does that mean that there's no place for another man in your life at all?"

Bev shook her head. "No, I've dated over the years, but nothing serious."

"And?"

"And I want you to know where I stand. I like you a lot, Ray . . ."

"A lot, in spite of my age?" He looked into the depths of her eyes.

Bev didn't waver. "An awful lot, and I haven't said those words to any man in a long time."

"I'm glad to hear that."

"But we both have to remember that after Dana gets better and all of this is over . . ."

"*This* what?"

Bev smirked. "I see that you're a man who hears what he wants to hear."

Ray nodded. "Not always, but right now it's suiting my purpose."

"Then the *this* that I'm referring to is the attraction that's developed between us, this flirting thing . . ."

Ray laughed. "That's one way of putting it."

"However you want to put it, it's going to have to come to an end eventually. After all, I live in Chicago and you live in L.A., and that can prove to be difficult."

Ray took her hand in his and entwined their fingers. "Oh, I don't know about that. People have long-distance relationships all of the time. Planes fly, plus we have a personal connection."

"Darnell and Thad."

"Actually, I was thinking of Nia, your granddaughter and my godchild. That's a lifetime connection as far as I'm concerned."

Bev liked what he was saying, but she had to remain focused. "I know that we'll see each other occasionally, just as we have over the years, but . . ."

"I plan on seeing you more than occasionally." He brought her hand to his lips. "I want a relationship with you, not a few quickies in passing. You mean more to me than that." He ran a gentle finger down her cheek. "I'm a forty-three-year-old man, divorced . . ."

"I didn't know that."

"Yep, married at twenty, divorced at twenty-two, and I have no children."

"Do you want kids?" That wasn't an option for her. Her child-bearing days were over.

"Not particularly," Ray said honestly. "The kids that I mentor are good enough for me. But I do want you." He traced the contours of her mouth. "The first time that I saw you I knew that, and my feelings have only grown deeper and stronger the better that I get to know you."

Bev could hardly breathe. His words were overwhelming. Sitting back, she gave herself a moment to think before replying. Ray Wilson could make quite a difference in her life. Would she be foolish not to explore the possibility? Yet . . .

Ray watched as she fingered the ring on one of the gold chains around her neck. He wondered what she was thinking. Couldn't she see that they could be good together?

"There are a lot of excuses I can give you why this might not work."

"I think you've exhausted them all." He gave her a crooked grin. "Don't let the past hold you prisoner, Bev." He drew her to him. "Give the present a chance."

His mouth took possession of hers, and Bev opened to let him in. This kiss was different than the first one that they had shared. It wasn't tentative. It wasn't searching for the answers to her desires. It was confident and meant to inflame. Ray's heart was in this kiss, but just as Bev started to respond he drew away.

"Your body isn't the only thing that I want," he breathed hotly against her ear. "It's your heart I want, and I won't settle for anything less."

CHAPTER 13

"We're not sex-starved teenagers. We need to take our time with this." Ray tried to concentrate on the highway leading to Dana's house as he and Bev discussed the evolving relationship between them.

Bev was pleased with what he was saying. "I'm glad that you think like that. In this day and age when you meet one minute then you're in bed with each other the next, I wasn't sure what you expected."

"Translated, I'm younger so you thought that I'd think differently about sex."

"You're perceptive. I like your style."

Ray merged easily onto a connecting highway. "We've got to be honest with each other, Bev, or we won't work, and with that in mind I want to ask you something."

Bev shifted in her seat to give him her full attention. "What is it?"

"It's about Darnell. What do you think she'll say about us getting together?"

"Well, she is still ticked off about you coming to Stillwaters with Dana."

"I know that."

"But she's a realist, and she knows better than to meddle in my business. I'm the mama."

They both laughed at the latter statement.

"I don't have to tell you how Thad will feel about us." Ray eased onto the exit leading to their destination.

"He'll probably throw a party." Bev chuckled. Her son-in-law had been one of Ray's staunchest advocates in his friend's efforts to attract Bev's attention.

"That's true, but what about the rest of your family? After all, they think that Dana and I are together."

"Not any longer," Bev informed him. "Your creative friend—who happens to be my dishonest sister—took care of that before she left town. Don't tell me that you didn't know that the two of you broke up? That's what she told everybody."

"Everybody but me," Ray sneered sarcastically.

"But you look like a saint to my family being there for Dana and being of such help to all of us in spite of *the break up*."

"I'm glad to hear it. Does that mean that you and I can start a relationship without me getting lynched by the town folk?"

"I guessssss." Bev giggled like a schoolgirl. God! She felt good. She really liked this man.

Ray turned into Dana's complex. "You do know that your Grandy scoped us out as getting together a while ago, don't you?" Ray's eyes twinkled as he recalled the farewell that the older woman gave him when he left Stillwaters. "She's a wise woman."

"And a remarkable one, too." Nothing surprised her when it came to Grandy. Bev looked away from Ray for a second to glance out the front windshield. She shifted forward in her seat with concern as she noticed the rotating lights from a police cruiser ahead of them. "What's all of this?"

"I don't know." Ray slowed the car, preparing to stop. "But it looks like they're at Dana's house."

After getting out of the car and approaching the police officers, Bev and Ray were told there had been an attempted burglary at her sister's house. The cleaning service had discovered that a window pane had been broken in the French doors leading to the ground floor patio and the door had been left ajar. Her Uncle Gerald and cousin Gerry, who were staying in Dana's condo, had been in the house only long enough to put their bags down. A call to them at the hospital revealed that whatever of value each of them might have brought they had with them. Their luggage appeared to be untouched.

Bev and Ray conducted a cursory walk-through and informed the officers that they could find nothing disturbed or missing. After their departure Bev and Ray searched the place again and confirmed their original assessment. They agreed with the officers' theory that the cleaning service might have scared the burglar away.

While Bev moved toward the walk-in closet in her sister's bedroom, preparing to search through it for more journals, Ray leaned against the doorway and watched her.

"I can't understand why the alarm wasn't set," he wondered aloud.

"Nobody knows the code." Bev started taking shoe boxes down from the shelves. "One of the cleaning people told me that even they didn't have the code. Dana would just disengage the alarm on the days they were scheduled to come."

Ray thought back to the first time that he and Bev had come to Dana's condo. There had been no alarm set that day, either. "You'd think she'd be more cautious," he mumbled, mostly to himself. Intent on achieving her goal, Bev wasn't listening. He sighed.

"I'm going downstairs to wait for the people to come and install the new glass."

Bev barely noticed when he left the room. Restlessly, Ray wandered through the first-floor rooms, finally settling in Dana's office. The presence of the computer that had been left untouched had been verification for the police that the burglary had been merely an attempt. Turning it on, Ray went to the internet with the intention of checking his e-mail. A sudden thought occurred to him. He wondered if the Stillwaters family had a website or blog. When he typed in the first two letters of their name, the words Stark Enterprises appeared on the screen menu. Ray hesitated. What was this?

Curious as to whether this was one of the companies that might belong to the Stillwaters family, he entered the website address. A well-designed site appeared on screen. According to the homepage, the company sold wholesale paper products and had offices in several countries. The CEO's name was Russell Ingram. Scanning his memory, Ray didn't remember meeting anyone in Stillwaters with that name. He went to another page.

"What have you got there?"

Startled, Ray looked up. Bev was peeking over his shoulder. He hadn't realized that she was in the room.

"I didn't mean to scare you." She squeezed his shoulder, and then returned her eyes to the screen. "What's that?"

"It's a website that Dana had on her computer. It's called Stark Enterprises. Does anybody in the Stillwaters family own this company?"

Bev's eyes scanned the screen. "No, I've never heard of it. Is it an entertainment company?"

"No, they sell paper products." Losing interest, Ray switched his attention to her. "Did you find the other journals?"

"Not yet. I thought I'd look in here." She straightened and looked around at the chaos in the office. Unlike the other rooms in her house, which were well-kept, Dana's office was bedlam. Papers and folders were stacked on file cabinets, chairs, and a desk. Nothing appeared to be in any order.

"It's hard to believe that this room is in the same house," Bev marveled. Her sister was an enigma, there was no doubt about that.

She tried to open one of the file cabinet drawers. It was locked. Abandoning the computer, Ray helped in the successful search for a key that was located in a magnetic holder on the back of the cabinet. After unlocking the drawers, Bev resumed her search. Ray was about to return to the computer when the doorbell rang.

"That must be the glass replacement people." Bev moved toward the door, but Ray spoke up.

"You keep on looking. I'll take care of it." Clicking the computer off, he headed out of the room.

"Thanks," Bev called after him. "And don't let them wander through the house."

As the workman repaired the glass, Ray sat and read Dana's latest copy of *Variety*. He was closing the door behind the worker when Bev came out of the office. She was carrying three brightly colored journals and she was beaming.

"Congratulations! You'd make a great detective." Ray caught her around the waist. Bringing her body against his own, he kissed her softly on the lips, nipping the sides of her mouth.

Bev savored his sweetness. "I must say, Mr. Wilson, you do know how to suck face."

He loosened his hold on her. "I'm glad you like it, Mrs. Cameron. I mean to please."

"And tease." She kissed the tip of his nose. Taking his hand she led him out the front door.

Ray was in nirvana as he followed her. "I hope that it's helping me work my way into your heart."

Looking back at him over her shoulder, Bev threw him a seductive smile. "It is."

"You don't have an iPod?" Bev looked at Ray incredulously. "You've got a Blackberry but no iPod? How can you live in the twenty-first century and not have an iPod?"

"I guess I'm just a dinosaur." Ray shrugged.

And a sexy one, too, Bev thought. She studied his clean-shaven profile. This was the first time that she'd actually noticed how thick his lashes were, and she was becoming addicted to his wide smile. There was a masculine quality about Ray's persona that made her feel safe. With a satisfied sigh, she turned her attention to her surroundings.

They were near the hospital where they were going to visit Dana and meet the latest contingent of the Stillwaters clan. They had been arriving all day, or perhaps a better word was invading. There were cousins from four different branches of the family who had come to L.A. to support Ginny and Bev. Each planned to sit with Dana until no longer needed, and it looked as though that might be soon. Ginny had been nearly giddy with happiness when she had called Bev to report that Dana showed signs of awakening. Bev hadn't mentioned the attempted burglary to her mother, and had asked her uncle and cousin not to do so, either. Everyone was in a good mood and she didn't want to inject any negativity. Even she felt better than she had in a long time and one of the reasons for that change was sitting in the car beside her.

Bev wasn't the type of woman to dwell long on regrets. There was no further need to brood over the time that had been wasted in not nurturing a relationship with Ray. Instead, she thought about the things that she had discovered about him, how funny, attentive, and caring he was. She wanted to enjoy the present with him, and looked forward to a future getting to know him better.

Ray couldn't help noticing how playful and upbeat Bev had been all day, especially since they had left Dana's house. Her sense of humor was proving to be as sharp as her mind. He enjoyed every minute that he spent with her. This woman was everything that he wanted and needed. There was no way that he was letting her out of his life.

After parking the car, Bev and Ray headed hand-in-hand toward the hospital, jostling and teasing each other, unaware that the happiness that they radiated was causing passing strangers to smile. It was in the hospital lobby as they were passing the information desk that Bev and Ray became aware of one of those strangers. She was a well-dressed woman who was asking the desk attendant about Dana's condition.

Her sister's name caught Bev's attention. She approached the woman.

"Excuse me, did I hear you ask about Dana Mansfield?"

It was when the stranger turned to face Bev that she noted how attractive she was. The woman appeared to be in her mid-thirties, and her caramel-colored complexion matched her caramel-colored eyes perfectly. Her small, oval-shaped face was framed by reddish brown hair that was cut in a contemporary hairstyle, and every hair was in place. Her eyebrows were professionally shaped, her makeup was flawlessly applied, her nails were manicured, and her toes were pedicured. The diamond studs in her ears were expensive, and the heart-shaped diamond in her engagement ring and the circle of diamonds in her wedding band were very large. Everything about the woman screamed money—lots of it—even the exotic perfume that she wore.

Bev and the woman scrutinized one another thoroughly before the younger woman spoke.

"Yes, I did ask about Dana. Do you know her?"

"I'm her sister, Beverly Cameron." Bev stuck her hand out. "And I recognize your voice. You're Renee Ingram, aren't you?"

A tepid smile replaced her quizzical expression. "I am." She shook Bev's hand. "It's nice to meet you.

Bev turned toward Ray. "This is a friend of ours, Ray Wilson."

Renee and Ray exchanged greetings. He recognized her last name as the same as that of the CEO of Stark Enterprises, the company that was on Dana's computer. Storing that bit of information in the back of his mind, he returned his attention to the conversation between the two women.

"I called earlier to see about Dana's condition," Renee was explaining. She stated that she was staying at her beach house in Malibu but had business in L.A. and had stopped by the hospital to see if she could get an update on her friend.

Bev was touched. "How nice of you. Ray and I were just going to see her. You're welcome to come with us."

Renee shook her head. "I don't want to impose."

"It's no imposition at all. Just follow us. I'm sure that my mother would love to meet you."

Bev steered her toward the bank of elevators that would take them upstairs. Luckily, they got one that took them up nonstop.

"My mother called me a little while ago and said that Dana was showing signs of waking up," Bev told Renee happily as they arrived at their destination and stepped into the hospital ward.

Excited by the possibility of Dana's recovery, neither Bev nor Ray noticed the look of anxiety that crossed Renee's face as the three of them headed down the hall to the patient's room.

CHAPTER 14

It was the next day and Bev and Ray were having lunch at a restaurant near his home when her cell phone rang and she received the good news that she had been waiting for. After disconnecting, she looked up at Ray. Her smile was effervescent.

"Dana's awake."

Abandoning their meal they hurried to the hospital, where they found the family jubilant. Ginny was beside herself.

"She's responding," she reported to Bev with tears glistening in her eyes. "Whatever the doctor asked her to do, she did it. There doesn't appear to be any brain damage."

"Is she talking?" Bev was as emotional as her mother as she silently thanked God for sparing her sister's life.

"She tried," Gerry answered. He had been sitting with Dana when she awakened. "But she couldn't quite manage it."

Bev and Ginny hugged, grateful that their small branch of the family still remained intact. Four years ago they had lost the head of their family, and the pain was still fresh. If the same had happened to Dana, neither woman could be certain of their recovery from that.

The next few days were a whirlwind for Bev. She ran her Chicago based business on the telephone and through e-mails, while continuing to monitor Dana's progress with stints at her bedside. The feeding tubes were removed and her sister began to speak in a soft, hoarse voice that was barely audible. She couldn't remember what had happened to her, but she was determined to get better and impatient to go home.

Bev and Ray had established a routine when they were together. The car service took Bev and Ginny to the hospital, and he spent his mornings working at his Beverly Hills office. However, his afternoons belonged to Bev, and so did his evenings.

Ginny spent most of her time at the hospital, leaving Bev and Ray alone most of the time. Those were the times that they most enjoyed.

Ray was a connoisseur of L.A.; there seemed to be nothing that he didn't know about it. Because of Darnell and Thad's occupations, Bev had been to this town many times and had never been impressed. Yet through Ray's eyes she saw the City of Angels in a whole new light.

He took her to the La Brea Tar Pits, which she had never visited, and gave her a history lesson about ancient dinosaurs. She had been to the Museum of Art many times, but a display of Greek sculpture took on new dimensions when Ray explained the dynamics of some of the pieces, topping it off with a few fables about Greek gods. Bev was impressed. One evening he picked her up from the hospital and took her roller skating, then to a Mediterranean restaurant where, after a delicious meal, they both took belly dancing lessons.

The more Bev was with him, the more she wanted to be with him. Ray Wilson was a Renaissance man. He was highly intelligent with a variety of interests. He wasn't adverse to new experiences or ideas. Communicating was something in which they both believed, and they talked constantly about everything. They were both well traveled and delighted in exchanging stories about their adventures. When they discovered that they both spoke French, they spent an entire day speaking nothing else.

Bev hadn't felt so alive with a man in a very long time. Ray was opening doors to her heart that she thought had been nailed permanently shut. There were parts of her that wanted to continue to resist him, but she was determined to defy them. She wanted to see what was on the other side of the door that had recently opened.

Ray wanted the same thing. Being with Bev was exhilarating. In his lifetime he had been with a lot of women and had enjoyed quite a few relationships, but Bev was different. The bits and pieces that he had found in other women hadn't equaled the whole for which he had been looking. She encompassed all that he desired. The time that he spent with her was his fantasy come to life. What she had come to mean to him was hard to put into words, but he could feel it in his heart.

It was useless trying to conceal the blossoming relationship from her family. The affection that had developed between them was visible to all. Ginny had spotted it the day that Dana awakened. Bev informed Ray that her mother said that the two of them looked like they were "glowing."

"I told her that was because we were," Bev relayed with a mischievous grin.

"I like that answer," Ray informed her. The two of them were in his family room, relaxing on the sofa. "Not that we need it, but I think that we have your mother's approval to become a twosome."

"Why do you say that?" Bev looked down at him as he lay with his head in her lap.

"Because before we left the hospital that day she kissed me on the cheek and told me to 'glow on.'" Ray closed his eyes and enjoyed the pampering as Bev stroked his brow. "Now I know what she meant."

"And are you doing like my mommy told you?" She tweaked his nose.

Ray purred, "I sure am trying."

"Good." Bev burrowed deeper in the sofa and let the soft sound of the jazz that they were listening to move through her. "When I was little more than a girl and pregnant with Darnell, I used to do this, sit and listen to music and think about what the future would bring."

Ray opened his eyes to look up at her. Her countenance reflected such peace.

"What did you think that might be?" he asked softly.

Bev gave a plaintive sigh. "I hoped that it would bring a healthy baby, a long and happy marriage, and a prosperous life." She looked beyond him back into the past. "I guess two out of three isn't bad."

Ray could hear the pain in her voice. He knew that she was thinking about the death of her husband.

Bev returned her attention to Ray. His mellow expression had changed to one of concern.

"What's wrong?"

Ray pulled himself upright. "How do you think that your life would have been different if your husband had lived?"

The question caught Bev off guard. No one had ever asked her that. She rarely discussed her late husband, except with Darnell. After his burial no one ever mentioned him again. It was if he had never existed, and she became comfortable with that. She had her memories, and that was all that she needed. But Ray was asking that she turn those memories into something more concrete, and she wasn't sure that she wanted to discuss that part of her life with him. They were in the early stage of their relationship. It was a fragile time. Avoiding this subject might be best.

Ray noted her hesitancy. "Of course you don't have to answer that if you don't want to."

Bev considered his words. "I'm not sure how to answer your question." She paused to gather her thoughts. "It's hard to speculate on something that never happened. When Darnell was growing up she used to ask me about her father and I would try to give her some semblance of who he was. I think that she used to fantasize about how it would be if he had lived." The thought of that had always saddened Bev. "I would have given anything if she had gotten to know him and vice versa, but at least she has a picture of him and knows how he looked."

"A picture?" Ray raised a curious brow as he wondered what the love of Bev's life looked like.

As she answered him, Bev retreated to her unconscious habit of playing with the ring on the chain around her neck. "She has the only picture of him in existence. Colton was notoriously camera-shy." She smiled nostalgically as she recalled his aversion.

Ray was sorry that he had brought the subject up. The romantic mood that they both had enjoyed only moments ago had vanished. He welcomed the reprieve when Bev's cell phone rang and she got up to retrieve it from her purse. He used the opportunity to gather the dishes which had held the snacks they had devoured earlier and took them to the kitchen.

As he loaded the dishwasher, his mind was on Bev. It seemed that she was all that he thought about lately. Making her happy had become his priority. Wanting her mind, body, and soul had become his obsession. He wanted her to want him as much, but Colton Cameron continued to stand in his way. He didn't like it, but he felt helpless to do anything about it. It was up to Bev to make the decision to move the ghost of his memory out of their way. Patience was the key. All he could do was stay the course.

Closing the dishwasher door, he turned in time to see Bev's long-legged stride as she entered the kitchen. She glided across the room gracefully as she completed her phone call. Ray couldn't take his eyes off her. This woman was more than worth the wait.

Disconnecting, Bev walked up to him and put her arms loosely around his waist. "You look like you could use a hug."

"From you, always." Ray pressed her to him and they stood for a moment enjoying each other. He rubbed his cheek against the softness of her hair. "Was that your mother calling?"

"Nope, it was Renee. She and her husband are heading back home to New York today, so she was calling to check on Dana's progress."

"She's a good friend." Ray liked her. She had called about Dana's condition several times since they encountered her at the hospital. "How long have they known each other?" With an arm around Bev's waist he walked her back toward the family room.

"According to Dana's journal they were friends in college and they ran into each other again about a year ago. It seems that Mitch was doing some work for her husband's company."

"Stark Enterprises?" Renee had confirmed for Ray that it was indeed her husband who was the CEO of the company whose website he had found on Dana's computer.

Bev nodded. "Uh-huh."

"Oh, I didn't know that." Ray settled on the sofa they had previously occupied and pulled Bev onto his lap.

Tossing her head back in delight, Bev's melodious laughter echoed through the room at the unexpected positioning. "What am I going to do with you?"

Ray's twinkling eyes turned serious. "Whatever you want."

Bev caught the change in tone and saw the look of hunger in his eyes. It told her clearly what he wanted. In the past she had dismissed that look. But now—

"You're turning me on, Mr. Wilson," she confessed.

"I sure hope so, Mrs. Cameron."

"You're making me want you in ways that I would never have imagined a short while ago." Bev traced the outline of his lips.

"I'm glad to hear that." He licked the tips of her fingers.

Bev drew a slow unsteady breath. "Sooo, since that's the case, I command you to make love to me." She exhaled.

"Are you sure?" Ray's heartbeat quickened. The outline of the ring that she wore around her neck could be seen through her clothing. He knew to whom it belonged. "Are you ready?"

Bev understood the meaning of his questions. He needed reassurance that he could trust her emotions, but could *she* trust them? Her answer to both of his questions was simple.

"Yes."

No further time was wasted as they nibbled on each other's lips, nipped at each other's ears, and giggled like horny teenagers as they anticipated the inevitable. Hands roamed, familiarizing themselves with places that begged for exploration. Buttons and zippers were released. Ray removed the chains from around Bev's neck—all of them—and laid them aside. He freed her from her lacey bra and then greedily suckled her breasts. Her moans of pleasure were like a sonata to his ears.

"Let's move into my bedroom," he suggested, picking her up smoothly.

"You like playing Hercules, don't you?" Bev kissed his neck and tightened her hold on him, recalling the injured foot that had put her in his arms previously.

"Just wait until we get in bed," he grinned. "All of the Greek gods come out in me then." Swiftly they moved up the stairs.

"It's been a while for me," Bev confessed as they entered his bedroom suite and he placed her on his bed.

Ray's eyes swept her shapely frame. She made a sensuous sight in her state of half dress. "Glad to hear it, but I can't understand how anyone could keep their hands off you."

Bev felt brazen under his scrutiny. "I've got to tell you that lying in a man's bed with my breasts exposed isn't something I do every day."

"I sure hope not." He lay down on his side next to her.

"Strangely enough, I don't feel nervous. A little self-conscious maybe, but not embarrassed like I thought I would feel."

"That means that you're comfortable with me." Ray caressed her cheek. "And I'm glad, because I want to tell you that you're beautiful. Everything about you is beautiful."

"Thank you." She was proud of having taken care of herself and was aware that her body looked good for a woman in her fifties.

"And I'm going to share something else with you." Seductively, Ray slowly circled her nipple. "I'm not quite the hound that you might think that I am." He placed a soft kiss on the hardened bud. "I've been celibate for a year."

"Oh, really?" Even in her distracted state Bev couldn't mask her surprise. Bringing his mouth to her own, she kissed him and whispered, "So, you must be hungry. Does that mean that I have to worry about your *appetite*?" She glanced at the bulge in his pants.

Ray felt dizzy with desire. "Should I worry about yours?"

"Probably." Bev kissed him again, but deeper this time. She drew away. "Now show me what I should look forward to getting."

She helped him remove his shirt. Ray worked out regularly, and his torso was a testimony to his efforts.

"Nice." Bev liked what she was seeing. "Real nice."

She helped him remove his pants and briefs. Lightly she skimmed her fingers over his engorged member, and then with adept hands showed her appreciation of the preview with unmerciful dexterity.

Ray bit his bottom lip, enjoying the pleasure. "My, my, aren't you bold."

Bev grinned wickedly. "Would you rather that I be timid?"

"No, I think that you're perfect the way you are." He clasped her busy hand before he exploded. Straddling her, he rubbed himself against her moistened triangle, enjoying their sexy repartee. "Do you think that you can handle all of this?"

Bev's eyes moved slowly up and down the topic of discussion. It was impressive.

"I'll try my very best."

"You do that." Burying his nose in the crook of her neck, Ray inhaled her fragrance. "Bev," his voice quivered. "From now on, that's what I'm going to call your scent." He slipped his hand inside her underwear, and a second later she lay beneath him nude.

"Mr. Magic, that's what I'm going to start calling you," she gasped in reference to her vanishing panties.

"I can only hope that I don't disappoint," Ray said, deliberately misinterpreting her meaning.

"I'm quite sure that you won't."

She was right. Ray was an experienced lover. He prepared her for him with kisses and caresses so erotic that he had her drenched with need. He used his full lips and his tantalizing tongue so provocatively that there wasn't a place on her body that was left untouched. She was begging for relief and he answered her call. Again and again Bev exploded. Lost in a kaleidoscope of vibrant colors, she had barely recovered when Ray covered his shaft and entered her tenderly. He was in complete control. Her body was incinerated. He stoked her with a skill that she didn't know existed. The pleasure was unbearable, and, just when she felt that she could take no more, it got better. She screamed. She convulsed, and then she imploded.

No, Ray Wilson did not disappoint.

CHAPTER 15

As Bev lay in bed next to Ray she felt so content that she could hardly move. In her lifetime, no man had ever made love to her as he had, and that included her late husband, whom she knew had loved her dearly. Ray had given her the best loving that she had ever had.

She didn't know if she had gone to sleep afterward or simply passed out, but she was aware that her world had tilted. She kept trying to tell herself that Ray's expertise as a lover was because he'd had so much practice with so many women. While that might be true, she had sensed that their joining had really meant something to him. He had made love to her, not merely had sex with her. There was a difference. His heart and soul had been in their lovemaking. Ray had held nothing back. She had given him what she had to give, but she was sure that he had given her all that he had.

Bev was right. Ray had made love to her with everything in him, he had wanted her to know how much he cared. As she lay sleeping beside him, he skimmed his fingers lightly down her back, and then placed a kiss on the curve of her spine. His heart was full. Bev Cameron was a very special lady, and he wanted her to be his. He wondered if she ever could be, or would her heart always belong to another?

Bev felt Ray's touch. It was difficult for her not to react, but she continued to feign sleep. She needed time to think about the two of them and where they could go from here. Having made love with Ray meant that she had started in a new direction, but she couldn't help wondering if her heart would follow.

She turned over on her back, opened her eyes, and found Ray staring down at her, his chin in his hand. She expected him to be smug about their lovemaking, and as far as she was concerned he had the right to be. But the smile that he bestowed on her showed no hint of conceit.

"Hey, there. How are you feeling?"

Bev stretched contentedly and yawned before answering. "Fine."

Ray flashed a grin. "Oh, you *are* that."

Bev rolled onto her side and propped her head on her hand, mirroring him. "My, my, my, you are a flatterer, aren't you?"

"I aim to please."

"You did that." Bev let her words leave no doubt about their meaning.

"Touché," he said, and he meant it. His body was still tingling from the effect that Bev had had on him. "You're one hell of a woman, do you know that?"

She winked. "It's in the genes."

Ray took her hand and entwined their fingers. He liked the feel of her, the scent of her, and the sound of her voice.

"Tell me what it's like to belong to a family where failure is not an option."

Bev gave a heavy sigh. "According to Dana's journal, it's hell." The sparkle went out of her eyes and the warmth left her smile. Withdrawing from his arms, she scooted up in the bed and propped a pillow behind her back.

"I never thought of the ambition that my family has as negative, but my sister thinks it is. She wrote about her pride in our mother earning her place as next in line to head our family, but she thinks that Grandy's shoes are too big to fill."

"Why?" Ray scooted up to sit beside her, trying hard to concentrate on her words and not her naked breasts.

"Because in a time when women weren't thought of as anything more than baby makers, Grandy nearly single-handedly made a fortune that's been passed down to four generations and expanded beyond one's wildest belief, *plus* she did it as a widow with six mouths to feed."

"Maybe she did it *because* she had six mouths to feed."

"No doubt, but according to Dana it was for revenge."

Bev pulled the sheet up to cover her breasts, but Ray barely noticed. Her last statement had caught his attention. He prompted. "How so?"

Bev wasn't sure that she should continue. If she did she would make Ray privy to Stillwaters family lore that few outside of their clan had heard. The story that followed confirmed her trust in him.

"After Grandy recovered from having the triplets, she started planning her return to the homestead that my grandfather had bought for his family. She was determined to not only claim her land, but also the business that bigotry and hate had destroyed. She was going back with or without the help of the Freedom or the Stillwaters families. Nobody could stop her. Grandy can be a very stubborn woman."

Bev stopped and glared at Ray, daring him to say what she knew was on the tip of his tongue. He could barely contain his amusement.

"What?" Ray looked at her innocently. He was practically biting his tongue in his effort not to make the comment about stubbornness running in the family. Instead he said, "I'm listening."

Bev rolled her eyes at him and continued. "The Stillwaters and the Freedom families decided to go back with her, and God help the man, black or white, who might stand in their way. Both families sold their businesses and combined their fortunes, but before they could make the trip back, both Great-Granddaddy Stillwaters and Great-Granddaddy Freedom fell ill. So, Grandy took control and hired an attorney to secure her claim on the family land and on the lumber mill. She also wanted to purchase the surrounding land for the rest of the family. It was bought in the name of the S and F Land Holding Group."

"Which is now the S and F Financial Consortium," Ray muttered.

His comment startled Bev. "How do you know that?"

"It's a major investor in Darnell and Thad's . . ."

"Production company." Bev said, completing his sentence. It seemed that Ray knew more about her family than she thought he knew. "You're right, but it started out under another name. The rebuilding of the mill was greatly anticipated by the town where my grandfather's killers lived."

"Which town is that?"

"It's the one that's about ten miles away. You have to pass it before you reach Stillwaters. Ironically by burning down the mill the stupid fools destroyed one of their town's major industries. The legal representatives that Grandy hired went there on behalf of S and F and informed its esteemed citizens that the mill would open as soon as the murderers of William Stillwaters were brought to justice, and not one minute sooner. S and F wouldn't do business in a town that harbored murderers."

Ray was riveted. "How long did it take to bring them to justice?"

"One day to round them up, one month for them to be tried for murder, convicted, and sentenced to life. It was a first in the history of the county that white men were convicted of killing a black man. The mill opened after they were sentenced and the town has been thriving ever since, and it was all because of our sweet and gentle Grandy."

Ray's mind was on overload. *Sweet?* He had no doubt about that. *Gentle?* From what he had just been told he wasn't so sure about that description, but one thing was for certain, Esther Stillwaters was tough.

"I've always heard that still waters run deep," Ray mused. "It's often the quiet, unassuming ones that you have to watch."

"I can agree with that." Bev paused before continuing. "Grandy earned her place as the head of this family. It was she who planned every detail of what happened in that town. She was twenty-three years old. Our family never thought of what happened as an act of vengeance. If we had wanted that, believe me, the Freedom and Stillwaters families would have gone into that town with guns blazing and we would have taken no prisoners. What happened in that town was justice, long overdue."

Ray found it hard to grasp all that he had been told. He had admired Grandy from the beginning, but now— "That woman is an icon."

"To say the least." Bev nodded in agreement. "It was she who led the two families back to the land that her husband had purchased. After they recovered, my two great-grandfathers and the other men and boys in our family built the wall that surrounds Stillwaters with their own hands. Grandy buried her husband and son in the cemetery that I showed you. She then left her six children in the care of her family and went north to Oberlin College in Ohio for four years, where she earned a degree in business."

"You're kidding!" Ray could hardly believe the woman's daring.

"No, I'm not. She was one of the first minority women to earn a degree in that area. Of course in those days that more or less meant secretarial work, but not for her. She used what she had learned to build an empire that has sustained our family ever since."

The room was silent as both absorbed the enormity of what Esther Freedom Stillwaters had accomplished.

For a moment Bev wondered if perhaps Dana was right about trying to live up to such a legacy. But the thought quickly dissipated as Bev continued.

"Each member of our family has been issued the challenge to follow in our matriarch's footsteps and under less daunting circumstances than Grandy faced. Each of us has picked up the gauntlet and has achieved success. Excuses are not acceptable."

Bev turned to Ray. "I love Dana, but if she can't appreciate such a heritage, that's her problem. I know for certain there are no murderers in our family."

Ray's mind was still reeling from the story that she had related. He didn't say it aloud, but the more he learned about the Stillwaters family the more convinced he became that she was right.

Lying back on the bed, Bev stretched again, enjoying how sinuous her body felt. It was a wonder what good loving could do. "What time is it?" she asked absently.

He glanced over his shoulder at the clock on the table next to the bed. "It's four."

"What?" Bev sat straight up. "I had no idea that it was that late. I need to call the hospital." She looked around for her clothes.

"While you were sleeping I called your mother. She said Dana is doing great."

That didn't stop Bev from clambering out of the bed. She started gathering her clothing. "I meant to call my office, but everybody's gone home by now. Why did you let me sleep so long?"

"Uh, I wouldn't call what we were doing sleeping." Ray plumped the pillows up behind his back and relaxed as he watched her rush around the room. She was nude. His groin twitched.

"I need a shower," Bev wailed, frustrated that she had let so much of the day slip by. "Is your bathroom through there?" She indicated a set of double doors across the room.

"Yep," Ray drawled lazily, slightly amused by the whirlwind of activity. He would have preferred that they continue to lie there and talk.

Bev headed toward the bathroom doors, opened them, and disappeared. A second later she peeked back out into the bedroom and looked at Ray. "Well, I'm running the shower. Are you joining me in it or not?"

As far as Ray knew, he broke the world record for getting out of bed.

Bev and Ray went to the hospital together to check on Dana. She was awake but still wasn't very alert. The family continued to sit at her bedside, and Bev was prepared to take her turn while Ray went to his office to catch up on business. They made plans to meet for dinner later that evening. Those plans quickly changed as each of them received unexpected telephone calls from two different sources. Bev's call came from Janice Brady, her long-time assistant in her Chicago office.

"We've got a problem."

Janice proceeded to tell her that one of their best clients was threatening to withdraw all of his funds from Bev's company. He had investments with them in the millions of dollars. Her intervention called for a face-to-face meeting with him. She had to be in Chicago ASAP. She booked a flight that would leave L.A. that evening. It was while she was at Ray's home hastily packing that he received his telephone call. Thad was on the other end.

"Man, I need a tremendous favor." There was desperation in his voice.

A pipe had burst in one of the bathrooms in their family home in Carmel. Their housekeeper, Mrs. Sharon, had reported the problem and had made an appointment with a plumber and a contractor to make the necessary repairs. However, a family emergency made her unable to be at the house when the repairs were to be made. They were scheduled for the next day, and a delay could mean additional damage to the house. Normally, Thad or Darnell's personal assistants might take care of the situation, but neither was available.

"I would never ask you to do this if there was anyone else we trusted in our house," Thad told him. "Nedra and her family are in New York . . ."

Ray stopped him there and volunteered to fly to Carmel. "If you can't count on a friend, who can you count on?" He called the airplane charter service that he used and booked a flight to leave L.A. thirty minutes after Bev's flight.

As Ray and she said their goodbyes at the airport, both were struck by the melancholy that gripped them at their parting.

"You know what," Bev told him softly, "I'm really going to miss you." She couldn't believe the intensity of her feelings about their parting.

He placed a quick kiss on her forehead. "Don't sound so surprised. I've grown on you."

She chortled, "Like bright, green ivy—all fresh and good."

"I like that," Ray hugged her to him. "I'll miss you, too." His heart was full.

After fervent kisses and ardent promises to call each other on their arrivals, they reluctantly separated. Bev watched as he moved in the opposite direction until he disappeared from sight. She felt bereaved. Turning, she went through the gate to catch her own flight, wondering when this man had become so important in her life.

Having arrived in Carmel, Ray opened the front door to the Cameron-Stewart home and disengaged the silent alarm. Dropping his overnight bag, he stood in the sumptuous entranceway and looked up the lavish stairway where Bev had been standing the first time that he saw her. She had been looking down at him with utter distain, but even under those circumstances he still had been mesmerized by her majesty. She had looked like a Nubian queen, and she still did.

As he trotted up the stairway, he couldn't get her out of his mind. They had parted only a short while ago and he missed her already. Moving down the hallway, he gave a wistful sigh. There had been a time in his life when *he* was the one who was being missed by a woman who craved him. When had that changed? Now he knew how it felt.

Turning into his goddaughter's beautifully decorated bedroom, he passed through it into the adjoining bathroom where the broken pipe had made a mess. Briefly surveying the damage, he left the room and headed back down the stairs to wait for the plumber. But instead of sifting through the work that he had brought from home, Ray found himself wandering through the opulent house aimlessly, glancing at his watch now and then as he calculated the time when Bev would arrive in Chicago. After a stroll around the grounds, he decided that he could wait no longer. Whipping out his cell phone he pressed her number, realizing that her voice mail might be the only response to his call. He was right. Disappointed, he left a message

"It's me. I'm in Carmel. I just wanted to make sure that you landed safely. Call me." He hesitated, wanting to leave an endearment. Instead he disconnected.

"Coward!" he uttered aloud.

The sound of the buzzer from the front gate startled him out of his self-flagellation. The plumber was here. As he went to answer the summons, Ray found comfort in the thought that maybe it was too soon to say how he really felt about her. When he did tell her he hoped that it wouldn't be over the telephone. When he said the words "I love you," he wanted to say them to her face to face.

CHAPTER 16

Bev's plane had arrived at O'Hare Airport on time, and she was in a good mood when she walked into Freedom Financial Services.

"You sure are looking chipper," Janice noted after greeting her boss with a hug. "I wish that I could be so calm about the possibility of losing millions."

"It's only money," Bev quipped as the two of them headed down the hallway.

"How's Dana doing?" Janice followed Bev into her office.

Bev had kept the office updated about her sister's medical progress through Janice, who was her friend as well as her employee. She had been with Bev for over a decade. At sixty-six, Janice looked as though she were in her forties. As stylish and sophisticated as her employer, she was the height of efficiency and solely responsible for keeping the office running so smoothly. Bev didn't know what she would do without her.

"She's getting better, thank God." Bev slipped into the white leather swivel chair behind her glass-top desk. "She's talking a little bit more each day."

"Does she remember what happened?" Janice took a seat in one of the fashionable chairs opposite the desk.

"All she knows at this point is that she's waking up in a hospital. It's going to take time, but we're hopeful that she'll be as good as new after some therapy."

"I'm glad to hear it."

The two women engaged in some small talk before getting down to the business that had brought Bev back to the office. Janice explained in detail the reasons that the client had expressed for wanting to withdraw his investment funds. Bev assessed the situation and went over a few strategic scenarios with Janice. A Plan A and Plan B were devised, and Bev spent the remainder of the day analyzing data and making telephone calls. By nightfall she had a solution to the dilemma that was causing her client concern. She made arrangements for lunch with him the next day to make her presentation. She was exhausted by the time the last call was made.

Janice stuck her head in the open office door. "Are you ready to go?" She was dropping Bev off at her Hyde Park home.

"Finally." Bev turned the light off in her office and shut the door behind her. It wasn't until she was following Janice down the hall toward the elevator doors that she remembered that she hadn't called her mother or Ray to inform them of her arrival.

Checking her messages, she saw that she had missed calls from both. By the time that she and Janice had gone downstairs and climbed into Janice's car, Bev had contacted her mother and her daughter. As Janice drove out of the parking garage and headed toward the Dan Ryan Highway, Bev called Ray.

"Hey there." She couldn't help smiling when he answered his cell phone.

"Hey there," he echoed. Ray had been sitting in the kitchen using the laptop that he had brought with him and thinking about her. "Guess who's been on my mind."

"Hmmm, let me guess."

"No need." Ray rose and wandered across the room to the patio doors where he stood looking out at the sweeping cypress trees. "Just look in the mirror and you'll see who I'm talking about."

"I just might do that, as long as you look in yours."

Ray liked the sound of that. They spoke for a few more minutes before saying their goodbyes.

"I miss you already." Ray's confession was husky with memories. So was Bev's.

"I miss you, too."

They disconnected.

"Humph." Janice's grunt brought Bev out of her stupor as the older woman threw her a look. "It sounds like a new relationship is in bloom. What's his name?"

Bev chuckled. "You wouldn't believe me if I told you."

Janice had met Ray in the past, and she was more than aware of the years of acrimony between them. For the past few years Janice had served as a sounding board for Bev's complaints about Ray.

"That means that I know him." Janice pulled into a parking spot in front of Bev's two story house. Turning the ignition off she turned to Bev. "Don't I?"

"Yes." Bev gave her a smug smile. "But I still don't think that you'd ever guess."

Janice didn't hesitate. "Ray Wilson."

"How did you know?" Bev couldn't believe it. Was the woman a psychic?

Janice threw her a dismissive wave. "Oh, please, it didn't take a genius. You were in L.A. and he lives there. He's a friend of your sister's, plus he's had the hots for you since forever. Who else could it be? I'm just glad that he finally won you over."

"You are?" That was another surprise. Janice had never registered an opinion about Ray one way or the other. "Why? I wasn't aware that you even liked him."

Janice shrugged. "I really don't know him, but the few times that I've been in the same room with the two of you I've noticed the chemistry . . ."

"What chemistry?" The woman wasn't a psychic, she was psychotic.

"The one he tried to be cool about and that you denied all together. So, how do you feel about him?"

Bev hesitated. "I'm still trying to figure that out."

"Because of the age thing." It was a statement, not a question.

"You're much too wise for your age," Bev said in admiration. "I'll admit that I tried to make it a problem in the beginning . . ."

"But he wouldn't let you, and you're still trying to come up with an excuse." Boldly, Janice made her point by thumping the ring hanging on the chain around Bev's neck. "How foolish you are to let a chance for happiness slip away." As she pulled up in front of Bev's house, she released the passenger door lock. "Go get some rest.

You've got a long day tomorrow." With that she indicated that Bev should exit. There would be no further discussion.

Perturbed, Bev got out of the car without a farewell. She didn't know whether to be angry with Janice or not. The woman had always said what was on her mind, but how dare she have the nerve to put her hand on Colton's ring!

As she unlocked the front door, stepped inside her foyer, and disarmed the alarm, she thought of a thousand things that she should have said to her. She muttered them aloud as she stomped up the stairs, entered her bedroom, and dropped her bag at the door. By the time she walked across the room to belly flop on her bed she was stripped down to her underwear, and still fuming.

Turning on her back, she listened to her uneven breathing. Gradually, she grew calm and clarity returned. She knew that it wasn't Janice who had fueled her anger. It was the truth that she had spoken. She wasn't used to being considered foolish. She took pride in the decisions that she had made over the years. Each one had helped mold her into the woman that she had become.

Lying alone in the silent darkness, she recounted the accomplishments of which she was so proud. After her husband died, she had raised her child alone, attended college all the way through graduate school, and started her own business. She owned this house and the one she had built in Stillwaters. She owned property all over the place. Hell, she was worth a fortune! By all definition she was a very successful woman. Fear and foolishness were not part of her DNA. Yet lately she had been experiencing both. She was scared to let go and foolish not to do so. Janice had been right about that. But how could she give Colton up? He had been her life.

They had met in Chicago at the Museum of Science and Industry. She was there researching a school project. He told her he was there because he liked the place. She had found him to be courteous and polite. It took her three months to fall in love. He claimed that for him, it was love at first sight.

Her parents liked him. He was well spoken, well mannered, and respectful, but that had not been enough. Colton was five years older, plus he had graduated from high school and had no plans to further his education. In the high-achieving family from which Bev had descended, that was unacceptable. Yet her parents hadn't interfered in their relationship, although they made her aware that they were concerned about its intensity. They had a right to be. A week after Bev graduated from high school, she and Colton flew to Las Vegas and got married. She was eighteen years old.

As young as they were, they lived well. Colton worked in construction, and he worked steadily. His jobs often took him away from her for days, but money was plentiful and so was their love. Bev had planned on enrolling in college the coming semester, but then she discovered that she was pregnant. She and Colton were ecstatic. Life was perfect. And then he was suddenly gone.

Even now the tears flowed silently down Bev's face. The depth of her grief at the time couldn't be contained.

Over the years, the memories of her life with Colton had wrapped around her heart like a blanket, keeping her warm and secure. They had been perfect together. *He* had been perfect. It was so hard to let go of those memories—to let go of him.

Ray sat at the computer staring blankly at the screen. He was trying to concentrate, but the call from Bev had rendered that nearly impossible. "*I miss you, too,*" had been her whispered reply. That was all he could think about. The love bug had bitten him a long time ago, and it seemed that it just kept on chewing.

Sighing, he turned his attention back to the computer screen. He had moved to Darnell's downstairs office, where he could hook his laptop up to her printer. There was business that he had brought with him and he knew that he should attend to it, but he chose procrastination. Remembering how he had tried to Google the Stillwaters family and had been interrupted, he tried again. Their story was fascinating and he wanted to learn more, but while the achievements of individual members of the family were well documented, there was no information on the family as a whole. He tried to find the website for The S and F Financial Consortium. He knew that there was some sort of monetary connection to the family, but again he had no luck. There was no website. Thad had been correct when he had informed him that the Stillwaters clan was discreet. Losing interest in that effort, he decided to look up Renee Ingram, who was proving to be such a good friend to Dana. Not only had she monitored Dana's progress by telephone and visited the hospital, but she had sent a beautiful flower arrangement. Everyone had been touched by her concern.

Having confirmed that she was the wife of Russell Ingram, CEO of Stark Enterprises, he discovered that she was quite the socialite. The mother of a young son, the family lived in Westchester, New York, and she had headed several charitable events supporting national and international causes. Ray clicked on another article and, to his surprise, there stood Mitch, posing with the young couple. Renee was standing between him and her husband. Ray recalled that Bev had informed him that Mitch had worked for Stark Enterprises, and he was about to read the article when he was interrupted by the ring of the buzzer from the entrance gate. The plumber had returned to finish his repair. Hitting print, he hurriedly snatched the single sheet of paper from the printer and went to answer the call.

Early the next morning another call summoned Ray. Bev was on the other end. There was a smile in her voice that made it obvious that she was aware of the time difference.

"It's six in the morning," Ray groused, barely awake.

"So why aren't you up and at 'em?" She laughed as she made her way down the stairs of her home to the kitchen.

"Shouldn't you be jogging or shadow boxing or something? I've already taken my bath and dressed. My housekeeper stocked my refrigerator with goodies, so I'm getting ready to eat breakfast and start my day. I'd say that you're lagging behind."

"You think?" Now wide awake, Ray rolled out of bed and slipped into his robe. The sound of her voice was just what he needed. "And what are your plans for today?"

"I'm going to have lunch with my disgruntled client and talk him into staying with my company." Bev left no doubt about that.

"You're going to work that Bev magic, huh?" Ray felt sorry for whoever it was. If she whipped it on the client like she had whipped it on him, the poor guy didn't have a chance.

As Bev and Ray got ready for their day the smiles on of each of their faces confirmed the affection that had developed between them.

"When are you flying back to L.A.?" It was Bev's plan to fly back as soon as she could settle her business.

"Let's see, today is Friday." Ray slipped his feet into his house slippers. "I probably won't get back there until Sunday evening." He started to rise from the bed when he froze. "You are going back, aren't you?" It wasn't until that moment that the possibility that she might stay in Chicago occurred to him.

"As soon as I can wrap things up here, I'll probably fly back on Sunday, too."

"Great."

Bev could hear the relief in his voice. "Why are you waiting until Sunday? I thought that the contractor was coming to fix the drywall in the bathroom today."

"That's right, but I plan on borrowing one of Thad's cars and driving up to Tiburon to check on my house."

Bev knew that he had purchased the house from Thad, but she had never been there. "Do you get there often?"

"I try to get there at least once a month. It's my resting place."

The chit-chat continued and then goodbyes were said, but before they disconnected, once again, Bev whispered the words to Ray that warmed his heart. "I miss you."

With that she was gone, leaving him standing in the middle of the bedroom in her daughter and son-in-law's house as hard as stone.

Bev moved around her ultra-modern kitchen humming a vintage Aretha Franklin song, "Call Me". It had always been one of her favorites, and that it had popped into her head hadn't surprised her. Each word now seemed to hold a special meaning since it was the song to which Ray and she had danced.

She missed him more than she could ever have imagined. He was the last person that she had thought about when she fell asleep last night and the first one she thought about when she awakened this morning—not her sick sister, not her overstressed mother, not her daughter who was working thousands of miles away, or her granddaughter who was with her parents, but Ray Wilson. It was disturbing. Family was always first.

At this point, Bev wasn't ready to analyze the change that Ray seemed to be making in her life. Instead, she chose to go about the mundane chore of fixing her breakfast in an effort to soothe the ache that she felt at being apart from him. How in the world had this happened? When had he become so important in her life that she physically ached for him, and how had it happened so quickly? Had she been lonely and searching and unaware of it? She wasn't a twenty-something girl looking for some elusive soul mate. She had found hers years ago, and they had lived their lifetime. She was too old for this. Her life was full. Her business was thriving. Her child was happy. Her grandchild was perfect. What was it about Ray that made her crave the man so? Maybe she was just horny.

Gathering her belongings to leave the house, Bev made a decision. She planned on remedying both situations—missing him and wanting him. Dialing her cell phone as she walked out the door, she started the process of closing the distance between them.

After talking to Bev earlier, Ray was walking with an extra spring in his step as he entered the kitchen of the Cameron-Stewart home. To his surprise Mrs. Sharon had stopped by the house to check on him. He now found her standing at the island, engrossed in reading a paper lying on the counter.

She looked up as he entered. "That's for you." She nodded toward a stack of pancakes and a glass of orange juice. Ray stopped short.

"Mrs. Sharon, you didn't have to fix me breakfast." The aroma assailing his nostrils made him grateful that she had.

She smiled. "I know I didn't have to, but I wanted to. You did all of us a huge favor, and it's the least that I can do. I've got to be leaving soon and get back to Salinas to my daughter, so you sit and eat."

Ray did as he was told. "Thank you, and congratulations on your first grandchild. It must be exciting."

"Yes, it is." Mrs. Sharon pushed away from the counter. "But we're still worried since she's so little. They've got her in an incubator."

"I'm sure everything is going to work out fine." Pouring syrup on the pancakes he cut into the delectable offering and savored the first bite. "Delicious."

"Glad you like them." Mrs. Sharon smiled at the compliment as she moved around cleaning up after herself. "I was reading that article that you left over there." She indicated the one about Stark Enterprises that Ray had printed out yesterday. He gave it a cursory glance.

"Oh, yeah, I meant to read that and forgot." He kept eating.

Mrs. Sharon placed some pots and pans in the dishwasher. "I didn't know that you knew that man in the picture."

Ray looked at the picture of Mitch, Renee, and her husband. "Actually, I only know one of the men, Mitch Clayton. He was Dana's fiancé." He knew that Mrs. Sharon knew Darnell's aunt. "I don't know the other man. He's the husband of the woman in the picture, Renee Ingram. I met her recently. She's a friend of Dana's."

Looking confused, Mrs. Sharon wiped her hands on a dish towel and went to look at the article in question. "Oh, no, I'm not talking about those two guys, I'm talking about that one."

Ray's eyes followed her finger. It pointed to a separate picture, a smaller insert, below the photo of the happy looking trio. It was a single photograph of a distinguished-looking man staring into the camera. The caption below the photograph read Charles "Moody" Lake, former CEO of Stark Enterprises. He looked up at Mrs. Sharon for further clarification.

"That guy rented the house across the street a few years ago."

"That's a coincidence." Ray popped a forkful of pancakes into his mouth and chewed.

"I remember that he came over to introduce himself to me once and wanted to meet Darnell, but I didn't let him. I think he was a fan. After that I started to notice him when I was coming and going. He would walk down to the beach nearly every day."

Ray scanned the article. It was a fluff piece about a charity event sponsored by Stark Enterprises. The information about Mr. Lake was only five lines. "It seems that Mr. Lake met an untimely death. It says here that he drowned while on vacation in Hawaii."

"Yeah, I saw that. Poor man." She gathered Ray's empty dishes and headed toward the sink. "But I think that they made a mistake about when he died, because the date that they have in there sounds like the same time that he was renting the house across the street. That's the one that the owner rents out to vacationers when he's gone." Rinsing the dishes, she put them in the dishwasher, and then looked around the kitchen. "Looks like I'm finished in here. What time is the contractor due?"

"Around now," Ray answered as he finished the article.

The bell at the gate rang. He and Mrs. Sharon shared a hopeful look, and then turned their attention to the kitchen monitor.

"It's my friend Laura," Mrs. Sharon said, identifying the visitor. "She's going with me to Salinas." She started toward the exit, then stopped and looked back at Ray.

"I just thought about something. What was the name of that guy in the picture?"

Ray glanced at the caption again, "Charles 'Moody' Lake."

"Hmmm." Mrs. Sharon grimaced as she tried to recall the past. "I don't think that's the name that he gave me." She left the kitchen.

With one last glance at the article, Ray tossed it in the trash. He was disappointed that their visitor hadn't been the contractor. The sooner the man arrived, the better. Ray planned on leaving for Tiburon as soon as the workman completed his task. After that he would be going back to Los Angeles and back to Bev.

CHAPTER 17

Ray was about to leave the kitchen when Mrs. Sharon re-entered, followed by a tall, stately looking woman with an engaging smile. Mrs. Sharon made the introductions.

"Mr. Wilson, this is Mrs. Laura Smith. Laura, this is Mr. Ray Wilson."

Laura and Ray exchanged greetings as he was walking out of the kitchen. Mrs. Sharon called after him.

"Where is that article that we were talking about? I wanted Laura to see the picture of that man. She's the housekeeper in the house across the street, the one that I told you that he was renting. "

"I threw it away." Ray went to the trash can to retrieve it. Smoothing the wrinkles, he placed it on the island counter as Mrs. Sharon and Mrs. Smith gathered around.

"See, isn't that the man that rented the house a couple of years ago? I only met him once, but I'm sure that's him."

Mrs. Smith agreed. "Yes, that's Mr. Waters. I'll never forget him. He was such a quiet, gentle man of great character and charm. He was one of the nicest people we ever had renting the place." She looked at the caption. "It says here that his name was Charles Lake." She looked up at Mrs. Sharon, confused. "That's not the name that he gave us."

"I *knew* that he used another name!" Mrs. Sharon gloated triumphantly, glad that her memory hadn't failed her.

"Good going." Ray gave her a wink and started to walk away.

"Now this other guy, he used his right name."

Laura's words stopped Ray's retreat. He turned back to her.

"What other guy? " Ray pointed to Mitch. "Him?"

"No, *him.*" Mrs. Smith pointed to Russell Ingram. "He was a nice young man, so polite."

Ray's interest was piqued. "You mean he was staying in the house, too? Was his wife with him?"

Mrs. Smith shook her head. "No, she wasn't, and Mr. Ingram only stayed overnight. As a matter of fact, he and Mr. Waters went to San Francisco together the next day and Mr. Waters decided to fly back home after that."

"I guess business was calling." Ray shrugged as he opened a cabinet door and withdrew an empty glass.

Laura continued to examine the article as Mrs. Sharon urged her to look at the timeline for Moody Lake's demise.

"Yes, it's wrong. Mr. Waters . . . Lake . . . or whoever was staying at the house then. These newspapers can't ever get anything right. I keep precise records on everyone that stays at that house, and I'm sure he was with us during this time." She addressed Ray, who was pouring another glass of juice. "He did leave unexpectedly, that's true, but . . ."

"Unexpectedly?" Ray sipped his juice as he wondered about the contractor's arrival.

"After the two of them went to San Francisco together, Mr. Ingram called me and said that some urgent business had taken Mr. Waters back to the East Coast and that he wouldn't be returning. He sent a courier service to pick up Mr. Waters' things, and that's the last we heard from him. He still had a month to go on his lease."

"Some people have money to burn," Mrs. Sharon piped in as she headed for the exit. "Come, on Laura, we have to go."

Mrs. Smith followed her. "I'm really sorry to hear about his death," she said to her friend's retreating back. "He was really nice."

"And nice looking, too," Mrs. Sharon added. The women left the room tittering in agreement.

Ray glanced at the wrinkled piece of paper on the counter. It seemed that there had been a bit of intrigue in the life of Stark Enterprises' late CEO. Maybe he had used an alias so that he could have a clandestine rendezvous with a woman here on the West Coast.

The buzzer at the front gate took him to the security camera. The contractor had finally arrived. Good! He was more than ready to get this project finished so that he could head for Tiburon. Yet eight hours later he was still in Carmel.

"He said that he had to come back tomorrow," Ray informed Thad. He tried to keep the disappointment out of his voice. "It seems that he has to put the finishing touches on the drywall before he can paint."

"Aw, man, I'm sorry. I didn't know that he was going to take up so much of your time."

Ray could tell over the telephone that Thad felt bad. That hadn't been his intent.

"Aw, it's all right. I can hang." He managed to convince himself as he reassured his friend. Ray then called Bev, but got her voice mail.

"Hey there, it looks like I'm going to be in Carmel another night before I head up to Tiburon, but I'll definitely see you on Monday. Call me."

After ordering take out, he ate his dinner alone in the dining area and later in the evening found himself back on his laptop. After checking his e-mails, once again he looked up Stark Enterprises. The conversation this morning had transferred his interest from Renee Ingram to Moody Lake. What was his story?

Although Stark Enterprises was not a huge international conglomerate that would draw a lot of media attention, there were a few articles about the untimely death of Moody Lake. In everything that he read, the date of death was consistent with what Ray had read previously.

Moody Lake had been on vacation at his beach house in Hawaii. He had been seen taking his boat out on the ocean to fish and he had never returned. His housekeeper had reported him missing. His body had never been found. No relatives were listed. Ray wondered who had inherited the man's estate.

The article about Russell's ascension to CEO of Stark Enterprises wasn't a long one. It mentioned that Lake's death had elevated Renee's husband to the top of his company's pyramid and identified Ingram as a graduate of an Ivy League university. It mentioned how long he had been with the company and stated that he had been handpicked by Lake to take over his position. Russell's parents were both mentioned. They appeared to be prominent and socially connected. His engagement to Renee was noted, and the date that they were to be married.

A specific quote from Russell Ingram gave Ray pause. It read:

"I had just visited Mr. Lake at his home in Hawaii two days before," the rising young executive said emotionally. "I took him some information that needed his attention. He was so relaxed and upbeat, so happy to be away from the business grind. His death breaks my heart. He was like a second father to me."

Ray reread the man's words, then read them again. If Mrs. Sharon and Laura Smith were correct about the dates that Moody Lake had been living in the house across the street, then Russell Ingram was telling a lie. He knew that Moody Lake wasn't in Hawaii. He had been with him in Carmel.

Ray sat back in his chair. What was going on? His cell phone rang and he glanced at the caller I.D. It was Bev.

"Hey there." A smile creased his face.

"Hey yourself." Bev was smiling as well. "I got your message. So you're still going to Tiburon?"

Ray took his glasses off and gently rubbed his eyes. "Yes, I'm going to go ahead and drive up there. I want to check on the house. I'll just stay overnight and then fly back to L.A. on Monday."

For her own reasons, Bev was glad to hear that. "And suppose you don't want to come back on Monday?"

"If you're there, I'll be there."

His words warmed her. "Smooth talker."

"I sure am."

"You've got smooth moves, too." The thought of them tightened Bev's core.

"I'm glad that you remember." His tone was heated.

"You're a hard man to forget." That wasn't just a compliment, but reality. Ray Wilson was the kind of man who could leave a permanent imprint on a woman. She could testify to that.

Bev's meeting with her client had turned out to be an unqualified success. She had presented a win-win alternative to his investment portfolio and he had agreed to stay with her company. Both had left the meeting feeling good about the deal.

She wasn't sure that the execution of her next endeavor would be as successful, but her first step was to get the address of Ray's vacation home in Tiburon. Bev reviewed her options. She could call her daughter and get the address easily, but how would she explain why she needed it? Her budding relationship with Ray wasn't something that she was ready to share with Darnell and Thad. She could call Ray and ask him the address, but that would spoil everything. She was driving back to her house when the answer to the dilemma came to her. Excited, she parked the car and called his L.A. office.

"Wilson Associates." The voice on the other end of the line was very professional.

Bev was equally as formal. "Yes, this is Beverley Cameron, Thad Stewart's mother-in-law. Is this Donna?"

"Yes, Mrs. Cameron." The voice registered recognition. Bev had been to Ray's office with Darnell a couple of times.

"Well, Donna, I need Mr. Wilson's address in Tiburon. He's informed me that he'll be there this weekend, and I would like to send him a surprise for being so nice to our family during these trying times." She knew that Ray had kept his office abreast regarding his whereabouts. His associates were aware of Dana's illness, and there was no hesitation on the young woman's part in providing the information that Bev needed.

As she pulled back into traffic Bev began to have doubts about what she was planning—a surprise visit to Ray's home in Tiburon. That was something that she had never done before with any man. She wasn't certain that it was the right thing to do. Was she being too forward? Would he feel smothered by her sudden appearance? What if he wasn't alone when she got there? That was a consideration. She had come to trust him, but those kinds of things did happen. Maybe he really didn't miss her as much as she missed him. She didn't want to look like a fool.

A thousand questions filled her mind. Each one tried to fuel her doubt about their budding relationship. Yet as she remembered Ray's telephone call and the words that they spoke to each other, those doubts gradually faded. She was going to proceed with her plan to visit Ray in Tiburon. Whatever happened would happen. This was one time that she was willing to take a chance.

CHAPTER 18

Ray was awakened by the sound of the buzzer at the front gate. It turned out to be the contractor trying to get an early start.

While the man worked, Ray showered, dressed, and went downstairs to fix breakfast, the articles that he had printed out yesterday in hand. As he ate he reread the quote from Russell Ingram, curious about the discrepancy in his statement regarding Lake. Something was definitely wrong. Then there was Mitch. How long had he worked for this Ingram fellow, and for Stark Enterprises? He couldn't remember him ever mentioning either.

Of course, if he were honest, Mitch and he rarely discussed business. When it was discussed, it was Mitch asking about Ray's dealings. Being an entertainment attorney was a glamorous profession, and people were always interested in what he did. Ray couldn't deny all of the amenities that came with his career. They had been exciting when he was younger—the celebrities, the movie premieres, the parties. He was glad that he had chosen the specific career that he did; it had made him a wealthy man. But, as he had grown older, his work had become less of a priority. He was looking for something else in his life. He was looking for a special someone.

Ray's mouth turned up into a smile at the thought of Bev. He couldn't wait to see her. His mind tried to drift to what would happen between them when they were together again, but the scenario was so erotic that he had to force himself not to think about her or suffer the consequences. It was better to return his attention to the computer screen and the growing mystery of Moody Lake, a.k.a. Waters.

What was Ingram's lie about? Did he have something to do with Lake's disappearance? Ray continued reading. According to two eyewitnesses who knew Lake, he had gone out on the ocean alone. But had it really been Moody Lake? Had anyone seen his face? He reread the section of the articles that held the witnesses' comments. They stated that they had seen his *boat* headed out to sea. Their comments didn't reveal whether they had seen his face or not. It was possible that if Lake's face hadn't been seen, anyone with a similar build could have posed as him.

His eyes swept the rest of the article, and one sentence drew his attention: *Mrs. Hiromoto, the housekeeper, reported that she had last seen Mr. Lake when she left work on Wednesday.* How could the woman see someone in Hawaii who was in Carmel at the same time? Somebody had to be telling a lie. Was it Ingram, the housekeeper, or both? Logic told him that it was the latter. His pulse quickened. What in the world had he stumbled onto?

Had Russell Ingram's desire to head Stark Enterprises been so great that he might have wanted Lake dead? Mrs. Sharon and Mrs. Smith had no motives other than truth and they were positive that Lake had been on the Peninsula and not in Hawaii. Mrs. Smith had verified that Ingram had been with him the last time that Lake was seen alive. It was possible that Russell Ingram did have something to do with Moody Lake's disappearance, and if so, it hadn't happened in Hawaii. He wondered if Mitch knew about Ingram and that possibility. He had been an attorney for the company. Was he more than that? How close was Mitch to Ingram? Did Mitch know what was going on? Dana's words to Ray flashed though his memory.

"What I've found is very serious, and right now you're the only one that I can turn to. The only one I can trust."

Maybe Dana hadn't been up to one of her tricks when she called him. Maybe she *had* discovered something and it had something to do with Mitch's death.

Ray leaned back in his chair, closed his eyes, and concentrated on recalling every detail of his last conversation with Dana. He knew that she had to be home when she called him because that was where she had fallen down the stairs after tripping over—

Mitch's briefcase! That had been at the top of the stairs. Bev had tripped over it. At the time she had mentioned that the same thing might have happened to Dana, and Ray had the offending item at his house. Perhaps Dana had been bringing the briefcase with her when she was on her way to see him. Perhaps she had put it down, gone back to her room for something, then, forgetting that it was there, stumbled over it and taken a tumble. Did the briefcase contain something that she wanted him to see? He had gone over all of the papers in it and had found nothing out of the ordinary. There had been nothing to do with Stark Enterprises. How did Mitch fit into this whole picture?

Ray sighed as he thought about Mitch and how little he really knew about him. He had been to his house in the Hollywood Hills numerous times, but it had always been for social occasions. He couldn't remember being invited there for any other reason. He had gone on double dates with Mitch and Dana quite a bit over the past years. Laughs had been plenty, but conversations had never been deep. He and Mitch had known each other for years and they had called themselves friends. Yet he had known nothing about Mitch's family, and Mitch had never asked him about his. They each knew where the other one had gone to law school, but they didn't know each other's middle names. They had friends in common—all associated in some way with the law. They played golf together and occasionally attended other sports events. If he really was honest with himself, he had to admit that he really didn't know the real Mitch Clayton at all. Maybe that's why he hadn't questioned his suicide. He hadn't known him well enough to doubt that he would take his own life.

It came as a surprise to Ray that Mitch was suffering from cancer. Dana had informed him of that. Mitch had never said a word to him about it. Their relationship had been nothing like the one that Ray had with Thad. They knew everything about each other. They were confidantes. Ray didn't know who Mitch's confidante had been. Dana, perhaps? Maybe she had been right about Mitch having been murdered, except that she had been looking in the wrong direction.

As Ray sat debating the possibility that there was some sort of rational explanation for all of this instead of something sinister, another ominous thought occurred to him. He typed the housekeeper's name, Mrs. Irene Hiromoto, into Google to see if he would get any hits. He did—her obituary. It stated that her cause of death had been a heart attack. She had died a month after Lake's disappearance. She had been forty-nine years old.

Had it been a coincidence? Every instinct that Ray possessed screamed no.

"Mr. Wilson?"

Ray nearly jumped out of his chair at the disembodied voice coming from the front of the house. He chuckled at himself for having been spooked by the intrigue that he seemed to have uncovered. After alerting the contractor to his whereabouts, Ray went to inspect his work, paid the man, and saw him to the door. He called Thad to inform him that the repairs had been completed. Ray then prepared to head to Tiburon with a lot more on his mind than the short time that he would spend in his vacation home.

Bev could barely contain the tears that threatened to flow as she read the latest entry in Dana's journal. Her flight to San Francisco had been delayed, so she had opted for this as reading material rather than a magazine. She was glad that she had. Bev no longer harbored any guilt for having invaded her sister's privacy. She had learned so much about Dana's life from her journals. There had been revelations that she doubted that her sister would have ever shared. Her entries had confirmed what Bev had always suspected. Dana loved her family, but she felt that she had failed to live up to their legacy and had embarrassed her parents and sister with what she described as her "antics." She felt that if she had been stronger, she would not have been an abused wife in her first marriage. Instead of embracing the strength that it took to leave that relationship, she berated herself for having chosen an abuser the first time and an adulterer the second time. She labeled her choices and her subsequent divorces as a disgrace to her branch of the family, and she seemed unable to forgive herself. Dana had been hell-bent on making her relationship with Mitch work, no matter what she had to do. She took her family's rejection of him as a personal reprimand for having made yet another bad choice.

In every journal, there had been page after page of self-deprecation. Bev wondered how her sister's confidence had become so diminished. Their family worked hard on instilling pride and dignity in each of its members. Where had it gone wrong for Dana?

Bev concentrated on the journal passage that she was now reading. It described what Dana believed that she had learned from being a part of the Stillwaters family:

We are a family whose foundation is based on hate and revenge. My grandmother wanted revenge for the death of my grandfather. She blamed people outside of our race for his death. That's why I don't have a chance of getting my family to approve of Mitch. So, once again, I'm the pariah. With Mitch, I'm the first one to consider marrying outside of my race. I know that's not going over well among the anointed ones, but never in my wildest imagination did I ever think that the hate that's been passed down would turn into cold-blooded murder. It breaks my heart and angers me at the same time.

Bev's heart sank. Esther Stillwaters had tried so hard to teach every member in her family the principles of self love, self pride, and self determination. How in the world had Dana gotten a message of hate out of that? Were there others in the family who thought as Dana did?

Closing the journal, Bev discreetly swiped at her tears as she looked out the window. Dana had been wrong about the family's objection to Mitch. His race had never been the issue. It had been his character. If Dana weren't so sick, or if it really mattered, Bev would tell her sister that the one and only time that she had met Mitch he had made a move on her, making suggestive remarks that were so graphic she was forced to give him a piece of her mind. The irony of the situation was that he had understood the dynamics between Dana and Bev perfectly. He had been smug when he informed Bev that Dana wouldn't believe her if she was told that he had approached her older sister. He was as certain of Dana's loyalty to him as he was of her jealousy and animosity toward her sister.

"Anything that you say against me will only turn her against you," he had told her.

She had made the mistake of testing his challenge, certain that blood was thicker than water. She had avoided informing her sister about his outrageous behavior, but she had verbalized her objection to the man. Doing so had been a gamble, and it was one that she had lost.

Over the loudspeaker the captain apologized to the passengers for the delay, and announced that they were cleared for takeoff. Bev relaxed in her seat. She wasn't sure that she would read anymore of Dana's journal entries. It was too difficult. Dana had emerged as a highly intelligent woman, but an extremely confused one. Her sister seemed to enjoy the role of victim. She liked being miserable. Bev felt sorry for her.

That made the course that Bev had decided to take even more important to her. She was choosing happiness. Never before in her orderly life would she ever have considered getting on a plane and flying unannounced to a man's home to surprise him. It just didn't happen with Bev Cameron. She was used to controlling a situation. The results in this case were beyond her control, but she was going for it anyway.

She had already reserved a car that she would pick up at the airport, and then she would drive to Tiburon. She had even bought a new negligee that she hoped Ray would remove very slowly. That thought brought a salacious smile to her face. She was becoming so bad.

By the time the airplane had cleared the runway and climbed high into the sky, Bev had replaced negative thoughts about Dana's journal with positive thoughts of Ray. She wondered what he was thinking about now. She couldn't wait to get to him.

"That's right, Stark Enterprises," Ray repeated into the speakerphone as he sat staring at the screen on his laptop. "I've read that Mitch did some legal work for them. The company's headquarters is in New York, and it's headed by a guy named Russell Ingram. Did you ever hear Mitch mention the company or its CEO before?"

Ray's fascination with what he had uncovered about Ingram had propelled him back onto the computer instead of on the road for Tiburon. Now he was talking to James Starr, a friend of his who had been a detective in New York City and presently owned a security consulting firm based there. He had met James through Mitch when the three of them played golf together. He and James had hit it off right away and still paired off on the golf course whenever they saw each other. His name had popped into Ray's head as he was going over the information that he had gathered earlier. James had known Mitch much longer than he had and might possibly have answers to some of the questions that were haunting Ray. But instead of responding to Ray's inquiry, there was a prolonged silence on the other end.

"James?" Ray frowned. "What's up?"

There was another beat before he responded. "Why are you asking?"

The tone in James's voice was measured. Ray was on instant alert.

"I was on the internet and ran across a picture of Mitch with the C.E.O. of Stark Enterprises, and the caption said that Mitch was an attorney for the company."

"And?" James stretched the word out making it clear that he wanted more detail in Ray's explanation. "What has this got to do with entertainment law?" He sounded more defensive than curious. "Anyway, Mitch is dead. What difference does it make if he worked for the company or not?"

There was a lot being left unsaid in this conversation. "What's up, man? What aren't you telling me?" Ray probed.

Once again, Ray was met with a measured silence. He could hear James thinking. He had something to relay, but was weighing whether he should do so or not. Ray remained silent until James made up his mind.

"Ray, all that I can say to you is that I have heard of Stark Enterprises, and if the caption that you read said that Mitch worked for the company, then he did."

That was it. No matter how much Ray tried, James would give him no further information. The two men disconnected, leaving Ray to speculate about what hadn't been said.

He knew from past conversations that James had worked as an undercover officer in the narcotics unit when he was with the police department. Could that mean that his reluctance to talk about Stark Enterprises indicated that the company was involved in the illegal drug trade? Ray came to only one conclusion about that, yes, and James's reluctance to discuss Stark Enterprises more likely than not meant that the company was under investigation.

Ray took a shaky breath. "Oh, boy."

What had started as mere curiosity on his part was developing into something he wasn't sure that he wanted to pursue. James had been right. Who cared if Mitch worked for the company? He *was* dead. Yet an hour later Ray found himself still in Carmel on his laptop.

He had settled in the kitchen this time, with a half-eaten sandwich sitting on the counter as he researched the name Charles "Moody" Lake. The latent detective in Ray identified him as being implicated in whatever had happened—or was happening—at Stark Enterprises. An extended search had yielded no more than Ray had discovered before about the man. Even his obituary was sparse. It listed his place of birth as upstate New York—but there was no city or town mentioned. It stated that he was in his fifties and mentioned his rise from messenger to the head of Stark Enterprises, his contributions to charity, and his demise in Hawaii.

The mystery of Moody Lake's life was as compelling as the mystery of his death. Ray stared at the picture of him on the computer screen. Who was this man? There seemed to be little information about him. Why had he been in Carmel under an assumed name? Had he been running from someone? Ingram, perhaps? If so, the younger man had found him.

Was Stark Enterprises a legal front for illegal activities? Had Lake been into drugs? Most drug kingpins liked to remain discreet, and Lake fit that description.

Ray continued to stare at the man's picture. The more he looked at him the more he got the feeling that there was something familiar about him, especially around the eyes. It was the eyebrows and the ears, too. The slope of his eyebrows reminded him of someone. Who? He leaned closer to the screen to examine the picture. He traced the eyebrows with his index finger. Where had he seen that slope before? It was very pronounced, and those ears—he traced the ears.

Licking his lips, Ray slowly leaned back in his chair as the answer dawned on him. His goddaughter Nia had those eyebrows, and she had inherited them from her mother.

As a matter of fact, her beautiful little face looked as though it had been genetically split in half. From the bridge of her nose to her chin, she looked exactly like her father, having inherited his nose, his perfectly centered dimples, his mouth, and his chin. From the bridge up she looked just like her mother. She had inherited her great-grandmother's eye color, but Nia's eyes were large and expressive like Darnell's and they were framed by the same thick, luscious eyelashes and sloped eyebrows. She even had her mother's ears.

Ray closed his eyes and visualized the face of his best friend's wife and child. He opened his eyes and looked at Moody Lake's picture again. What was that man doing in Carmel using a different name? Why didn't he want anyone to know who he was? Yes, Stark Enterprises was an international company, but its CEO didn't have worldwide recognition. The paparazzi hadn't been camped on his doorstep. Why the secrecy? Was there more to his presence on the Peninsula than a simple vacation? Was he protecting someone? Having a rendezvous with someone?

"I remember that he came over to introduce himself to me once and wanted to meet Darnell . . ."

Mrs. Sharon's words echoed in Ray's head. He studied Moody's picture again.

Had the man been a stalker? Had he planned on harming Darnell? He enlarged the photo. The slope of the brow, the shape of the ears kept leaping into the forefront. What crept into Ray's consciousness caused his head to pound. What he was thinking was impossible. Quickly, he turned off his computer, disconnecting himself from the source as if it were complicit in the formation of his illicit thoughts.

Ray backed away from the counter on shaky limbs. No more Stark Enterprises, no more Russell Ingram, no more Moody Lake. He had to get back to the realm of sanity, because what flashed across his mind had been insane, and he refused to go there.

CHAPTER 19

"Hi, baby." Bev was nearly breathless with excitement as she strolled through the San Francisco airport with her overnight bag slung across her shoulder.

She was headed for the car rental agency. Darnell had called just as Bev disembarked from the plane. Her daughter was unaware of her mother's plan to surprise Ray, and she planned on keeping it that way. As a matter of fact, Darnell wasn't aware of the change in the relationship between her mother and Ray. Bev knew that Ginny had noticed how the vibes between Ray and her had shifted and she assumed that her mother would have said something to Darnell, but it was becoming apparent that she hadn't. That made Bev wonder why. No matter, she felt too good to care.

As far as Bev was concerned, if she had wings she would fly. Never would she have thought that in this stage of her life that she would feel this happy about a man. She wanted to share her joy with someone, but when Darnell said—

"My, don't you sound happy today. What's up?"

Bev answered, "Oh, I'm just enjoying life."

"That's good. When are you flying back to California?"

It was clear that she thought that Bev was still in Chicago, and Bev didn't correct her assumption.

"I plan on being back in L.A. on Monday." Bev quickly changed the subject. "How are my grandbaby and son-in-law doing, and how is the production going?"

Those were safe subjects and Darnell took the bait, telling her about her family and the progress of the new film. She was chattering happily until a voice over the airport loudspeaker caught her attention.

"Who's that? Where are you?"

"I'm out and about doing my thing." Bev was deliberately evasive. "I've got to go now. Kiss my grandbaby for me." She disconnected before further questions could be asked. Sometimes it was best not to let your children know all of your business, especially your grown children. It made life less complicated. This was especially true when it came to her daughter, who was always getting to the *bottom* of things.

Darnell was no shrinking violet when it came to expressing her opinion, no matter the subject. She was definitely her mother's child. Bev was sure that when her daughter found out about Ray that she would have plenty to say. So be it. She would tell her when she was ready for her to know. That is, if somebody else didn't beat her to it.

With her shoulders squared and head high, Bev stepped up her pace. She was a woman who danced to her own tune, and this weekend she and Ray Wilson would be singing her song together.

Ray felt like a fugitive from justice as he moved along the highway toward Tiburon. The crime had been committed in Carmel and he was carrying the evidence with him in his head. He had gone into entertainment law to avoid having to delve into the abyss of depravity that too often accompanied criminal law. Yet here he was, mired in what appeared to have been a murder and wandering off into flights of fantasy about the apparent victim. Right now he needed the diversion offered by his home in Tiburon, with its close proximity to the beach and its magnificent view of the San Francisco skyline.

Ray wasn't sure what he was going to do with the information he had uncovered regarding Ingram and Lake. He needed time to think. There was a lot to consider. If he was correct about the CEO of Stark Enterprises, Renee Ingram's world would be turned upside down. He would hate to be the source of upheaval in her life. She was such a nice person. If he had simply let well enough alone he wouldn't be facing this dilemma.

When he reached Tiburon he planned on calling Bev so that he could hear her sweet voice. Then he would take a hot bath, climb into bed, and sleep through the night. On Monday he would board a plane and head back to L.A. That sounded like a plan to him.

As she turned off the highway onto the Tiburon exit, Bev could hardly concentrate. She couldn't wait to see Ray's face when he opened the door and saw her standing there. He should be home by now. He had told her when he expected to arrive at his house. That had been hours ago. He had further informed her that his only plan for the evening was to rest. She figured that he could do plenty of that after they were finished with the business that she had planned for them. They would both need their rest.

The GPS system that she had brought with her guided her through Tiburon's streets and finally to the tree-lined neighborhood in which Ray's house was located. The houses in this area were elevated on sloped hillsides and were obscured from the street by terraced lawns. The landscaping was elegant with trimmed shrubbery, exotic flowers, and flowering fruit trees. There were no addresses on the mailboxes, which had proven to be a godsend for Thad when he lived on this street. Fans found it difficult to find his house. It might have proven to be an obstacle to Bev as well if Ray's receptionist hadn't told her about the custom-made gate that identified the property. It separated the stone steps leading upward to the house from the street below. At the left of the gate was what appeared to be a garage built into the hill beneath the house, but it was only a facade. The faux double doors with the frosted windows opened to reveal a driveway that wound its way up to the house.

Bev parked the car across the street from Ray's home. Flinging her overnight bag over her shoulder, she stepped out of the car and dashed across the street, wondering at the lack of sidewalks in such a prosperous area. Pulling on the ornate handle of the wooden gate, she discovered that it was locked. She hadn't planned on that, but she should have expected it. A vine-covered speaker and buzzer were located next to the gate. It looked as though her surprise scenario would have to be adjusted a bit. She had hoped to see the look of shock on his face when he opened his front door, but from the look of it that might not happen. It didn't matter, she was here and she couldn't wait to see him. She pressed the buzzer and waited.

Ray crossed the Golden Gate Bridge, awestruck, as usual, by the natural beauty of the Bay Area. Unlike others who might live in this region, he wasn't immune to its intoxicating allure. He was seriously considering moving his law office up here. That possibility had been in the back of his mind since he purchased his house in Tiburon, and each year it grew stronger as life in the Hollywood bubble grew less appealing.

On his journey north, he had taken Highway 1, known as the Pacific Coast Highway, and he had enjoyed the leisurely drive. He had even packed his cell phone in his overnight case and put it in the trunk of the car. This was one of the few times that his life had been unencumbered by time restraints or other obligations, and he was glad that he had made that decision. It had done wonders for his psyche, helping him to temporarily forget the pressing issues that he might have to face in the coming days. He'd needed this brief respite for his peace of mind.

Glancing at the gas gauge he became aware that there was something else that he needed. Thad's expensive sports car wasn't mileage friendly, and there had been many fuel stops along the way. Ray turned off the highway onto the Sausalito exit, doubtful that he would make it home if he didn't feed the gas tank.

As she sat in the car parked across the street from Ray's house, Bev tried hard to fight the disappointment that she felt at his not being at home. She had called his cell phone with the hope that he had stepped out for an errand, or perhaps was inside his house asleep, tired from his trip north. His voice mail answered. Leaving a message for him to call her, she had disconnected in dismay. She had tried the buzzer at the gate one more time with the hope that if he were asleep inside he might hear it. The silence that met her attempt dashed that hope.

The joy that she had harbored during her journey to Tiburon threatened to erupt into tears now that she was here, but she wouldn't allow it. She was a grown woman, not some adolescent child. She had built her surprise visit with Ray into an event that hadn't materialized the way that she had planned. No big deal, but she couldn't help wondering where he was. She knew that there were any number of places that he could be, but it was almost certain that he wasn't in his house.

Mentally, she listed her options. She could continue to wait until he returned, camping out here in front of his home like some groupie. This meant that she could still surprise him, but stakeouts weren't her style. Or, when she did talk to him—that was if he returned her call today—she could tell him where she was, nip the element of surprise, and still be with him as planned. That was the most logical plan, but what if he didn't call until late this evening? She didn't plan on being some homeless refugee. Maybe she could get a hotel room nearby. Somehow that plan didn't appeal to her, either, but she had to think of something to salvage this fiasco. Starting the car, Bev drove away.

Nobody knew that she was here. Her plan had been a gamble from the beginning, one in which she would win or she would lose. The latter had been the result, and she would take her emotional lumps. She would see Ray on Monday. She could live with that. Meanwhile, she had to come up with a plan to make lemonade out of lemons.

Ray's progress was slow as he drove into Sausalito. The picturesque hamlet drew tourists like flies to honey, and this weekend was no different. The streets were thick with people. His slow progress made him wonder if he couldn't have made it to Tiburon with the fuel that he had. There was a line of cars at the first gas station that he spotted, and he made the mistake of not stopping. In an effort to get to the next station, he tried to take a detour to avoid being caught in the line of traffic that would take him through the main street where tourists were even more abundant, but he got trapped in the caravan of cars. He ended up exactly where he didn't want to be, on Sausalito's main street. Frustrated, he sat behind the wheel of Thad's fancy car as it inched along at a snail's pace.

Bev was determined not to let her disappointment ruin her day, and she had come up with a plan. The Stillwaters family owned a building in San Francisco in which Darnell had a furnished condo. Bev had a spare key to the place. Usually the condo was subleased, but it was empty at the moment. Bev had decided to stay there overnight. She had originally reserved a chartered plane to fly Ray and her to L.A. on Monday, but she decided to cancel that reservation and spend Sunday driving down the coast to Los Angeles. She hadn't done that for quite some time. She would spend the night in Santa Barbara, then arrive in the City of Angels on Monday morning, return the rental car, and take a cab to Ray's house, meeting him there. Her trip to Tiburon need never be mentioned.

Satisfied with that decision, she found a parking space off the beaten path and hiked down the hill toward her intended site, the bustling main thoroughfare of Sausalito. Central to her recovery plan was shopping in as many of the stylish boutiques lining the boulevard as she could until she spent herself into feeling better about today's events. She turned the corner and stepped onto the main thoroughfare just as the car that Ray was driving inched by.

CHAPTER 20

Bev was having a ball. In her opinion there was nothing better in life to counter temporary depression than shopping, and she was taking her prescription with a vengeance. Most of the packages that she was carrying were filled with clothing for her granddaughter.

Months ago Darnell and Thad had presented Bev with a plaque that dubbed her the Doting Grandmother of the Year. They said that it was in honor of her obsession with buying Nia everything on earth that a baby did or didn't need. Thad had threatened to submit Bev's name to the Guinness Book of Records for having purchased more baby products than any human being on earth. Bev had informed them both that it was their fault that she was such a spendthrift when it came to Nia. It was their combined genes that had produced the most beautiful baby in the world. That had stopped their teasing, and all they said now when presented with new gifts for the baby was thank you. Smiling at that thought, Bev moved on to the next shop, enjoying herself to the hilt.

Ray's frustration at his slow pace through the streets of Sausalito led him to take drastic action. At the first opportunity he made a sharp left off the main drag and climbed uphill on a one-way street that was taking him further away from a gas station and closer to empty on the gas gauge. Parking the car, he got out and started trekking downhill toward the crowded downtown street that had caused him such aggravation. If he couldn't beat them, he would join them. There were worse places in the world to kill time then in Sausalito, where its quaint shops, eclectic art galleries, and breathtaking views attracted tourists from all over the world. He had way too much on his mind. Perhaps this was his clue to slow down, chill out, and enjoy simply being. He would pick up some junk food, walk down to the Downtown Plaza, and sit and watch the tourists coming and going on the ferry from San Francisco. He hadn't done that in years. He brightened at the thought of it as he joined the throngs on the city's streets.

Two hours passed before Bev took a break. Surrounded by packages, she kicked her shoes off beneath the table as she relaxed at an outside café and feasted on a sumptuous crab salad sandwich, washing it down with a cold glass of lemonade. Finishing her meal, she leaned back in her chair and sighed with satisfaction. What a day.

Observing her numerous purchases, she dreaded having to hike back down the street and uphill to her car carrying her bundles and seriously considered an alternative. In retracing her steps to her vehicle, she had to pass the Downtown Plaza where the ferries docked, and it was much closer than the street where she had parked. She could easily board a ferry to San Francisco, catch a cab from Fisherman's Wharf to Darnell's condo and come back tomorrow and get the car. The thought was a bit extreme, but it sure would save her lots of steps and some arm strain. Actually, it was a solution for the extremely lazy, but what the hell. She was on a mini vacation, and that's when people did crazy things. Gathering her bags, she mentally reviewed her choices as she paid her tab and headed up the street.

In the picturesque Plaza, Ray folded the newspaper that he had been reading. He hadn't felt this relaxed in years. He had spent hours doing nothing but reading, snacking, and people watching, all against a San Francisco backdrop that was picture-postcard perfect. Who could ask for anything more? Tossing his trash into a receptacle, he took one final breath of sea air and headed back to his car.

As Ray exited the Plaza, Bev entered it from the opposite direction. She was still weighing whether to take the ferry or not. She hadn't ridden on one in ages, and it might be fun. Shifting the packages, the possibility of boarding the next one headed out became more of an intent as her arms grew weary. She stood watching the passengers disembark from the latest ferry to arrive. A boisterous group of teenagers caught her attention as they pushed and shoved each other playfully.

Ray strolled back into the Plaza headed for the trash receptacle where he had accidently discarded the newspaper that he had been reading. It had an article that he had meant to save.

Bev watched the frolicking teenagers as they entered the Plaza. Their joy was infectious. They reminded her of her young cousins in Stillwaters.

Preoccupied with his intended purpose, Ray found the newspaper resting where he had tossed it. He started to retrieve it, but the piercing squeals of a group of boisterous teenagers distracted him.

Bev continued to watch the adolescents. She turned. Ray looked up.

In that instant, the newspaper was abandoned. The bulging packages were dropped to the ground. All else faded into the background except one another.

"We're supposed to be in Tiburon," Ray reminded Bev as they strolled along the waterfront in Sausalito.

"I know." Bev leaned in to him and she tightened her arm around his waist. "But how can we leave heaven?"

Ray agreed. Being with her, no matter where they were, was like floating on cloud nine. He was beyond happy that she had left Chicago and flown to the Bay Area to surprise *him.* He knew that such an action was outside of her comfort zone, which had to mean that he was very special to her. He had no doubt that he loved her, and if she could find it in her heart to return his love his world would be complete.

He had hardly been able to believe his eyes when he looked up and saw her standing there in the Plaza. Their fervent greeting had turned all eyes from the animated teenagers causing a ruckus to the passionate couple's reunion. Bev and Ray had been oblivious to everything around them except each other.

She had explained the reason for her presence in the area and the grin that Ray had bestowed on her was still etched on his face. Taking her burdensome packages back to her car, they had decided that they weren't ready to leave the ambience of Sausalito. They spent what was left of the day hand-in-hand exploring the special places that Bev and he had missed as solo explorers. They talked and laughed at everything, thrilled at doing simple things together. As evening descended, they dined at a first-class restaurant and then caught a jazz act at a nearby club. It was now past midnight, Sunday morning, and there they were still in the hamlet and strolling along the marina, reluctant to end the magic in what they had dubbed their special place.

Both of them were exhausted. It had been a long day for each. Stifling a yawn, Bev took refuge on a bench overlooking the Bay. In the distance, the lights of San Francisco sparkled. The sound of the water lapping the shoreline threatened to lure her to sleep.

Ray sat down beside her. Putting his arm around her, he drew her closer to him as she rested her head on his shoulder.

"I used to be able to go until sunup, sleep for a couple of hours, jump up, shower, and work nonstop for the rest of the day," Ray reminisced. "It's obvious that those days are over." Every bone in his body was screaming for relief.

"Father Time creeps up on all of us." Bev patted his leg and gave another extensive yawn. "Now what we have to do is decide our next move. I don't know about you, but I'm not sure I have the strength to walk back to my car and follow you to Tiburon. I know that it's not that far, but I'm too tired to drive. How about you?"

"No can do." Ray stretched his legs out. "We can always bunk out here and call it a night." He patted the bench. "It's kind of hard, but at this point I can manage."

"At this point, that doesn't sound half bad." Bev yawned again, and then hugged the sports coat he had loaned her snugly against her body. They sat in silence for a moment, reluctant to move. She interrupted the night sounds.

"I have an idea."

Ray turned to her and in the moonlight saw the twinkle in her eyes. "What?"

She gave him a mischievous grin. "We passed a four star hotel a couple of blocks back." She jabbed her thumb in that direction.

Ray got the message. "Uh-huh, and if that one is full, I'm sure that there is at least one that isn't."

"Yep." Bev nodded. "And I don't know about yours, but my credit card travels. I'm willing to go half and half."

"Oh, I think that mine can handle the whole thing." Ray stood and pulled her to her feet with both hands. Suddenly he was filled with new energy. So was Bev.

"Then let's go. After all, we're wearing our pajamas."

Her words shot straight to Ray's groin. "You're so bad, but I like it."

"I try to please."

"Indeed you do."

When they arrived at the sumptuous hotel, they were in luck. There was one room left, a suite on an upper floor. As Ray registered them at the front desk, Bev slipped her hands into his jacket pocket to pull it tighter around her. It was then that she felt something small and hard against her hand. Curious, she withdrew the object. It was a diamond earring—heart-shaped and expensive. She was examining it when Ray, the card key in hand, turned to escort her to their room.

"What's that?" he cocked his head and peered at the article she was holding.

Bev held it up to him for examination. "It's an earring. I found it in your pocket."

"*My* pocket?" Ray took it from her and peered at it curiously as they headed for the elevator. "Hmmm." He tried to remember the reason it had been in there. "This cost a chunk of change."

Bev watched his baffled expression as he held it to the light, and then rubbed it gently between his fingers. While her son-in-law and other men that she knew had pierced ears and wore at least one earring, Ray didn't. She waited patiently for an explanation as they stepped into the elevator. It was as they ascended to the second floor that Ray remembered the earring's source.

"This is Dana's. I found it on the floor in the living room of her condo that day that we went over there to get her night clothes. Remember? It was the day that you hurt your foot."

"Oh, yeah." She recalled that day, and all that had happened, vividly. That was when Ray had first kissed her. How could she forget?

"I must have been wearing that jacket and slipped this into the pocket." He looked down at the diamond lying in his open palm. "I forgot all about it, but I do remember something else that happened that day." He wiggled his eyebrows suggestively. Indeed, he did remember the kiss that they had shared. He handed her the earring. "Why don't you put this in your purse and return it to her jewelry box." The elevator doors opened. "Meanwhile—" Picking Bev up, he stepped into the hallway with her in his arms. "We've got business to take care of."

She smothered her laughter in the crook of his neck as he waltzed in circles down the hallway to their room. Once the door closed behind them they wasted no time stripping down to their *pajamas.* They showered together, not knowing whether it was the water or their steamy lovemaking that fogged the etched glass of the shower stall. They mapped each other's body with searing kisses and touches that brought both to shattered completions.

Bev's body throbbed with pleasure as Ray enfolded them both inside of one of the fluffy robes that the hotel provided and then he walked them into the bedroom. She smothered his face with kisses, enjoying everything about this man.

He led Bev to the king-sized bed, where they lay draped in each other's arms. Anticipation between them was running rampant as they snuggled together in perfect contentment and promptly fell asleep.

They awakened in the same position when the sun tried to sneak past the closed blinds later that morning.

When they realized what had happened, all they could do was laugh.

"I guess we're officially a middle-aged couple." Ray wiped at the tears of mirth in his eyes.

"No doubt." Bev rolled out of his arms onto the floor and crossed the room, headed for the bathroom of their opulent suite. She couldn't remember the last time that she had felt so good. Oh, yes, she could! It was the first time that she and Ray made love, or maybe it was when she saw him in the Plaza, or maybe it was when they were strolling through the streets of Sausalito. She felt good whenever she was with Ray. He had brought so much into her life.

Ray lay in bed thinking exactly the same thing about her. Bev was a dazzling ray of sunshine. The presence of a woman's earring in his jacket pocket could have meant loads of trouble from any other woman, but it hadn't appeared to faze her. She had listened to his explanation and moved on. No sweat, no drama. She had trusted him, and he hoped never to betray that confidence.

Refreshed, Bev re-entered the room and crawled back into bed beside Ray. He drew her to him. "I just want to thank you for trusting me. You never questioned what I told you about that earring. Your faith in me means a lot."

Bev was surprised by his words. "Why wouldn't I trust you? You're the man who took my mother and me into his home and treated us with kindness, even when I wasn't sure that I liked you. When my family was preoccupied with worry about Dana, it was you who saw to our every need. Shoot, you even served as my Sir Galahad when I hurt my foot, and I don't know many men who would have dropped everything that they were doing to fly out of town for a friend to see about his busted toilet." She waited until he stopped laughing at that one. "You're a good man, Ray. You really are, and you deserve my trust."

Her words brought a lump to his throat. He didn't try to speak. Instead, he kissed her thoroughly, putting into action what he couldn't express in words.

Bev lay back on the bed, ready to make love to Ray. Running her hands down his muscled torso she opened her arms to him and he entered them.

"You know that what's between us isn't merely sexual, don't you?" Ray flicked the tip of his tongue over her moist triangle.

"I know." She was barely able to respond as his lips roamed. She had never allowed a man to do to her what he was doing. Of course she had never been with a man quite like Ray. The pleasure he was giving her was indescribable. Every nerve in her body was screaming for release, and Ray's expertise provided it. Bev saw stars.

"You're much too good at this," she rasped as she tried to recover.

"And I can get better." Covering his shaft, he proceeded to show her.

When he entered her Bev had no doubt that he would live up to his word. Wrapping her legs firmly around him, she allowed him to delve deep.

"You don't know the power you have over me," Ray gasped as he set a slow, unhurried pace. As he did so he looked into Bev's eyes. He wanted her to know what she meant to him. He wanted to alleviate any doubt about his love.

Conversation disappeared as the blistering heat building up inside of her threatened to scorch her very soul. Their synchronized movements intensified. Ray pumped like a man obsessed and Bev responded eagerly. The need for each other was uncontrollable. The rest of the morning they indulged in sensuous acts of pleasing one another in every way that they could think of.

It was an hour before check out time and, amid a tangle of damp, wrinkled bedding, Bev and Ray still lay in the hotel room wrapped in each other's arms.

"I'm as tired as hell." Ray caressed Bev's derrière as she lay sprawled across his torso.

"Ditto," was all Bev could manage to say. She was too exhausted to move and wasn't sure if she ever wanted to do so again. She had never been so satisfied in her life. A steady dose of this man could kill a woman, but it was guaranteed that she would die happy.

"Then I vote that we stay here until we gather the strength to move," Ray suggested. He could barely keep his eyes open.

Another "ditto" was Bev's reply as her heavy eyelids slowly closed and she succumbed to sleep. A few seconds later Ray joined her. A sliver of Sausalito sunshine managed to steal its way past the closed window blinds and shine on the naked lovers asleep on this bright Sunday afternoon. There was nothing unusual about the two of them and the scenario, except that they both slept with smiles on their faces.

CHAPTER 21

"I bet that you were spoiled rotten," Ray teased Bev as they sat across the table from one another before the open French doors that led to the balcony beyond. They were still in the suite that they had rented in Sausalito. It faced the Bay, and they were enjoying the incredible scenery beyond. The setting was very romantic, and they had been reluctant to give it up. Their erotic romp had left them so exhausted that they had made a decision to stay put. It was now late evening and they had yet to leave the hotel. They'd ordered room service, slipped into their fluffy robes, and were now enjoying a delicious meal, as well as each other.

"I won't lie to you," Bev confessed. "When I was growing up, what I wanted, I got. I was one of the few Stillwaters children who didn't have any brothers and sisters. That is, before Dana came along, and I lived up to the stereotype of being an only child. It got so bad that my cousin Gerry threatened to stop playing with me."

"You must have been a holy terror." Ray could imagine it. Bev had a stubborn streak a mile long.

"I prefer thinking of myself as having been behaviorally challenged." Bev grinned, spearing a piece of quiche and sticking it into her mouth.

Ray chuckled. "Or maybe you were just special."

"I like to think so." Bev chewed and swallowed, then sat back and watched Ray fondly. "Did you know that I think that you're special, too? I'm crazy about you."

Ray almost choked on his food. He coughed and sputtered until Bev was ready to come out of her chair to his rescue.

"Are you all right?" Her eyes were wide with alarm.

Ray nodded his head in the affirmative, waving away her concern. He gave a final cough and took a deep breath.

"You caught me off guard. You should give a guy a warning before saying things like that, although I do like hearing it." He sat back and observed her closely. "Now you can tell me exactly what 'I'm crazy about you' means." Crossing his arms across his chest, he waited for her reply.

Bev knew by his stance that he expected her to dodge his question. He was wrong.

"It means that I like your intelligence and kindness, your consideration and loyalty. I like your gentleness, and—" She hesitated. Leaning toward him, she rested her chin in both hands.

Ray was about to burst with anticipation. "Okay, *and* what?"

Bev made him sweat. From the grin on his face she could see that he was pleased by what she had already said. If that was true, then her next words should make him ecstatic.

"And you can get down in the bedroom."

Ray laughed out loud. "I'll never get tired of hearing that one." Leaning across the table he gave her a peck on her lips. "Thank you."

"I thought that would stroke your ego." She resumed eating.

Ray studied Bev as she finished her meal. Her words had touched him in ways that she would never know.

"Now I'm going to tell you something to stroke yours." He gave her the same dramatic pause that she had given him before continuing. "These last few weeks with you have been the best of my life, and I think that you're wonderful."

Bev gave him a pleased nod. "Thank you very much."

"I want you to know that everything I've thought about you all of these years, all of the daydreams I've had about you, have been fulfilled."

Bev licked her lips nervously. She was beginning to feel uncomfortable as Ray's mood became more serious.

"And having said that, I want to ask you something."

Bev swallowed. She wasn't sure that she wanted to know what that *something* was.

"I want to know if you coming here to be with me means that you're committed to us being together? I don't plan on dating anybody else. I don't want to see anyone else. I'm yours exclusively."

Bev didn't shrink away from what he was saying. He was being honest, and she owed him the same. She knew that what he was asking was different from the conversation that they'd had before. He wanted something deeper from her, something that she hadn't been sure that she could give him the last time that they'd had this conversation. Truthfully, she had hoped to have more time together before they progressed to this stage, but things happened when they were supposed to happen, and she had increased the stakes when she had shown up unannounced.

"It seems that every time we make love we have this conversation." Bev tried levity, but Ray didn't laugh at her attempt. She reached across the table and took his hand. "I haven't been good at commitment for a long time, Ray, but on my way here all I could think about was you. Having any man on my mind like that hasn't happened to me in a long time, and I'm glad that man is you."

Ray liked her reply. He kissed the palm of her hand, and then, reaching across the table, he brought her face to his and devoured her mouth. The heat between them spiraled. It didn't take long for the robes to be discarded, the dishes tossed aside, and the table to became the setting for a different kind of feast.

It was nightfall and Bev stood on the balcony of the hotel suite looking across the inky waters of the Bay at the twinkling lights outlining the San Francisco skyline. She would have appreciated the beauty of the scene if she had been aware of it, but the postcard moment faded into oblivion as she wondered if she was in love or in lust? Never in her life had she experienced anything like the erotic romps that she'd had been having with Ray. She couldn't recall having had such sexual fulfillment with a man before, not even with Colton, and she felt like a traitor even forming that thought.

She had been a sexually inexperienced girl when she was with her husband. He'd had to teach her everything. He was a conservative man, a traditional man in every way. Ray wasn't, and her satiated body was grateful for the difference. Yet, lust wasn't love. She knew what love was, and what she had described to Ray about her feelings for him, that was—what?

As was her habit, Bev's hand went to her throat to finger Colton's wedding ring. She stilled. It wasn't there.

Surprised, she stepped from the patio into the bedroom and inspected the room. After their table-top loving, Ray and she had hiked to their respective cars to retrieve their overnight bags so that they could change clothes. Had she been wearing the chain then? She couldn't remember. Maybe she took it off before going into the bathroom for a shower. Her eyes fell on the nightstand. She normally placed it there. It was empty. She snatched up the shoulder bag that she had been carrying and dug through it frantically. Ray entered the bedroom from the sitting room and noticed what she was doing.

"What's going on?"

"I'm looking for Colton's ring."

Bev didn't seem to notice that Ray had stiffened, but he did notice the fear in her voice and the anxiety on her face. Both bothered him.

A moment later she relaxed as she found the chain and ring in a zipper compartment. She placed it around her neck. Reaching back into the purse she withdrew the diamond earring that she had retrieved earlier. Turning to address Ray, she found him standing at the open French doors. His back was turned to her.

Bev went to him, studying the earring as she did so. "You know, there's something about this that looks familiar."

"What did you say?" Ray asked absently. He turned to her with a sad smile, but again she didn't seem to notice.

"This earring, there's something about it that looks familiar." She held it up for his inspection.

Ray took it from her fingers. "Maybe you saw Dana wearing it."

"Hmmm." Bev peered closely at the diamond that Ray was holding. "That just doesn't look like her. It's kind of gaudy."

He held it up to reflect the light inside the room. "It has to be a couple of carats. Your uncle and cousin are staying at her place, maybe it belongs to one of them."

Bev looked at Ray. "My uncle is in his seventies and does not have a pierced ear. As for Gerry, he's my age. I don't know what he'd be doing with one, but I can assure you he'd never wear a heart-shaped diamond. This is a woman's earring."

Ray handed it back to her. "Well, I don't think it belongs to the cleaning people." He moved past Bev back into the room. She followed him, still trying to solve the mystery.

Ray picked their overnight bags up off the floor. They had decided to spend the night at his house in Tiburon—finally. He headed toward the door with Bev trailing him as she continued to stare at the object.

"Hmmm, heart-shaped," she muttered to herself. The memory eluded her. As they walked down the hallway headed for the elevator, she slipped the diamond back into the zippered compartment of her purse.

It was Monday morning and the day was a glorious one as Bev and Ray sped along Highway 1. She had suggested that they cancel the plane reservations that each had made to fly down to L.A. and drive down instead. Ray had agreed. He sensed that there was something more to her wanting to drive south than their spending more time together, although that was an added bonus.

They enjoyed being together even more than either of them had anticipated. After dining in Sausalito, they had arrived at his home in Tiburon and had spent another sensuous night of lovemaking. Bev was in awe of her heightened sexuality. From everything she had read, her appetite for sex should have waned around her age. It hadn't. Ray had fed it in his bathtub, on the balcony outside of his bedroom, and, this morning, in his bed. If anybody ever asked her, she would highly recommend that every woman over fifty take a dose of lovemaking with a younger man as a cure for many of their ills.

In her case she was lucky to have found a man with whom she was compatible in more areas than just the bedroom. He had already displayed his interest in music, art, and politics. During this time together, she discovered that Ray held extensive real estate interests, just as she did, and they spent a lot of time discussing the various aspects of that business. They didn't agree on everything in their menagerie of mutual interest, but she was never bored with their conversations. Ray Wilson was quite a man, and this additional time spent with him was helping to alleviate any doubts in her mind about that.

They had stopped at Half Moon Bay, eaten lunch, and were back on the road when Bev made an observation.

"I saw your reaction back in Sausalito when I brought up Colton's ring," she told him quietly.

Ray didn't mask his surprise. "I didn't think that you'd noticed."

"I notice everything about you, even when you aren't aware of it." She caressed his cheek. "You've become that important to me."

Ray could feel his body react to the touch of her hand. If this wasn't love, then it must be insanity. "You're driving me crazy, do you know that?"

"But am I driving you to a feeling of insecurity?"

Ray chose not to answer, but his silence said volumes. Bev knew that this was about her late husband, and she wondered how she could fix this. Could she verbalize how she had felt about Colton? Would he, could he, understand?

"I need to apologize about making you feel that way. It has never been intentional." She laid her head back against the headrest and remembered the past. "I never got a chance to say a real goodbye to Colton. One day he was there and the next he was gone, and all I had left of him was his wedding band."

Ray knew that it must be difficult for her to talk about her late husband. He didn't want to cause her pain, but he couldn't fight his curiosity about Colton Cameron and his hold on Bev. So he remained quiet and his silence reaped the results for which he hoped. Bev kept talking.

"Colton had to go out of town on a construction job. He was to be gone a week, and neither one of us was looking forward to it. Our baby was due in a couple of months and he didn't want to be away from me for a second. He was so excited about the baby; you would have thought that he was pregnant instead of me. He was worried that something would happen before he got back and he called me every day that he was gone, sometimes two or three times a day. Finally, the job was done and he was coming home. He called me that morning to say that he would be driving straight through and that he would be home that evening. Night came and went and so did the next morning, but no Colton. I was going out of my mind.

"A week passed, a month, and there was no trace of my husband and no indication as to what had happened to him. My parents hired a private detective to see if he could be found, but no luck. Colton had vanished into thin air. Although nobody said it, I still believe that there were members of my family who thought that he might have walked out on me. After all, he was a young man with a wife who didn't work and had a baby on the way. That was a lot of responsibility, but he was up to it. Colton made a good living. We had no money problems. There was no way that he would have left me. Then one day I got a phone call from the state police. A car had been found at the bottom of a lake with a body inside." Bev swallowed the lump that still lodged in her throat at the memory. "It turned out to be Colton. He had been in a one-person car accident."

"You identified his body?" Ray held his breath, hoping against hope that she hadn't had to go through such an ordeal. Yet, Bev's identification would have confirmed Colton's death beyond a shadow of a doubt.

She shook her head in answer to his question. "No, I never saw my husband again. My Uncle Gerald identified him and I went into labor. The shock proved too much for me. Uncle Gerald brought Colton's ring to me while I was in the hospital. After I recovered, we had a graveside service for him and I barely got through that. In the end, I had two things that proved that he ever existed, his daughter and his wedding ring." Pausing, Bev looked out the window.

They drove in silence, each with thoughts that they didn't care to share with the other. Bev was remembering a young man who'd had so much to live for but who died much too soon, while Ray's thoughts were of a body submerged in water for months, and which might not have been recognizable. He wouldn't let his thoughts go any farther than that. It was Bev who interrupted the uneasy calm.

"So, Ray, I'm not trying to hurt you by holding on to Colton's wedding band. It's just a part of my past that I can't seem to let go."

Ray turned to her with a pensive smile. "I'm sure that it's difficult."

"Every time I think about how his young life was snuffed out, it breaks my heart. I would have given anything—he would have given anything—for him to see his daughter just once. And I know he would have given his life to get to know her." She gave a heavy sigh. "Maybe someday I'll be able to release all of this."

Ray thought it best not to address that. She could figure out where he stood on the subject. It was her hurdle to clear.

The mood in the car had turned from joyful to solemn, and was about to take another turn. Reaching into her purse, Bev withdrew her cell phone and called her mother to check on her sister. Ginny reported, happily, that Dana was greatly improved. She was talking and the nurses had her walking with assistance. It would take time, but Dana was on her way to a full recovery.

"Does she remember what happened?" Bev asked, thrilled at her sister's progress.

"No," Ginny replied, "but who cares? All that's important is that she's better."

Bev couldn't argue with that. Ginny reported on members of the family who were still there in support, and informed her that Renee Ingram had been kind enough to call. It was after her mother disconnected that Bev's memory was jolted. Placing her cell phone back inside her purse, she withdrew the diamond earring.

"I know who this belongs to," she announced triumphantly. "Renee Ingram. She was wearing heart-shaped earrings that day she came to the hospital. I remember noticing that they matched her engagement ring."

"Mystery solved." Ray smiled over at her, relieved that the energy in the car had shifted.

"I guess," Bev frowned as her eyebrows knitted. "Except that I've got one question."

"What's that?"

"When was Renee at Dana's house?"

CHAPTER 22

Bev disconnected her cell phone and held it thoughtfully before turning to Ray.

"Renee says that the earring does belong to her, that she must have lost it when she was visiting Dana."

"That makes sense." Ray sped up to pass a truck ahead of them. It had been his suggestion to call Renee. The diamond in that earring was worth a small fortune, and he knew that whoever it belonged to must have missed it.

"I guess," Bev answered, but there was still something about the earring that disturbed her. As she started to put her phone away, it rang. Darnell was on the other end.

"Hi, sweetheart." Guilt threatened to tug at Bev's conscience. In her effort to be with Ray she had all but forgotten her daughter. "How is everything going? How are Thad and Nia?"

That question always got Darnell going. Her husband and daughter were her favorite subjects. She was busy telling Bev the latest when the sound of a truck horn drifted through the closed window. It caught Darnell's attention, much as the announcer's voice had in the airport when Bev was headed to Tiburon.

"What was that? It sounded like a car horn. Are you on the road? Where are you?"

Bev decided to go on the offensive. "I'm on my way to L.A., and what's up with you? I haven't heard from you."

"We did some late shooting this weekend," Darnell answered smoothly, then went right back to the original subject. "So where are you, in Chicago headed to the airport? What time do you arrive in L.A.?"

Bev avoided specifics. "Oh, it shouldn't be long." As soon as she said it, she knew that she had made a mistake. Her daughter had always been extremely bright, and she had to be fed facts. Suspicion tinted Darnell's tone.

"I wouldn't call crossing a time zone soon. What time is the plane leaving Chicago and arriving in L.A.?"

Bev was getting annoyed. What was this, the Inquisition? She was going to squash this. "I'll get there when I get there, Darnell. You haven't even asked about your Aunt Dana. I just talked to your grandmother, and she said that they've got Dana walking."

There was silence on the other end. Bev knew that wasn't good. That meant that Darnell was thinking, and when that happened that meant that she was putting the pieces of a puzzle together to come up with a whole.

"I know about Aunt Dana," Darnell said slowly. It was clear that she was still weighing their conversation. "I spoke to Grandma before I called you. She said that you told her that you were headed to L.A.—" Her voice drifted off

"I'll call you when I get there," Bev reassured her, treading the minefield carefully. Darnell might need to know the truth about Ray and her, but she wasn't ready to tell her until *she* was ready. Meanwhile, a car honked its horn trying to move Ray out of the passing lane. Bev said a hurried goodbye. "Kiss the baby for me." Disconnecting, Bev slumped in her seat.

Amused, Ray gave her a sideways glance. "You know that it's not going to take long for her to figure out what's happening with us."

"I know." Bev was sure about that. "At times having a gifted child isn't all that it's cracked up to be. My daughter is a little too smart for her own good."

"Then why the secrecy? Is it because it's me and not some stranger? Or do you think that knowing that her mother has a love life will shock her?"

"Maybe I am hesitating because it's you. I'm not sure." She sighed. "I know that she likes you. She never would have agreed to naming you Nia's godfather if she didn't."

"Tell me about it." Ray had been honored. Winning Darnell over had been almost as difficult as attracting her mother. "Then may I offer a reason that I think you're not telling her?"

"Sure." Bev was curious.

"If you tell her, your secret won't be a secret anymore. It's out in the open. It becomes real. It's not as thrilling or exciting knowing something that somebody else knows."

"My mother knows about us." Bev was defensive because she knew that he was right.

"And she approves." Ray knew that Bev was disturbed by his insight, but this needed to be settled. "I suspect that the reason that she hasn't said anything to Darnell is because she feels that it's not her place. But I don't plan to be a secret much longer. I doubt if you would like it if the situation were reversed."

Bev knew that he was right—again. "You're just too smart for your own good." Her words were said in jest, but there was truth behind them.

"That's what you get for falling for an intelligent man," Ray crowed. He laughed when Bev thumped him playfully on the head.

She slid down in her seat, resigned to the eventual revelation of her secret pleasure. "I don't want to share you yet."

Ray reached across the console and took her hand. This woman touched him in so many ways. "I'll tell you what. Do you remember those houseboats that we saw in Sausalito?"

"Yes, I do." Bev smiled at the memory. During their wanderings around the artsy hamlet, they had strolled down the rows of colorful houseboats moored on the dock, delighted with the idea of living in one of them and concocting fanciful stories about those who actually did.

"When we're uncovered as a couple, we'll rent one of those houseboats . . ."

"The bright yellow one trimmed in startling blue," Bev piped in excitedly. "It had a For Rent sign on it."

"Okay, that one, and we'll pull the ramp up so that no one can come aboard."

"I like that." Bev's eyes were shining. "Then we'll set sail into the sunset—or whatever you do on a houseboat—so that I can keep you all to myself."

"And vice versa." Ray squeezed her hand.

Bev gave a wistful sigh. "Meanwhile, if I know my daughter—and I do—she'll figure everything out. She won't need any help from me. I'm sure of that."

Sitting in her elegantly decorated trailer on the set of the latest movie that she would star in with her husband, Darnell Cameron Stewart was thinking hard about her last two conversations with her mother. Bev had been a little too evasive. Something smelled fishy and she was going to find out what it was. Her musing was interrupted when Thad entered the trailer.

"Hey, baby." His tone was seductive. He and Darnell had a two-hour break before having to return to the set, and he knew exactly what he wanted for lunch.

However, Darnell had other things on her mind. "Sweetie, would you do me a favor and call Ray? See if he's in L.A. yet and ask him if he drove your car down there instead of leaving it in Tiburon."

Thad dropped down beside her and loosened the tie that he had been wearing in the last scene. He knew the love of his life well. He wasn't fooled by the sweetness of her tone. He cut to the chase.

"What are you up to?"

Darnell didn't pretend to be insulted as she used to do when they were first married. Thad knew that trick. He was becoming too good at reading her.

"I think Ray is with my mother."

Thad hesitated. "Uh, they're staying in the same house, Darnell."

"Which, if you remember, I told you was not a good idea, but you said that it was none of my business."

"Which it wasn't." He reached for her to pull her onto his lap, but a preoccupied Darnell got up from the sofa and began to pace the room. Thad sighed in acquiescence. The quicker he complied with her plan the quicker they could get to his plan. Taking out his cell phone, he dialed.

Ray had Bev retrieve his cell phone from the console so that he could keep his eyes on the road. She looked at the name on the display window.

"It's Thad. Darnell's behind this call. She's zeroing in on us."

Ray chortled at her declaration. "Let it go to voice mail. I'll call him back later."

"Good," Bev replied. "Let her sweat, but I'll bet you $100 that she'll have it all figured out before we hit L.A."

"You're on."

Back at the trailer, Thad left a message for Ray to call him. Darnell stopped pacing. Bracing himself for his wife's next move, he settled back to enjoy the action. He had no doubt that his lady must have been a private detective in her former life. His only hope was that her effort wouldn't take too long.

"Voice mail, huh? Well, we'll see about that." Darnell whipped out her cell phone and called her mother's Chicago office. Eventually the call made its way to Janice, who greeted the younger woman cheerfully.

"Hey, how are you doing? How's the movie going?"

"Great!" Darnell's greeting was equally as friendly. "The production is on time and we've been happy with the results so far, thanks for asking. Listen, I called you to see if my mother got off okay. She was scheduled to leave from there today to fly back to L.A., wasn't she?"

"Yes, she was, but she left on Friday from home after the meeting with our client." Janice sounded concerned. "Haven't you been in contact with her?"

Darnell avoided the question. "We've been busy here. I just thought that she wasn't leaving Chicago until today."

"All I know is that she told me on Friday that she was off to California. Can't you get her on her cell phone?"

Darnell could hear that Janice's concern was growing. She sought to ease it.

"Don't worry, I'm going to call her. I just wanted to get her schedule straight. Thank you." Disconnecting, Darnell looked at Thad smugly. "I knew it! Mama's headed for L.A. all right, probably from Carmel or Tiburon!"

She shared her accumulated evidence—the car horns, Bev's evasiveness, and what Janice had said during their conversation.

Thad was delighted, "So my man finally did it! Yes!" He pumped his fist in the air.

"*Yes*, what?" She glared at him. "My mother is supposed to be in L.A. with her sick sister, not holed up with *your* agent, and maybe in *our* house! God! Who knows what they were doing, and on *our* furniture!"

Thad laughed, prompting Darnell to throw a pillow at him, which only evoked more laughter. Sighing in disgust, she speed dialed her mother's number.

When the phone rang, Bev glanced at caller I.D. and then at the clock. It had been thirty minutes since her daughter's last call. She glanced at Ray.

"I think she broke a record, and you owe me $100." She answered the call with a sing-song, "Hellooooooo."

Darnell wasn't amused. She knew that her mother knew that she knew what was going on. The preliminaries were skipped.

"I know that you're with Ray, Mama, so don't try to deny it, and you're in a car not on a plane. Is it one of Thad's cars?"

"No, we're in a rental car, sweetie. Thad's car is in Ray's garage in Tiburon." Lord have mercy, her child was good! She would have made one hell of a detective, except for one little thing. "And let me suggest that you change your tone, or I'm going to hang up."

Darnell was properly chastised, but not deterred. "All right, I get the message. But may I ask if that's where you spent the weekend?" If so, at least they hadn't been in her house doing whatever, but her mother wasn't too cooperative.

"You may ask." That's all that Bev felt compelled to say. After all, she was a grown woman. She didn't have to answer to her own child.

Darnell held her temper. She knew just how far Bev would let her go. "All right, Mama, but I want you to know that your secrecy about you and Ray has hurt my feelings."

"Just like your secrecy about you and Thad hurt mine," Bev countered.

For a moment, Darnell was left speechless. Her mother was right. She and Thad had been together for months before she found the courage to tell her mother about their relationship. At the time, Bev didn't like the movie star's playboy reputation and thought that Darnell was too good for him. Now Bev and Thad were crazy about each other.

When Thad sat beside Darnell and draped his arm around his wife, she knew that the gesture was to show his support for her feelings. But the look that he gave her was a silent message to her that it was time to let this go. Darnell knew that Thad was good at seeing both sides of an issue, and it wouldn't be difficult for him to take Bev's side on this.

She took a deep breath and surprised her mother, her husband, and herself with her next words. "You're right, Mama. All I'm trying to say is that you didn't have to keep the fact that you and Ray have a relationship from me. I like him. I would have loved it if you had shared that information."

Bev was stunned. She put her cell on speakerphone. "Uh, will you say that again? I want Ray to hear this."

Darnell did as asked. Her words put a smile on Ray's face.

"That's good of you to say that." He meant it from the bottom of his heart. Winning Bev's affection was the golden medal. Winning her daughter's acceptance was the silver. What more could he want?

Darnell was gracious. "Ray, there is nothing that you won't do for us. You're a good friend, a great human being, and the best godfather that Nia could ever have. I have no doubt that my mother is in the best of hands. She sounds happy, and that's all I want for her."

"Me, too!" Thad shouted loudly, making sure that his presence was known.

Bev and Ray laughed. The four of them carried on a conversation for a few minutes. Bev and Ray made plans to join the younger couple in Virginia for the wrap party when the film was finished. It was Thad who ended the banter.

"We've got an hour before we have to get back on the set," he informed Bev and Ray. "We've got to go."

"And do what?" Darnell started to protest, but the warmth of Thad's lips on her neck answered that question. She ended the conversation quickly.

"Bye, Mama. Bye, Ray." The line went dead.

It was early evening when Bev and Ray pulled into L.A., and, despite being exhausted, their first stop was the hospital. They both wanted to see Dana's progress for themselves.

As they walked into Dana's room, Ginny greeted them as though they had been gone for a year, and much to their surprise Dana was propped up in bed welcoming them with a smile. She opened her arms to her sister, and an emotional Bev went straight into them.

"Oh, Dana," she sniffed, making no effort to hold back the tears. "You don't know how hard I prayed for this moment. I love you, sis."

"I love you, too." Dana's speech was slow, but her words were said clearly. She looked past Bev to the man standing behind her with misting eyes. "Hi, Ray."

"Hi yourself." He took her hand and squeezed it. "You look like a million bucks, kiddo."

"Sure," Dana said skeptically, but she seemed grateful for the compliment.

A tearful Ginny stood back observing her two children saying words to each other that she had not heard them utter in decades. She touched Ray's shoulder.

"Let's go out and give these two a little privacy, okay?"

Ray agreed. It had taken a drastic event to make these sisters realize what they meant to each other, but God had given them a second chance. Who was he to stand in the way of progress? He followed Ginny out the door.

Dana was listening quietly, with occasional comments, as Bev brought her up to date about what had happened since her hospitalization. For the first time in their lives they chatted like sisters who were friends. Bev's praise of Ray's actions during this period of crisis was so exuberant that the obvious became clear to Dana right away.

"The two of you are together, aren't you?"

"What makes you ask that?" Bev answered cautiously, uncertain about Dana's reaction.

"It's no problem. He's a nice guy and he loves you."

"Oh, I wouldn't say the L word." Bev was embarrassed. Neither she nor Ray had ever professed love for each other.

"I will," Dana said flatly. "He's in love with you, and you have to agree with me because I'm sick."

"You're pushing it." Bev chuckled uneasily and quickly changed the subject. "We've all been so worried about you. Your family loves you, Dana. Don't ever doubt that."

Tears began to well in Dana's eyes. "I know, Grandy has been calling me daily. She was even trying to come to L.A., but I told her not to. On top of that, I think that every aunt, uncle, and cousin in the country has been at the hospital, called, or sent me something." She nodded toward the flowers, cards, balloons, and stuffed animals that occupied every available space in the room. "The nurses told me that the hospital has been besieged."

Dana took a shaky breath. Bev could see that she had been overwhelmed by the experience.

"That's the Stillwaters family. When we love, we love hard. You know that Mama has been at the hospital practically nonstop. She's barely eaten or slept since you've been in here."

Dana nodded. "I know, and she told me that you've been here, too, and when you couldn't be, you kept in touch constantly." She grabbed Bev's hand. "You don't know how much that means to me."

Bev let her tears flow as she kissed her sister's cheek and laid her forehead against Dana's forehead. The emotions between them formed a silent bond that each had wanted for so long. Bev drew away and swiped at her tears as she drank in the sight of her sister.

She had lost weight during her ordeal. She looked wan and spoke slowly, as if unsure of her words. She had experienced some memory loss, but she was alive. She was alive! Through her sister's journals Bev had gotten to know her better than she had ever known her before, and had discovered a deeply insecure woman who was unsure of her place in a family that made demands that seemed to overwhelm her—a family that was there by her side no matter what.

"Look at us, we're some kind of ugly when we cry." Bev reached into her purse and withdrew a couple of tissues. She gave one to Dana and swiped at her own running makeup. The open purse reminded her of something. "By the way, your friend Renee Ingram has been calling about you. I know Mama must have told you how kind she's been. Renee even came by the hospital when she was in town. Oh, and look at this."

Bev withdrew the diamond earring and held it up for Dana to see. "Look what Ray found at your condo, her earring. Some rock, huh? She said that she must have lost it when she was at your house visiting."

"At my house?" Dana looked perplexed. "When she was at my house with me?" She looked at the earring and then at Bev. "I don't remember . . ."

"Oh, don't worry about that," Bev said and patted her hand. "No big deal. I'm going to send it back to her." She placed the earring back in her purse. "I've talked your head off, and you look tired. You get some rest. I'm going to try and get Mama to get some rest, too."

Exhausted, Dana offered no resistance as Bev smoothed the covers around her body. Bev could see that the problem with her memory was disturbing to her sister. She kissed her brow and headed for the door. As she stepped through it her sister called after her sleepily.

"I think that I do remember Renee coming over to my house. It was the day that I fell down the stairs."

CHAPTER 23

Ray sat in the private waiting room with Gerald Stillwaters while Gerry and Ginny went to the commissary to eat. It was good seeing Dana awake and alert. He was as excited about her progress as her family, who, according to Uncle Gerald, had caused quite a commotion in the hospital.

"I think we're the talk of Cedars-Sinai," Gerald told him with an amused smirk. "Every Stillwaters with a M.D. behind his or her name has been here, which has kept Dana's doctors on their toes, I can tell you that."

"I bet." Ray laughed with him at the implication.

"Along with the doctors in the Stillwaters family came our legal contingent—the attorneys and judges in the family. Hell, you could feel the hospital quake at its very foundation when they started showing up." Gerald cackled. "The chief administrator got so nervous that he's had the doctors declare Dana fit to go to a rehabilitation facility. They want the Stillwaters family the hell out of here!"

Gerald doubled over at that one. His delight forced Ray to smile. He liked this man with the quick wit and benevolent manner. He couldn't forget how welcoming he had been when he stayed with him in his home.

"What rehab place is she going to?" Ray wasn't familiar with any in L.A., although he figured that there were plenty of them.

"Oh, we're taking our baby girl home to Stillwaters." Gerald stretched his long legs out in front of him and settled back on the waiting room couch. "Ginny has already made the arrangements. One of our nieces is a physical therapist who'll help take care of her in Stillwaters. As we speak, Ginny's house is being set up with all of the equipment that will be needed for Dana's recovery. The doctor said that she'll be as good as new in a couple of weeks, but back home with us it'll probably be sooner. I'll be flying everybody out of here tomorrow."

"That soon?"

Ray's stricken reply caused Gerald to raise a quizzical brow. "I see that Ginny hasn't had time to tell you. Me and my big mouth. I'm sure she'll let you know that she'll be moving out in the morning." Gerald paused and looked at Ray closely. "And I suppose that means that Bev will be leaving, too."

Ray looked at him steadily, but didn't reply. Gerald gave him a thoughtful smile.

"You know, son, I don't mean to be nosey, but I can see what's happening between you and my niece, and I'm going to tell you up front that I like it, because I like you and I love Bev. She's like a daughter to me. She's been through a lot. You probably know this, but she was very young when she lost her husband, and she went through hell."

"She told me that you were the one who identified her husband's body."

"Yes," Gerald said sadly. "That is, if you want to call what I did identifying. It was more like I identified his wedding band. I don't know if you've ever seen a body that's been underwater for months, but it's not a pretty sight."

"I'm glad that I haven't had to do that."

"It was the hardest thing that I've ever had to do, especially since there was no face."

Ray froze. "What do you mean?"

Gerald glanced at the door to make sure that no one was entering before turning back to Ray. "The accident that Colton was in was horrendous. I never told Bev this, and I trust that you won't either, but Colton was decapitated when his car smashed into the tree and careened into the river. The impact was so hard that the car stripped bark from the tree. They found only parts of his skull later, but no jaws, so there were no teeth that could be used to identify him, and his body was too decomposed for fingerprints. The ring was all that we had."

Gerald went on to describe how all the family had conspired to save Bev's sanity during that trying time. However, the man's voice became background noise to the thoughts whirling through Ray's head. *There was no face. There were no teeth. The ring was all that we had.* The only proof that Colton Cameron was dead was a wedding band that could be removed and placed on the finger of someone else.

Bev noticed that Ray was as quiet and as preoccupied as she was as they drove to his house. Ginny had ridden home with them and was so excited about taking Dana home the next day that she didn't notice that she was the only one talking. When they arrived at Ray's house Bev was taken aback when she noticed that her mother had not only packed her own things for their departure, but she had also packed Bev's things. Seeing her belongings so neatly placed by the bedroom door forced her to face a reality. Her mother's expectation was that she would be accompanying them to Stillwaters. It also meant that she and Ray would have to part, once again, and it would be different this time. A long distance relationship between them would actually begin and be put to the test.

She didn't say anything to her mother about the packed bags; she wanted to talk to Ray first. Not only to get his opinion regarding their parting, but to share with him something that was quite disturbing, Dana's last words to her before she left her hospital room.

Bev lucked out when her exhausted mother made the announcement that she had eaten dinner at the hospital and would be going to bed early. She bid goodnight to Bev and Ray and retired to her room for the evening.

Ray suggested that Bev and he order take-out, but she persuaded him to go out to dinner. She didn't want to take a chance that her mother might hear what she had to say to him.

They settled on a nearby restaurant. Conversation was limited until after they ordered; then Bev propped her elbows on the table, rested her chin on her folded hands, and looked at him expectantly.

"If you tell me what's on your mind then I'll tell you what's on mine."

Ray studied the face of the woman he had come to love more each day. She was not only beautiful, but astute. He wasn't used to a woman being so attuned to his every mood or caring about his thoughts and feelings as much as she did. Yet there was no way he could share with her all that was on his mind. She wouldn't believe what he was thinking anyway, especially since it bordered on pure insanity and was based on nothing more than speculation. But he could share with her something else that was heavy on his heart.

"You'll be leaving me tomorrow," he said sadly. "I knew that it was coming, but I didn't want to think about it."

"I didn't want to think about it, either," Bev agreed. "But it's best that I do go with Mama and see that my sister is settled. It looks as though we've laid the foundation for a whole new relationship, and I want to be there for her."

"And you should be." Ray took her hands and squeezed them affectionately. He would never have asked her to make any other choice. "But may I make a suggestion?"

"What?"

"You've got her journals. Make sure that you put them back before she makes her way back home and the fight is on." He expected her to laugh at his attempt at humor, but instead Bev's face crumbled.

"What is it? What's wrong?"

Bev withdrew her hands from his and folded her arms across her chest as she tried to regain control of her emotions. His words had reminded her of what Dana had told her, and she didn't know whether to be sad or mad at what she suspected. Taking a shaky breath, she shared what she knew so far with Ray.

"Dana said that Renee Ingram was at her apartment the day of her accident."

Ray was taken aback. "What!" His mind raced. "Was it before or after she fell?"

"I don't know, but why didn't she tell us that she had been there that day?"

Ray searched for a plausible explanation. "Well, when you called her about the earring she did say that she had been at Dana's house."

"Yes, but suppose she didn't lose that earring before Dana was hurt. Suppose she lost it after."

"What do you mean?" Ray looked confused.

Bev started to speak, but was interrupted by the waiter with their salads. After he placed them on the table and left, she continued.

"Do you remember when I told you that I had noticed Renee's earrings in the hospital when we first met her?"

Ray nodded slowly, and then it dawned on him what Bev was saying. "I found the earring before the break-in at Dana's place." His mind raced. "Renee broke into your sister's house."

"Bingo! After we saw her at the hospital." Bev was ready to fly to New York, Malibu, or wherever Ms. Thing was and kick her behind. "Now the question is, why did she do that?"

Ray fell back in his chair, reeling from what had been revealed. Then it hit him.

"Wait a minute! When we were driving to Stillwaters, Dana showed me the ring that she wore when she claimed that we were engaged. She told me that she had borrowed it from a friend whose husband had bought her another one with matching earrings."

"Renee." That clinched it for Bev, but now what? "Was she there when Dana fell, and if so why didn't she call 911? And, again, why did she break into Dana's house?"

The waiter interrupted them, this time with their dinner plates. "The food isn't to your liking?" The young man looked puzzled as he noticed that neither of their salads had been touched.

Both Bev and Ray looked at the plates before them as if they were seeing them for the first time. Food was secondary at this point. They asked that their salads be removed and waited patiently for him to place the dinner plates and leave. The conversation resumed with a revelation from Ray.

"Bev, if I share something with you, will you promise not to tell anybody?"

Bev was insulted. "I'm not going to tell anybody. Just tell me."

Ray proceeded carefully. "Uh, I spoke to a friend on the East Coast about Stark Enterprises and he indicated that there might be some sort of investigation going on concerning that company."

"About what?" Bev dug into her food. She needed substance for this.

"I'm not sure, but my friend used to work with the New York Police Department in the narcotics division."

"Oh, really?" Bev's eyes widened. "Do you think that the company might be involved with drugs?"

"I'm not sure," Ray said, looking at her steadily, "but remember that Mitch used to work for Stark Enterprises."

Bev stared at him. She lowered her fork to the plate. "So Mitch was involved in drugs, too?"

"I don't know, but I'm going to share something else with you that I was reluctant to mention before. The day of Dana's accident, she called me and said that she had done some snooping around and that she had found something."

"Found what?"

"I don't know, but she said that it was serious and that she wanted to show me because I was the only one she could trust."

Bev didn't have to ask him the next question; she knew the answer. "And you didn't want to share this with me because it might have been some sort of evidence that someone in our family killed Mitch."

"I wasn't sure. She told me that she would be at my house around six that evening." Ray rubbed his temples. He could feel a headache coming on. And why wouldn't it? He might have stepped into a hornet's nest, and all that he could hope was that neither Bev nor he got stung.

The two of them finished their dinner with minimal conversation as each contemplated the full meaning of what they had discussed. After finishing their plates they rejected dessert, but still remained seated. There were things that needed to be settled.

"Dana doesn't remember very much before the accident, and the doctors couldn't assure us that she would," Bev informed Ray. "That means that she might not remember what it was that she had to show you."

"Then how did she remember that Renee was at her place?"

"I don't know, a flash of memory maybe, but we do know that she was there. The only thing is, I don't really know what it all means."

"It means that she was in Dana's house for a reason, and that the last time she was desperate enough to break in."

"She might have been looking for the earring, but whatever it was I'm really disappointed in her," Bev lamented. "She seemed so nice."

Ray held the same sentiments. "It's hard to think that someone as classy as Renee could resort to something as ordinary as breaking and entering."

"Do you think that we have enough to go to the police and charge her with that?" Despite her disappointment, Bev was ready to bring her down, if for no other reason than the fact that she might have been there when her sister fell down the stairs but did nothing to help her.

"I say that we go back to Dana's house tomorrow and search it thoroughly until we find out if she was looking for something other than the earring."

Bev's determination was evident, and Ray didn't want to temper her enthusiasm, but—

"Since we really don't know what we're looking for it may be better if you go with your mother and sister tomorrow. I can hold down the fort here."

"But . . ."

"*But* as much as I want you with me, right now your sister needs you more."

There was no argument against that. Bev didn't try.

"Actually, it could work out. If her memory about why Renee was at her house or why she called you returns, I'll be there to hear it."

"That's my girl." Ray flashed her a smile. "I'll work on this front to see what I can find. Maybe together we can gather enough evidence to see if there's a criminal case."

Bev glanced at the clock on the bed stand. It was two o'clock in the morning and she was still awake. After having driven from Tiburon for hours, visiting Dana at the hospital, and the unbelievable exposés at dinner with Ray, her body was begging for rest. Yet since crawling in bed barely able to keep her eyes open, she'd dozed for barely three hours and had been tossing and turning ever since. She had to get some rest!

Turning on her side, she plumped the pillow in an effort to get comfortable. It didn't work. She tossed and she turned, her thoughts swirling with all of the things that had happened, not just within the last twelve, twenty-four, or thirty-six hours, but in the past couple of weeks. It seemed that in the blink of an eye her life had been placed on a roller coaster at its crest and all she could do was hold on. It was disconcerting. From the time she was a young widow she had always been in control—in control of her child's welfare, her financial and business affairs, and her romantic relationships. Men wanted her and they would usually do anything to have her. She had always been in the driver's seat when it came to accepting or rejecting them. That option was still there with Ray, but this time things were different. With the others it was meet them, date them, and bid them a fond farewell. Easy come, easy go. With Ray it was about falling in love.

Bev rolled over onto her stomach, buried her face in the pillow, and groaned. She was in love with Ray Wilson. She screamed her frustration with herself into the crisp linen, and then rolled back over on her back.

How had she let this happen? As unrealistic as it seemed she had never planned on falling in love again. After the parade of losers she had dated, it hadn't seemed so implausible and then Ray came along. He hadn't swept her off her feet as men do in the movies, although Lord knows in those early days he tried. Circumstances had allowed her to really get to know him and in doing so he had wrapped himself around her heart.

What she felt about this man surprised her. It had never occurred to her that she could fall for a younger man. She had always figured that such a man would have nothing to offer her. After all, she was the one with the life experience, the wisdom and guile that time had honed. Who knew that a man barely out of his thirties could be her equal and evoke such strong emotions in her?

The stereotype had always been that a younger man would only be interested in an older woman for her money. What else could they want? Mature women in American society were devalued; they couldn't possibly be interesting or sexy. That was the exclusive domain of the young. Bev had never bought into that reasoning. She was a confident woman—she was a Stillwaters—and she knew what she brought to the table. Any man that she dealt with had to bring the same. Ray had brought it, and she found herself a willing recipient. Age was irrelevant when it came to what she felt for him.

Bev lay still, closed her eyes, and listened to the rhythm of her heart. Ray's face appeared before her and the beat accelerated. Yes, he was there, all right, dead in the center of her being. She opened her eyes. Okay, what was she going to do about it? For her there were only two answers: accept it or leave it alone.

Giving up on her effort to fall asleep, she got out of the bed. Grabbing her robe, she left the bedroom and headed toward the kitchen. There was no need to be sleepy and hungry, too. She had eaten only a small portion of her dinner. Considering the discussion that she and Ray had about Renee Ingram, Stark Enterprises, and Mitch, it was a surprise that she was able to eat at all.

The moonlight shining through the skylights guided her down the stairway. On her way to the kitchen she passed Ray's office and noticed a sliver of light coming from under the closed door. She knocked softly and opened the door without an invitation to do so. Ray was sitting at his desk with an open briefcase in front of him. He was reading some papers. At her entrance, his head snapped up. He looked surprised.

"What are you doing up?" The question was asked to each other simultaneously. They laughed at the coincidence. Bev shut the door behind her and moved further into the office.

"Okay, me first." She propped herself on the edge of the desk. "What in the world are you doing up at this ungodly hour?"

Ray began to gather the papers lying in disarray on his desk. "I couldn't sleep. All of this stuff kept going through my head, and I remembered that I had taken Mitch's briefcase from Dana's house. I was going through some of the papers in it again to see if there was any hint at all about what he might have been doing for Stark Enterprises."

"Do you think that he knew about any illegal operations? You don't think that he was involved, do you?" Bev picked up a newspaper article that had been printed off the Internet and began to scan it. She didn't notice Ray stiffen.

"I don't know what he knew." He stacked the papers and watched anxiously as Bev looked at the article that contained the pictures of the Ingrams, Mitch, and of Moody Lake.

"So this is Russell Ingram." Bev studied the picture, especially the look of adoration on Renee's face as she gazed at her husband. "He's nice looking." Her eyes dropped to the head shot of the man in the picture below that one. She read the caption aloud, "Charles 'Moody' Lake, former CEO of Stark Enterprises."

"That's the man that Russell Ingram replaced as head of the company," Ray informed her.

"Hmmm," was Bev's only reply as she handed the article back to him.

Relaxing, Ray tossed the papers into the briefcase as he moved around the desk and propped himself next to her. "Now your turn. What are you doing up?"

"I was thinking about you." Bev's glowing eyes met his as she slowly removed the linen robe that covered her matching pajamas and let it drop to the floor.

Ray's body ignited instantly. His eyes swept her shapely frame. She was a vision in white as she sauntered to the door. The pajama top she wore was sleeveless, with a v-neck trimmed in lace that accented the swell of her breasts. The bottoms snaked down her long legs, ending in gathers above her bare feet.

The door lock clicked, and Bev turned back to Ray. "This should keep Mama out in case she wakes up." With hips swaying, she increased the heat in the room as she came to a stop in front of him and began to untie the belt to his robe.

"It looks like opportunity has knocked, and I plan on taking advantage of it." She removed his belt and tossed it aside.

Entranced, Ray caught her around her waist and drew her to him. "Woman, have I ever told you how fantastic you are?"

"Plenty of times. Now you can show me." With both hands, she slid his robe from his bare chest.

"Only that I could, but I don't have any protection." That didn't stop him from letting her help him out of his robe.

"You are a creative man." Bev ran her hands seductively over the wiry hairs on his chest. "I'm sure that you can think of something."

Ray wanted to run to his bedroom and grab a handful of condoms, but he was wrapped in her hypnotic spell. Instead, he gave her a kiss that was so erotic that it weakened Bev's knees. She nearly sank to the floor. Ray placed her on the desk and then slipped between her rubbery legs.

"Oh, goody." She gave each of his nipples a gentle love bite. "Desk sex."

"Or as close as I can get," Ray promised as he assaulted her neck with fiery kisses and hands that teased her breasts relentlessly. "But I'll do my very best."

"I'm sure that you will." Bev threw her head back, reveling in the sensations that possessed her. She slid her hand beneath the waistband of his pajama bottoms and moved downward, wanting to give him as much pleasure as he was giving her. Ray removed her hand.

"I'll never make it if you do that."

She gave him an understanding smile and then outlined his jaw with kisses. He unbuttoned the delicate mother of pearl buttons that ran down the front of her top. Her breasts spilled out. Ray licked the tips of each nipple.

Bev braced herself on the desk and moaned long and loud.

"This is only the appetizer." Ray's fingers snaked downward to her hidden cove. "I haven't gotten to the main course."

As he readied her for the ultimate tribute, he mapped her body with blazing kisses, blistering nips, and a scorching tongue, setting Bev ablaze.

Bev's screams ripped from the bottom of her soul as she writhed on top of the desk, flailing and convulsing with such fervor that she was unaware of having knocked the briefcase to the floor. The desk lamp followed, as did a clock, but neither of them cared as Bev shattered in release, and Ray enjoyed the pleasure that he was giving her.

His unselfish gift of love was costing him dearly. The pain in his groin begged for release. Recognizing his dilemma, Bev proposed to Ray that she return the favor. They conspired to go to his bedroom, which was further from where Ginny lay sleeping than Bev's room. It was their hope that she was still asleep.

"You probably raised the dead with all the noise that you made," Ray teased as he made an attempt to pick up the evidence of their wild tryst on his desk before they stole upstairs. Still throbbing, all Bev could do to help him was watch. As he picked up the open briefcase, a CD in a case fell out of it onto the floor.

He looked at it, bewildered, and then looked back at the briefcase. A compartment had opened up beneath the bottom lining of its interior, a secret compartment. Wide-eyed, he looked up at Bev, whose expression showed that she was equally as amazed.

"What in the world?" was all that Bev could think of to say.

CHAPTER 24

It was seven o'clock in the morning when Ginny entered Ray's kitchen ready to begin her day. Rejuvenated by a good night's sleep, she had planned on fixing a special breakfast for her daughter and Ray in celebration of Dana's release from the hospital. To her surprise both Bev and Ray were up and breakfast was waiting for her, but both of them looked exhausted. Ginny didn't speculate as to the reason when she offered a cheerful greeting and joined them at the breakfast table.

"I wanted to fix you two my super-duper cheese omelet, along with my applesauce pancakes."

Bev looked disappointed. "If I had known that, I would have awakened you a long time ago. I haven't had those in a long time."

"You missed a treat," Ginny told Ray as she dug into the breakfast that he had prepared. "But I've got to tell you that this tastes delicious."

Ray nodded his appreciation as he concentrated on trying to maintain a facade of normalcy. Bev and he had agreed that they didn't want to give Ginny the slightest hint that anything was wrong. He glanced across the table at Bev, who appeared to be preoccupied with her meal. He marveled at her demeanor. He wished that he could be as cool, calm, and collected amid the storm in which they had found themselves unexpectedly embroiled.

Bev didn't know if she could eat another bite. She wasn't sure if the butterflies in her stomach would allow it. Her temples were throbbing. She was so tired that she wasn't sure if she could make it through the rest of the day. She noted how easily Ray was conversing with her mother. She wished that she could be as nonchalant. Not only was she dead on her feet from lack of sleep, but she was a nervous wreck. She was certain that her mother would notice at any moment. Never in her life would she have believed that she would have any direct knowledge of a drug cartel. Sure, she had read about them, had seen movies and television shows about them, but most of that was make-believe. What she knew was for real! All she could do now was follow the plan on which Ray and she had agreed, and the first part of that plan was simple: finish breakfast. She scooped up another forkful of eggs, chewed, and swallowed.

Ginny Little was ecstatic. Her daughter was going home. She chattered happily as Ray drove Bev and her to the hospital to pick up Dana. Just like yesterday, she never noticed the uncharacteristic silence in the car.

There was a caravan of cars filled with Stillwaters family that followed the limousine carrying Dana and her mother to the airport. Before boarding Uncle Gerald's airplane, Bev and Ray engaged in a parting kiss that left no doubt in anyone's mind that they were much more than friends. Since Dana didn't appear to be disturbed by the apparent relationship between her sister and her ex-fiancé, neither was anyone else in the family. Bev handed Ray a small package before she boarded the aircraft. She told him to open it when he took the flight that he would be catching in a few hours. Then, with a soft kiss goodbye, she followed everyone else aboard.

As she watched Ray disappear from sight, she thought about the nightmare that they had stumbled into and shuddered. Neither she nor Ray knew what the outcome might be.

The sudden appearance of the CD had done what nothing else could have in the early hours of the morning. It cooled the sizzling ardor between Bev and Ray. All of their focus had turned toward the mysterious find.

Slipping it into the computer, they spent the remainder of the morning reading a record of illegal activities that was mind-boggling. Mitch had kept a detailed account of how he had been hired by Russell Ingram for some legal work regarding the misappropriation of funds involving the Stark Enterprises accounts. He had won the case. Impressed by his skills as an attorney, Ingram had put Mitch on retainer to deal with "special" cases.

Mitch had been aware of the kind of people for whom he worked. Bev and her mother had been correct about his character. Ethics were not a consideration. Money was his only motive, and Mitch's work on "special" cases hadn't started with Stark Enterprises. He had a history of corruption, and the depth of his duplicity was astonishing.

As they reviewed Mitch's chronicle of evil, Ray had questioned Bev about something that he remembered. "Dana told me that she thought that either you or your mother had Mitch investigated."

Bev shook her head. "I read that in her journal, but no, neither of us did that. After reading this, I wish we had." Mitch had turned out to be even worse than she or her mother had suspected.

He seemed to have taken sadistic pleasure in recording not only his client's misdeeds, but his own. Among his many indiscretions had been his numerous trysts with women. Being an engaged man hadn't tempered his attraction to the opposite sex. Dana had been only one in a long line of fiancées that Mitch had loved and left over the years, and he'd planned on leaving her, too, but death had claimed him before he could execute his plan. As they read further, they discovered that Renee Ingram was among his sexual conquests. The two had been embroiled in a torrid affair while he was engaged to Dana. It had lasted for months, but Mitch suspected that Russell had found out.

After reading that passage Bev had turned to Ray. "Do you think that Russell Ingram might have killed him? Maybe Mitch didn't commit suicide."

Ray couldn't deny that the prospect was likely, but there was more. The two of them had reeled from the revelations.

According to Mitch there had been trouble in the cartel, and Russell's boss had been blamed for losing a great deal of money. Mitch had suspected that Russell might have either murdered the former CEO or helped him disappear. He wasn't quite sure whether the younger man's loyalty had been stronger or his greed. He speculated that Moody Lake could still be alive, and if that were true the cartel would have two people to kill.

As the airplane soared above the skies toward their destination, Bev's eyes tried to drift shut. She was exhausted, but the barrage of questions wouldn't stop running through her head and let her rest. Did Renee know about the CD? Had she come to Dana's home to ask her about the incriminating item? Was that why she had broken into her house? Was she looking for the CD? There were so many questions and so few answers. But by the time that she and Ray had read the last lines there was one question that no longer had to be asked. Mitch *had* committed suicide. He had carefully laid out his plan to do so, and there was even an element of evil intent behind that.

After being told that his cancer was terminal, his last entry had been a rambling discourse about his life and the many sins that he had committed. He didn't appear to have regrets. He was an atheist. There was no fear of heaven or hell. He had lived, and he was going to die. Yet it was going to be on his terms, and he was hell-bent on leaving turmoil in his wake. He had told Renee Ingram that if her husband had found out about their affair, as he suspected, she didn't have anything to worry about from Russell. Her husband loved her and she would be safe. However, Mitch had informed her that he would be his target, and more than likely Russell would make his death look like a suicide. Mitch thought that leaving Renee with doubts about her husband was hilarious. His only regret was that he wouldn't be around to witness the chaos that his lies and deceit would cause. Mitch Clayton had been a real piece of work.

After seeing Bev off, Ray headed for Dana's condo to execute step one in the plan that he and Bev had hatched to maneuver out of the maze in which they had unexpectedly become entangled. Ray had pointed out to Bev that legally, the CD that they had discovered did not belong to either one of them. The assumption was that it belonged to Dana, since it had been found in a briefcase inside her house. Neither of them had gotten her consent to remove any items from her home, therefore, if a trial was held, anything on the CD could be ruled inadmissible. So it was Ray's job to return the briefcase to the condo and Bev's job to get the needed permission from Dana.

As he drove along the highway to fulfill his mission, Ray's mind wouldn't stop churning. The information on that CD was so explosive that he needed to get it into the proper hands as quickly as possible. Stark Enterprises was located on the East Coast, so the first name that he thought of was James Starr, who had already indicated that he knew something unsettling about the company. He would hand him the proof that might be needed with the hope that James had the connections to make something happen. Ray just wanted the CD out of his and Bev's hands. The last thing that they needed was any involvement with a drug cartel.

Then there was the matter of Moody Lake. Mitch had indicated that he could still be alive. These words had jarred Ray. He'd had the same thought, only his thinking went further. He suspected that Moody might be Colton Cameron. But Bev had looked at Lake's picture when she read the article and had not displayed a hint of recognition. Yet it had been her Uncle Gerald's words about Colton's accident and his identification of the body—or lack of it—that had kept Ray up last night. It had been those words that had sent him to his office this morning looking for any information on Lake that he could get. He had been on his computer searching before going through the papers in Mitch's briefcase. It had been Bev's sudden appearance that had stopped his one-man investigation, but the erotic results had been well worth it.

The thought of their sexy interlude brought a smile to his face. He wasn't sure that he would ever be able to work on that desk again.

Thinking of Bev reminded him of the package that she had given him. Curious, he pulled over to the side of the road and slipped it out of his jacket pocket. It turned out to be her iPod. She had used it during their trip from Tiburon to L.A., at times snapping her fingers and singing at the top of her lungs. She had taunted and teased him about being in the Stone Age for not owning one. A note was wrapped around the iPod. Unfolding it, he read the words scrawled in her precise handwriting: *Enjoy, and listen closely to the words of the first song.*

Slipping on the earphones, he turned the iPod on and pulled back into traffic. He should have stayed parked, because the first song that played nearly had him driving off of the road.

It was Aretha Franklin's old-school classic "Call Me" and the first refrain of the songstress soulful voice left no doubt in Ray's mind about Bev Cameron's feelings. The words were loud and clear, as were their meaning. She was in love with him.

The first floor of Ginny Little's house had been turned into a sanctuary for her daughter. Dana was using a walker, so the house had been made handicapped accessible. But there was one gesture of her mother's love that brought Dana to tears. Ginny had seen to it that all of the bedroom furniture from her younger daughter's L.A. condo was transported to the house in Stillwaters, recreating an exact replica of the room.

After seeing that her sister was settled, Bev retreated to her own house. She welcomed the solitude. The Stillwaters family rarely did anything small, and Dana had been welcomed by a banner mounted across the front of their mother's house, followed by a stream of visiting relatives led by Grandy. They had brought enough food to the house to feed an army, and, much to Bev's delight, she discovered that her refrigerator had been stocked as well.

Dragging herself up the stairs, she jumped into the shower and washed the day's grime off of her body. Slipping into a pair of pajamas, she sank into the comfort of the billowy mattress. Her body welcomed the relief. Nothing in her life had prepared her for a day like this—drug cartels, murder, infidelity, break-ins. What was next?

She was close to falling asleep when her cell phone rang. She had placed it on the table by her bed, and her first thought was to ignore its summons. She was too tired to reach that far, but fearing that the call might be one regarding Dana, she picked it up.

"Hello?" Her voice was sluggish from exhaustion.

There was silence on the other end for a moment, and then a voice—Ray's voice.

"I love you, too."

CHAPTER 25

It had been quite a week. Between being knee-deep in the middle of intrigue, running her Chicago business from her home office in Stillwaters, and helping attend to her sister, Bev had little time for anything else, except Ray. Their calls to each other were nonstop. They took turns calling each other in the morning to start their days. She usually called him in the afternoon and he called her at night. He had become a part of her life. It had gotten so bad that she found it difficult to fall asleep without his voice to soothe her. She was in love! Bev Cameron was in love! Added to that revelation was the flourishing relationship with her sister.

Dana was thriving. Her speech was improving, as was her gait. Much of her memory had returned, but she was still unclear as to what happened the day of her fall. For Bev, that was irrelevant when compared with the many advantages that her accident had garnered. The love and support of her relatives seemed to have turned Dana's former opinion of the Stillwaters family in a new direction, and she and Bev had never been so close. They chatted daily about everything, even Ray. Bev didn't share with her how she felt about him, but Dana was happy that he and Bev were together. They even examined their past sibling relationship and, out of that, began forging a new one.

Bev hadn't informed her that she had read her journals, and never would. She had given them to Ray to be returned to their rightful place. That she had breached her sister's privacy wasn't something of which she was proud, but reading them had given her insight into Dana's life that helped heal the wounds between them. Those journals had served a purpose for which she would always be grateful.

On this day, Dana and she were walking down Stillwaters Road together. It was the same tree-lined street that her sister and Ray had driven down months before. Dana was using a walker, and a daily stroll was part of her therapy. Her memory was slowing returning, and her engagement to Mitch was part of that.

Bev wasn't sure if this was the right time to broach the subject of the briefcase, but she decided to proceed. When she asked her sister if she remembered having it at her house, Dana looked at her blankly at first as she tried to recall.

"Yes, I think so. Why?"

"There's something inside it that's very important, and Ray needs your written permission to give it to the authorities."

Dana stopped walking and stood studying Bev. "What is this about?" The unspoken question was for Bev to remind her of the reason that the briefcase was important. There was a hint of recognition of the issue in her tone.

"There's a CD in that case that has some information on it that the police need to see."

"Something that Mitch was working on?" Her eyes wandered beyond Bev, trying to recall. "Yes! He left the briefcase at my house before he died. That's what happened." She turned to her sister with excited eyes. "There was a CD in there. There was something on it . . ."

"You remember!" Bev's hopes soared and sank at the same. "Did you read what was on it?" She didn't want her to be caught up in the intrigue.

Dana bit her lower lip, trying to recall details. "I read the first few pages and that was enough to let me know that something illegal was going on. I wanted somebody else to see it." She hesitated. "Hey, didn't I call Ray? Did he tell you that I called him?"

"Yes, he did. You told him that you had something to show him." She was relieved that Dana didn't appear to know everything that was on it. What Mitch had written about Dana and the other women in his life had been near the end, and it had been less than flattering. The man was a misogynist, a first-class jackass.

"That's what the call must have been about," Dana mumbled. "But then the doorbell rang—" Her eyes took on a faraway look.

Bev took over. "Was it Renee Ingram?" She didn't want to put words in her mouth, but she was eager for Dana to confirm her suspicions. She knew the moment that her sister remembered. The look on her face said it all.

"Renee was there when I fell down the stairs." Dana paused. "She pushed me!"

"She *pushed* you?" Bev was irate. Taking her sister by the arm, she guided her to the seat attached to the walker.

"Come on, sit down and tell me everything that you can remember." Bev settled on the grass in front of her as Dana told it all.

Dana and Renee had met through Mitch. The two of them had hit it off, and whenever Renee vacationed at the Ingram house in Malibu, she contacted her. After his death, Dana had shared with Renee her suspicion that it had been foul play and her plan to investigate her relatives to see if any of them were involved. Renee had even offered her old engagement ring to assist with the ruse.

Renee's visit to Dana's condo that day had been unexpected. She said that she had stopped by to pick up the ring that she had loaned Dana. From what Bev could discern, what occurred after that was a series of misunderstandings and coincidences that had nearly cost Dana her life.

"I was telling Renee that I was in a hurry," said Dana, "explaining to her that I might have found some evidence that someone else might have killed Mitch, and not somebody in my family. She asked me why I would think that, but not being sure of what I had, I wouldn't say. For some reason that really upset her and she kept demanding that I tell her what I knew. I mean, she was going off.

"I went up the stairs to get her ring, and she followed me. She was ranting and raving like a lunatic. She kept asking me what I knew and saying something about how I wasn't going to ruin her life and break up her family. Crazy stuff! I don't know what she was talking about. We were at the top of the stairs and I told her that I didn't know what her problem was, but she could get out of my house. I had someplace to go. She grabbed me by the shoulders, saying something about how I wasn't going anywhere. Then she pushed me, and that's the last thing that I remember."

That was it, all of the evidence that was needed to bring charges against Renee Ingram. Bev was disillusioned that the concern that the woman had shown so fervently during Dana's hospitalization had been deception based on self preservation. They hadn't heard from her since she was told that Dana's memory had been impaired. When she spoke to Ray that evening, she told him what her sister had revealed.

"Renee either came back to the condo for her ring, or she was looking for the evidence that Dana had told her about. But she didn't get what she was looking for. From the sound of it, she thought that her husband had something to do with Mitch's death."

Ray agreed. "That's what Mitch wanted her to think. Apparently, she must know that her husband is capable of murder."

Bev shuddered at the thought. "Dana promised me that she wouldn't share what she told me with anybody else yet. I asked her to trust me to take care of it, and she agreed. I sent the signed letter of permission to you by overnight express. You should get it tomorrow."

"Good, I'll look for it. Meanwhile, it sounds as though a lot has changed between Dana and you." Ray sounded pleased for her.

"It has." Bev couldn't be happier. "And when I told her that Mitch had written that he was going to commit suicide, she accepted it quite well."

"I'm glad to hear that, too. And you," his voice became seductive, "when do I get you again?"

She gave him a sexy chuckle. "I'll be flying home to Chicago the day after tomorrow."

"Give me a few days to take care of some business and then I'm coming to you."

Bev curled into a ball and purred, "I can't wait."

After talking with Bev, Ray lay in his bed and thought about how wildly insane his life had become. He was madly in love with the most wonderful woman in the world, and, between making deals with Hollywood moguls, he was secretly involved in the possible downfall of a drug cartel, the implication of its leader in a murder, and the likely arrest of the man's wife for attempting to do the same. Added to this was the possibility that the dead husband of the woman that he loved might also have been a killer, a drug czar, and really wasn't dead. There wasn't a writer in Tinsel Town that could have come up with this story. If he had read a script like this he would have rejected it as too bizarre.

He thanked God for Bev. It was she who brought some balance into his life. It was she who brought him a sense of calm. The sound of her voice was his lifeline. He had wanted to tell her that he loved her face to face the first time that he said the words, but that hadn't happened. It didn't matter, they both made up for it by repeating those three little words every chance they got. Ray wanted to shout to the world that he was a man in love.

Bev's son-in-law was having a field day when it came to teasing Ray about her. After Thad had fallen in love with Darnell, Ray had bragged with confidence that he would never let a woman possess his heart so thoroughly. Thad had no problem reminding him of that declaration. Ray took the ribbing good-naturedly. Considering what he had gained, a little teasing was a minor price to pay.

He lived for his daily talks with Bev; whether their conversations were short and mundane or long and steamy, there were few subjects that they didn't discuss, except one—her former husband. She hadn't mentioned him since their conversation during their drive to L.A. from Tiburon. Still, he remained on Ray's mind, especially in light of what Mitch had written. He could no longer rule out the possibility that Colton might be alive. For his own satisfaction, Ray felt compelled to solve the mystery of Colton Cameron.

He hadn't told Bev about his trip to Carmel earlier in the week. He had flown up and searched Darnell and Thad's house until he found a photo—a color snapshot of a man who appeared to have been caught off guard by the camera. Darnell had placed it alone on one of the pages of a family album that she kept in her office. Below the photo, she had written the words: "My father, Colton Cameron." Next to those words was written the year that the photo was taken, the same year that he had died.

Ray studied the close-up. It was of a handsome young man in his prime. There was a slight smile of surprise on his face, but his eyes were sparkling with humor. It was a good picture for a daughter to have of her father. He made a copy of the photo, returned it to its place of honor, and flew back to L.A. the same day. When he compared the picture of Colton Cameron with that of Moody Lake, he noted that there were similarities in the slope of their brows and the shape of the ears. Other than that, if there had been plastic surgery on Lake the doctor had performed his job well.

As Ray lay in bed contemplating what he would do next, he knew that his choices could be explosive. If Colton Cameron and Moody Lake were the same person the complications could be many, not the least being that the man was a killer. Someone had given his life so that Moody Lake could live, and the way that the victim had died had not been pretty. It took a special kind of sadist to decapitate another human being, to say nothing of the kind of character it took to head a drug cartel. If this man were Colton, he was a dangerous man. If he were still alive, who knew what he was capable of doing?

With that in mind, sleep didn't come easily for Ray. He got up from his bed and wandered downstairs. After pouring himself a glass of wine, he stretched out in a chair and tried to relax. It didn't work. All he could think about was Bev. How in the world had Colton Cameron left a woman like that, knowing that she was carrying his child? All indications were that he loved her and was looking forward to becoming a father. There must have been a hell of a reason for him to want to erase all traces of his existence. Ray concluded that if Colton and Lake were the same, he must have been deeply involved in illegal activities for quite a while.

Reportedly, he worked in construction. It was no secret that the industry was rife with criminal activity. Colton must have been involved. Something had happened and he'd had to run for his life, which meant that he had to end someone else's life in order to live.

Just how long had he been involved in such activities? This was a man in his twenties who might have pulled off a deception that had continued successfully for over three decades. It took ingenuity to pull something like that off. It took savvy way beyond the years of someone that young, unless that person had experience in the criminal world. He would have had to have underground contacts and lots of money. If he'd had assistance, he would have had to develop a level of respect from those who helped him that took years to hone. Who could Colton Cameron have been in the underworld that he would be able to pull something like that off? Were there people still alive who could confirm Ray's suspicions? Or had he killed them along the way, as he might have done to the victim in the river who took his place? Was Colton Cameron—a.k.a. Moody Lake—still alive under another name and with yet another face, still trying to make contact with his daughter, or with Bev? Would that mean that mother and daughter were in danger? More than likely it would be Ray who would be in danger simply because he loved the woman that Colton had loved.

Ray gave a distressed sigh. How could he rest not knowing? How could he rest if he knew? Did it really matter? He could end all of this speculation and anguish by walking away and ending the relationship with Bev. After all, she still wore her ex-husband's wedding band around her neck. Why should he stress over the man?

But he knew that he would never abandon Bev; he loved her too much. Whatever the outcome might be, he was going to be there. That was a definite.

Massaging his throbbing temples, he longed for the days when the only challenge that he could foresee regarding the two of them being together was her concern over their age difference. How trivial that had been.

Draining his glass, he made a decision. He would be flying to New York to talk to James Starr about the CD. While there he was going to contact another friend of his, a private detective. He was tired of living with this mystery. He was going to get some answers once and for all.

CHAPTER 26

Bev could have flown to Chicago without the airplane transporting her because she was floating on air. Why shouldn't she be? Her sister was doing well, her business was thriving, and she was in love. Ray would be arriving in a few days and she was giddy with excitement. Throughout their blossoming relationship, she had been on his turf. Now the tables would be turned. She wanted to introduce him to *her* town, Chi Town, not to mention what she wanted to do to him and with him. Bev gave a wicked grin at that thought.

As for the other matter, that had been taken care of in a manner that she never would have expected. Ray had called her from New York, where he had reported that his friend James had served as an intermediary and had taken the CD to the proper authorities.

"He didn't interject our names or Dana's," Ray told her. "We'll just be known as sources. They'll probably confiscate Mitch's computer, wherever that is, to verify that he actually wrote the entries, but that's not the best news that I've got to tell you."

He teased her and told her to tell him that she loved him and that he was the smartest man in the world before he would reveal the rest. Laughingly, Bev had complied.

"Just as I suspected, Stark Enterprises was already under investigation and warrants had been prepared. Ironically, the same day that James turned the CD over to the authorities, Russell Ingram and his cronies were arrested."

"What!" Bev was surprised.

"Yep." Ray sounded relieved. "And that's not the best part."

"Don't you dare try to tease me again," Bev warned him.

"All right then, I can tell you that Renee Ingram was included in the roundup."

"No!" Bev squealed excitedly.

Ray chuckled at her reaction. "It was alleged that she was privy to her husband's activities and had assisted in the laundering of money for the drug cartel."

Bev was amused at Ray's formal description of Renee's activities. It made him sound like the lawyer that he was, but no matter how it was put, Renee and her husband were getting what they deserved. She felt sorry for the couple's young son, but she wasted no pity on his parents.

"The newspapers here are having a field day describing the opulent lifestyle that Russell and Renee lived. Hell, they're in their thirties and own four houses. One newspaper said that a vase in one of their homes cost enough to feed a small country."

"I'm not surprised," Bev sniffed. "I could tell by her jewelry that Renee was flamboyant."

Ray could hear plenty of attitude in her statement. "Uh-huh, it seems that I remember your being her biggest fan when you first met her."

"I did fall for her act at first," Bev admitted, "just like you did, but you can't deny that it was her jewelry that helped bring her down. Grandy always told us that you don't have to flaunt your wealth. It's simply a tool with which you can help others and then you can enjoy the rest."

Ray told her that he would scan some of the articles about the arrest and e-mail them to her. Bev was eager to see them.

"I can't wait to call my sister and tell her about Renee's arrest."

"It sounds like the two of you are really getting along." Ray thought back to when he and Dana had driven into Stillwaters, and marveled at the difference in the relationship between the sisters then and now.

"We're becoming good friends." Bev didn't try to conceal the catch in her voice. "If anything good has come out of what Renee Ingram did, that was it. But I'm still a little confused.

Did the information on the CD help bring the cartel down or not?"

"James turned the CD in about an hour before the arrest, so everything was in motion before they got Mitch's information. But I'm sure that it will only make their case stronger."

"Then we won't have to worry about some drug dealers coming after us because we snitched, huh?" Bev said it in jest, but it had been an underlying concern.

Ray recognized that concern. "No, baby, we don't, and if anybody thinks that they could come and harm you they will have to come through me."

Bev melted like a stick of butter. "It sounds like I have my very own special Hercules."

Ray had reassured her that she did. He then went on to tell her all of the ways that he would perform like the strong man until Bev was drenched with desire. Even as she sat in her office thinking about what he had said, she could feel her body growing warm. When Janice knocked on the door briefly and entered the room, the look on Bev's face must have said it all.

"What are you doing in here?" Janice looked at her suspiciously. "And what put that smile on your face? Oops, excuse me, I know what." She placed the papers she had brought with her on the desk and crossed her arms. "Or should I say who."

Bev nodded for her to take a seat. "Ray and I are doing pretty well, thank you very much, and he's supposed to come visit me in a few days."

"I can see that you're excited." Janice smiled at her fondly. "I'm so glad for you. Ray seems like a nice guy, and you deserve the love of a good man in your life."

"Thanks, Janice. That's good of you to say."

"I mean it. I wish you the best." Janice got up and headed for the door. Opening it, she turned back to Bev. "Oh, I do have one little bit of advice for you, though."

Bev looked up and noted the twinkle in her assistant's eyes. She braced herself. "What is it?"

"Don't mess it up." She managed to shut the door before the balled-up wad of paper that Bev tossed hit her.

Ray watched from a distance as Thad shot a scene in his latest film. Since he was on the East Coast, he had called Thad and made plans to fly to Virginia to catch up on the film's progress. He would be staying overnight, providing him with the opportunity to visit with the Stewarts and to see his goddaughter before heading to Chicago.

The past week had been anxiety-ridden. The detective that he had hired was looking into the Colton Cameron matter, and Ray was anxious about what he might uncover. If the news delivered to him confirmed his suspicions in any way that Colton might have transformed into Moody Lake, then what would he do? He had to come up with a Plan B. Meanwhile, his visit with Thad and Darnell, culminating with his upcoming weekend with Bev, was much needed. He felt better merely being there.

The director ended the scene and called it a wrap for the day. Thad sauntered over to where Ray was sitting. The two men hugged.

"It's good seeing you." Thad flashed his trademark dimples.

"Looks like you're headed for another Oscar nomination." Ray liked the work that he had seen.

"You can tell that from one scene that took four takes?" Thad sniggered, unimpressed by the compliment. "But thanks anyway. Come on, let's go." He nodded toward the direction of his trailer and started walking. Ray followed.

"Are you going to go see the dailies?"

"Are you kidding? I'm dead on my feet. The only place that I'm going is to get some rest. They'll send them over to me. You can watch them with me if you'd like."

"I'll pass. I just dropped by to see you at work, and visit with Darnell and the baby."

Thad came to a dead stop, effectively halting Ray's steps. Ray gave him a shrug that silently asked him what was up.

"Man, I have known you since I was seven years old. You're as close to me as my own blood sisters, and you're going to stand there and lie to me about why you're here?"

Ray tried to be offended. "What? I did come here to see you guys."

"Yeah, and—" Thad lifted a brow, waiting.

"And I'm here!" Ray knew that Thad had seen right through him. He usually did.

"Man, you've got something else on your mind and you know it, so spit it out." He resumed walking. So did a tight-lipped Ray. "Is it about business, or is it personal?"

Ray glanced at him, but remained silent.

"Come on, man, I'm tired. So ask me what you want to ask me or tell me what you want me to know."

Ray felt defensive. "You're such a know-it-all."

"Obviously not, because I don't know what's on your mind."

Thad had always been intuitive, a little too much for Ray's taste. But he was right. Ray wanted to tell him about his dilemma with Colton Cameron and Moody Lake so badly that he ached, but he couldn't put him in the middle of what could be a minefield. Besides, Thad's wife was involved, and if he thought that she was in danger of being hurt in any way then he would go ballistic. No, it was best if Thad was left out of this. But he could try another tactic.

"If I ask you something, you've got to promise me that you won't share what we talked about with Darnell, okay?"

"Hmmm." Thad looked unsure. "I don't know about that. It depends on what it is."

Spotting a couple of chairs that had been placed under a nearby tree, Ray guided Thad over to them and they sat down. Thad looked at him and waited.

"I want to ask you if Darnell has ever talked to you about her father."

If Thad was surprised by the question he didn't show it. "Yes, she has. She even has a picture of him that she's showed me."

"Do you mind telling me what she said?"

"When she was pregnant with Nia, she used to talk about how she wished that she'd had a dad when she was growing up and that she was glad that she could give our baby one." He smiled at the memory. "And when the baby was born, I remember her saying that she wished that her father could have seen Nia."

"She really missed having one, didn't she?" He could identify. His own father had died when he was four years old. He had felt the same way when he was growing up.

Thad nodded. "But she would never tell Bev that. Darnell feels that she's being disloyal when she says something like that. She doesn't want Bev to feel that she wasn't enough. She would cut out her heart before she'd hurt her mother."

"So would I." That made two things that Darnell and he had in common.

"Is that all that you had to ask me?" Thad stood, joined by Ray. Once again, they started toward the trailer. "Ray, you know that Colton Cameron was a man who was loved by his family, but the man is dead. Don't let him reach out from the grave and spoil what you can have with Bev. She's got to let him go one day. Don't you be the one to resurrect him."

Ray thought about Thad's prophetic words as he was waved inside the trailer. How many times had he told himself the very same thing, but like a stubborn fool he hadn't listened. He prayed that he had not made the mistake of his life.

"So you and my daughter had a good time?" Bev scooted up in bed and placed pillows behind her back for support. She stretched, enjoying the feel of her body after the good loving that Ray had lavished on her most of the night and into the early morning.

He had arrived yesterday afternoon. She had picked him up at the airport and they had been sequestered in her home since they walked through the door. After they finally came up for air, Ray had begun telling her about his visit with Thad and Darnell. For the first time since he'd known her, Darnell and he had sat and talked for hours.

"It was the longest conversation that I've ever had with her." Ray lay on his side facing Bev. "I really don't remember a time when the two of us were in the room together and Thad wasn't there as some sort of buffer. But Thad conked out on us and when Darnell and I started talking and playing with the baby, one subject led to another and pretty soon we were talking about a little bit of everything. I really enjoyed it, and I enjoyed her." It was obvious that he was pleased, and so was Bev.

"She's an amazing woman." Bev had never been shy about praising her only child. She was intelligent, generous, talented, and kind, add to that beautiful, and what more could any mother want? "Her father would have been so proud of her."

Her words were met with silence. Sensing a shift in Ray's mood, Bev glanced down at him to find him toying with the blanket. Catching himself, he looked up at her with a crooked smile.

"Hey, I'm hungry. You gave me quite a workout."

"Touché." Bev tossed him a wink.

"What do you say that we go out on this town of yours and find some food for me to eat?"

"Sounds like a plan to me."

Scooting up beside her, Ray gave Bev a quick kiss before she scrambled out of the bed. "I've got dibs on the shower." She padded naked toward the bathroom, still amazed at how uninhibited she felt when she was with Ray.

"You know, I was thinking about a long, hot bath myself." Ray crossed his hands behind his head and enjoyed the view from the rear.

Bev turned and met his shining eyes. "I like the sound of that."

A few minutes later the two of them were relaxing in her garden tub, her back now supported by Ray's ample chest. The water was soothing and she felt nearly boneless. She liked this feeling of being in love. It had been long in coming, and she was enjoying every minute of it.

"It's a wonder that I don't go out of business, I'm taking so much time off to enjoy myself." Bev gave a long, satisfied sigh.

"That's the advantage of being your own boss." Ray felt just as relaxed as Bev. "We've worked hard all of our lives so that we could enjoy the fruits of our labor." He tweaked her breast. "And I'm sure enjoying this fruit."

As usual, Bev's body ignited at his touch. "I think I'll take a sample of the forbidden." Turning, she slid onto his member and groaned with pleasure at the perfect fit.

That was the way that Bev felt about Ray—they were perfect together. The rest of the weekend she shared her favorite haunts with him, from museums to blues club. When they weren't on the go, they spent much of their time together talking, and there was a lot to talk about.

Both of the Ingrams had been indicted on numerous charges. In addition, Russell had been charged with conspiracy to commit murder. Ray noted silently that Moody Lake's name wasn't among the suspected victims.

He didn't know whether to be relieved or not. However, Bev had an entirely different concern.

"If information from the CD is introduced as evidence, do you think that they'll reveal Renee's affair with Mitch?" She and Ray were strolling hand-in-hand along Lake Michigan.

"No, I don't think so. I don't see why that would be relevant to the case. This is about drug trafficking. I doubt if anybody cares about her extracurricular activities. Why?"

"I was thinking about Dana, and how she feels like such a loser when it comes to picking men. She knows that he was lacking in ethics because of his illegal activities, but I don't want her to know that he really didn't love her. That wouldn't make her feel any better."

Ray hugged her to him. "You're such a good big sister." He gave her a kiss on her temple. "Dana is lucky to have you."

"And I'm lucky to have her, too."

Bev had kept her sister abreast of the Ingrams' legal difficulties, and Dana had decided not to press charges against Renee. Based on the charges already levied against her, if she was found guilty the woman and her husband would be going to jail for a very long time. That's all that Dana wanted. Bev had been relieved that Dana had also made the decision not to share the circumstances regarding her fall with the other family members. There was no point in doing so. As far as her mother and the others were concerned, Dana's injuries had been the result of an accident. Case closed.

Bev was proud of her sister. She was making a remarkable recovery under the loving care of their mother and the other family members. Her negative opinion of the Stillwaters family had completely changed, so much so that she had decided to sublet her condo in L.A. and stay in town with her family for a while.

"Dana has come home in more ways than one." Bev hooked her arm around Ray's waist. "I couldn't be happier."

"That's all I want," Ray assured her. If she was happy, he was happy. His only hope was that it would last.

CHAPTER 27

Bev inhaled deeply as she sat on the patio outside of Ray's bedroom in Tiburon. She loved it here. The scenery was spectacular. The environment was invigorating, and she had always loved the weather in California, especially up here. It could get cool without getting too cold and it could get warm without getting too hot. The San Francisco Bay was nature at its best. Bev exhaled. As far as she was concerned, it contributed to making the weather in the Bay Area nearly perfect.

Adjusting her sunglasses on her face, she closed her eyes and sank deeper into the cushioned lounge chair on which she was relaxing. Life was good.

Ray had been right when he had said that a long-distance relationship between them could work. It had been four weeks from the day that he had arrived in Chicago to spend his first weekend with her, and they had become quite the frequent flyers. The miles were racking up.

As the mother of Darnell Cameron she had experienced the sort of life of which others could only dream. There had been premieres and parties, strolls down the red carpet, and front row seats at concerts and films all over the world. After Thad became her son-in-law there was more of the same.

Ray was part of that glamorous life. Attending social events to wheel and deal was part of his job, but she wasn't impressed by the glitz, and neither was he. They were both familiar with the giant egos in the entertainment industry, as well as the phonies and the hangers-on that inhabited its outer fringes. She and Ray attended only the events that were necessary. Their favorite pastime was to meet in Chicago or in Tiburon and simply enjoy being together.

They found plenty to do wherever they were. Earlier that day they had gone hiking on Mount Tam, after having toured Angel Island yesterday. Bev loved Ray's sense of adventure. Putting it plainly, she simply loved the man.

With a satisfied sigh, she snuggled against the pillows and was drifting off to sleep when her cell phone rang. Opening her eyes, she glanced at the intrusive culprit. It was laying on the table between the two lounge chairs on the patio, the other one having been occupied earlier by Ray. Bev frowned when she saw that there were two telephones on the table. Ray had left his when he went to run an errand, which meant that it was a certainty that the call was not from him.

Reluctantly, she picked up the ringing instrument. The call was from Darnell.

"Hey, sweetie," Bev sing-songed.

"Hi, Mama." Darnell sounded chipper. She and Thad had finished shooting their movie and were back home in Carmel. "Have you and Ray decided whether you're driving down here tomorrow or not?"

"No, we haven't." Bev wanted to say that she wished that her daughter would stop bugging her about it. She had called her three times during the weekend with the same question.

"But Mama, it's not like you've got to rush back to Chicago or something. You're taking a couple of extra days off to be with Ray. Don't you want to see your granddaughter?"

Implied in Darnell's question was that her mother was putting Ray before her grandchild. Bev resented the implication, but she wasn't going to be manipulated.

"Honey, I met you in Virginia for the wrap party and the three of us flew back to Chicago together. You guys spent a week with me. Two weeks ago Ray and I spent a weekend in Carmel . . ."

"Where you stayed in a hotel," Darnell whined. "You used to stay here with us."

Bev gave a weary sigh; her daughter could be such a child sometimes. "*I* used to stay with you. Things have changed. As your mother I'm not able to sleep under your roof with my boyfriend. I've never done it before."

"Oh, that's so twentieth century." Darnell sounded frustrated. "And you're with Ray this time, that's different. He's like family."

"So it's okay for me to make love in my daughter's house with a family member? That sounds like incest to me."

Darnell gave an aggravated grunt. "Very funny."

Bev was ready to cut this short. "I'm tired, Darnell. I need to get some rest. You're sounding more like a baby than the intelligent, mature woman that I know you are, so you need to take a step back and check yourself. I'm flattered that you want to see me more often, but I'm one person and I'm a busy one. I love you more than I love my own life. You're always in my heart, but I won't allow you to try and make me feel guilty because I have a life that doesn't revolve around you."

"Excuse me?" Darnell was insulted, and she didn't mask it.

"You heard me, and we'll discuss this at another time. Right now, I'm getting ready to take a nap until Ray gets back. Bye, sweetie." Bev disconnected, leaving her daughter wanting but unable to say more.

Bev had just repositioned herself in her lounge chair and closed her eyes when once again, the ring of the telephone disturbed her peace. A second frown creased her face. She thought that her cell phone had been turned off. Her eyes slid over to the table. She was right. The ringing was coming from Ray's cell.

She started to let voice mail get it, but decided that she could deliver a message to him. Picking up his cell phone she answered the call: "Hello."

As Ray stood in the restaurant where he was to pick up the meal Bev and he would dine on this evening, he was feeling on top of the world. He was so in love with Bev that it was sickening. He had never felt so vulnerable or so alive. He was actually thinking about marrying again, something that he had sworn he would never do.

He and Bev were so compatible. There wasn't a woman that he had dated—and there had been many—that had ever been as perfectly adapted to his lifestyle as Bev. Too many of the other women had been either needy or greedy. Bev was neither. It was refreshing.

The bumps in the road insofar as their relationship was concerned had not all been smoothed. It seemed that there was one development that neither Bev nor he had expected. Darnell had become jealous of the time that her mother spent with Ray. She had never had to share her before. Much to Ray's delight he had been told that Bev's previous relationships had never been as serious. Neither had they been long distance, which took a lot of time on both their parts. It was time that Bev used to spend with Darnell but was now spending with Ray. Until Thad entered her life with his flair for spontaneity, Darnell had not been the type of person who was easily adaptable to change. She liked order in her life, and her mother was her foundation. The bond between the two of them was strong. Sharing was proving to be a difficult adjustment. However, Ray felt that Bev was handling the situation well.

She had raised her daughter to be a strong, independent woman who was loved without question, but who wasn't coddled. When Darnell reached adulthood, Bev continued to support and encourage her daughter in her endeavors, but she lived her life and expected Darnell to live her own. Her daughter had met that expectation, even when she fell in love with Thad. Now when Darnell expressed her anxiety regarding her mother's time, Bev reminded her of both of their independent statuses. Meanwhile, she kept Ray out of it and he liked that.

Paying for the order, Ray was walking to the restaurant parking lot when he decided to call Bev to let her know that he was on his way back home. Sometimes he would find excuses to call her just to hear her voice and remind himself that she was with him. Reaching into his jacket for his cell phone, he discovered it missing. Frantically, he patted all of his pockets with no results. Stopping, he searched his memory until he recalled where he had left it. With a nonchalant shrug, he got in the car, started it, and pulled into traffic. He chuckled to himself for his initial panic about his missing telephone as he thought about how easy it was to become dependent on the instrument. Glancing at his car phone, he thought about using it to make the call, but dismissed the urge. He would be home shortly. Little did he realize the surprise that would be waiting for him when he arrived.

Bev was sitting in the living room when Ray walked into the house with his hands filled with the sacks of food her empty stomach had been craving, but she had lost her appetite. One telephone call had accomplished that. All she was hungry for now were some answers.

"Hey, baby." Ray flashed her a smile as he headed for the kitchen. "Our order wasn't ready when I got to the restaurant. I had to wait, but at least it's still hot."

He disappeared. Bev followed him.

Ray was busy unpacking the sacks when she reached his brightly painted kitchen. She remembered that he said that when Thad lived there this room had been painted a bright blue. He'd had it painted yellow, a happy, sunny color meant to influence the mood. It wasn't working on her. She stood with arms folded across her chest, glaring at him as he busily gathered the dishes and silverware needed to eat their meal.

"I started to call and tell why it was taking me so long, but I left my cell phone here." He set a place at the counter for Bev and for himself. "You didn't happen to find it, did you?"

"Yes, I did, and I answered a call."

It was the hard tone of her voice that caused Ray to pause and look at her. The expression on her face made it apparent that Bev was not happy.

"Oh, really? Who was it from?" He had no clue why a call for him would make her so visibly upset. Perhaps it had been from an old girlfriend. Her next words made him wish that the latter had been the case.

"It was the secretary for Nathan Webb, a private investigator. She said that he needed you to call his office regarding his investigation of Mr. Colton Cameron."

Damn! Ray could feel the breath draining from his body. He had never expected this to happen, but he held her eyes and waited to see what she would do.

Bev was incensed. How dare he investigate Colton! What gave him the right?

"Would you like to give me an explanation?"

Everything in her demeanor told Ray that whatever he told her wouldn't be good enough, and he knew that he could not share the truth. How could he explain that he suspected that after thirty-plus years her deceased husband might still be alive? She would think that he was joking. If he told her that he further suspected that Colton Cameron had murdered an innocent man and that it was an unidentifiable body that was claimed as his, Bev would think that he was insane. He would only solidify that thought if he added that the man whom she had loved and honored for so many decades had risen from the dead as Moody Lake, a drug kingpin who ran an illegal operation that spanned three continents. So what could he say? His silence served to fuel her anger.

"You're not going to answer me?" Bev tried to remain calm, but it was increasingly difficult as he stood before her looking contrite. She took a step toward him. "Are you so jealous of a dead man that you have to have him investigated?" Again she was met with silence. She stood before him face to face, arms outstretched. "Just give me one rational explanation as to why?"

Ray felt sick. He wished that this had never happened. Why hadn't he let it go when he had a chance to do so? But the least that he owed her was some element of truth. "There isn't a rational explanation."

Bev didn't have a counter to that. Ray held her eyes as he sank to one of the stools placed at the kitchen island. His eyes were clouded with pain. Her eyes were blinded by confusion.

"So, it just happened? You woke up one morning and told yourself that was the day that you were going to find out all about Colton? I hadn't told you enough? You had to know more?" Turning abruptly, she walked away from him in order to gather herself, and then she turned back. "I thought that you respected me."

"I do."

"I thought that we had the type of relationship where we could be open with each other."

"We have."

"Yet you didn't trust me enough to answer any question that you might have had about Colton."

Silence.

Bev gave a heavy sigh. This was a side of Ray that she hadn't seen before. Since they had been together they had discussed every subject imaginable. Why did he feel that he couldn't discuss her ex-husband, too?

"Have you even noticed that I no longer wear Colton's ring around my neck?"

"Yes, of course I noticed. You keep it on your dresser. It's hanging by a gold chain on that jewelry stand."

His words caused Bev to wince. Yes, the ring was in her bedroom, and it was visible, but when she was here with him she didn't bring it with her. Did he expect her to throw the ring away?

"I took it off because of you, Ray." Bev threw her hands up in frustration. "My God! What do you want from me?"

He didn't hesitate. "Your love and devotion to me alone."

It was clear by the sadness in his voice that he doubted that she had given that to him. Bev felt as if he had slapped her. She had given more of herself to this man than she had ever given to any other, except for—

She caught the thought that came into her head and became defensive.

"I've given you everything that I have to give." Her feelings were hurt. "How can you doubt that?"

"Have you?" He needed more from her, and this was the time to demand it. "I love you with everything in me. Are you ready to say the same thing to me?"

Bev bristled. "I thought that my actions assured you of that. Obviously, I was wrong."

She turned and left the room. As Bev climbed the stairs to his bedroom she fought back tears of disappointment. She had thought that he was more secure than that. How could he doubt that she was in love with him? Over the past few months she had flown back and forth across the country to be with him. There was no pleasing him! Perhaps Ray wasn't the man that she thought him to be. Maybe it was time to re-evaluate their situation.

That night they lay in bed together back to back, not wrapped in each other's arms. They said nothing to each other. They had nothing to offer one another, not even their bodies. Earlier, Ray had brought her dinner up to her and Bev had asked him again why he'd had her husband investigated. Just as before, he had no answer. The communication that had been the foundation of their relationship was nonexistent on this night. With Ray's silence it had begun to crumble. There was a gulf that was building between them and it was frightening to them both.

At the airport the next day Bev gave him a dispirited kiss goodbye. Ray responded with much more passion.

He watched her walk to the security gate with a lump in his throat and a knot in his heart and he wondered if he had lost her.

As Bev went through the gate, she glanced back at him. Ray looked as miserable as she felt. Could this be the beginning of the end for them?

CHAPTER 28

The weekend after Bev found out about Ray having her late husband investigated she changed their traveling plans. They hadn't spoken to each other daily as they had been doing for months. It seemed that when Ray called during the day, Bev's voice mail answered. Instead of returning his calls as soon as she was available, she did so at night and her excuse was always that she had been busy at work. Conversations between them that had flowed easily before were now awkward, rife with occasional silences where much remained unsaid.

Ray had anticipated Bev's call regarding their plans the next weekend. He was to fly to Chicago on Friday. The call from her came on Thursday night.

"I need to go to Stillwaters this weekend." Bev had worked all week to convince herself that she had to go rather than wanted to go. Therefore, it sounded almost plausible when she actually said the words.

"Is Dana all right? Grandy?" His questions were mingled with concern as well as doubt.

Bev could hear his uncertainty. She tried to reassure him.

"They're both doing fine, but I need to go there," and she did, if for nothing else but her peace of mind. There was a lengthy silence on the other end.

Ray knew that this could be the beginning of the end, and he blamed himself for it. All week he had conducted introspective self-analysis regarding his obsession with Bev's husband, and he was still doing so. Their being apart this weekend might be best for them both.

"Then get there safely, and don't forget to call me." Their signature tag line was like a knife in the gut for them both. It was to assure each that the other had arrived at their destination safely. They always looked forward to those calls, which were filled with the love that they felt for one another. Now they each wondered if the meaning of those words would ever be the same.

"I will," Bev whispered. She had expected more resistance to his not coming to see her and was disappointed that she hadn't gotten it. "Good night, Ray." She held her breath, waiting for his reply.

"Good night, Bev."

They disconnected and both took a relieved breath. At least neither one of them had said goodbye.

Ray received a call from Bev that Friday evening. Their conversation had been short. She'd advised him of her arrival. He'd asked about the flight and they had ended the call with the words "I love you." That hadn't changed, and Ray had decided that from his end it wouldn't. He had waited too long to win Bev's love and he was going to fight to keep it. He wasn't giving up easily and it was his hope that she wouldn't, either.

In evaluating his obsession with Colton Cameron, he had come up with some conclusions, and one of them was that he was afraid of the man. He wasn't frightened of him physically. His biggest fear was the hold that the memory of him had on Bev. Colton had been perfect in her eyes, and no one could compete with perfection. It was impossible to live up to something that didn't exist, and he didn't plan on doing so.

Having decided to be absolutely honest with himself in his week of self analysis, he knew that one of the reasons that he pursued the Colton/Moody transformation was that he was looking for the imperfections in her late husband. He would never tell Bev anything that was revealed regarding Colton, but Ray realized that knowing that Colton wasn't a man without faults would be very satisfying. His knowledge would be his defense against her memory of him. It might prove to be the only weapon that he had. Yet when he thought about the price of possessing such a weapon, the reality was that it might not be worth it.

The investigator had informed him that he would be sending the Colton Cameron report to him by messenger on Sunday. Ray would have the only copy. What he chose to do with it was up to him.

"Now let me get this straight." Dana looked incredulous as she scooted up in the lounge chair in which she had been relaxing so that she could get a better look at her sister sitting across from her. "You're rethinking your relationship with Ray because he's jealous of Colton?"

"Yes," Bev answered. "He's proving to be more insecure than I thought."

Dana scoffed. "Ray Wilson? Insecure? We are talking about the same man that negotiates multi-million dollar deals with the biggest players in Hollywood, aren't we? If so, insecure wouldn't be a word that I would use when referring to him."

"Well, that's how he is when it comes to Colton."

Bev rose from her seat and turned to look out onto Grandy's garden. She could hardly believe that she was talking to her sister about her love life. It was a testament as to how things had changed between them.

The conversation had started out innocently enough. On a walking excursion Dana and she had decided to visit Grandy. Dana was walking with a cane now, and from the look of it she wouldn't need that much longer. Bev had stated how impressed she was with her improvement. Her sister had asked how her life was going and then about Ray. Dana had caught Bev's hesitation in answering. She wanted to know what was wrong, and now here they were engaged in a question-and-answer session.

"I noticed that you're still wearing Colton's wedding band around your neck." She peered at her sister's back accusingly.

Bev lowered her hand from the ring that she had been fingering. "I don't wear it any more when I'm with Ray." She turned to glower at Dana, who wasn't intimidated.

"Yet you still wear it." Dana returned her stony glare.

"And as long as you do it will be a constant reminder that Ray's number two in your life." A voice came from behind them, and the two women looked up to see Grandy standing in the doorway.

"How long have you been there?" Bev went over to help her onto the patio, but she was waved away as the older woman took a seat next to Dana.

"I've been there long enough to understand what's happening." Grandy adjusted her body in the chair and settled back comfortably. "But first I have to say that it's good to see you ladies together, talking like sisters ought to be doing. It's long overdue."

Bev and Dana smiled at each other. Neither one of them could disagree. Bev took a seat across from her grandmother, hoping that the conversation that Dana and she had been having when Grandy walked in on them would be ignored. It wasn't.

"So Bev, you're about to lose a good man because you insist on continuing to play the role of the grieving widow." Grandy looked her granddaughter straight in the eye. "How long has it been now, thirty-three, thirty-four years?"

Bev was appalled. She wanted to rail against her grandmother's sarcasm, but she knew better. Grandy was the Alpha and Omega in their family. Disrespecting her just wasn't done. Ironically, it had been she who had been aware of her relationship with Ray even before other members of the family, and had voiced her hearty approval. Bev wanted to ask the woman to stay out of her business, but didn't dare.

"Ray and I are simply having some difficulty. That's all." Her tight-lipped answer indicated her displeasure with her grandmother's observation, but Grandy didn't appear to care.

Esther Stillwaters leveled Bev with a look that clearly stated that she must think that her grandmother was a fool. Folding her arms, Grandy closed her eyes. To those outside of the Stillwaters clan her grandmother appeared to be nodding off. Those within the family knew that this was a sign that words of wisdom were about to be dispensed. Bev and her sister waited quietly until she spoke.

"When I buried your granddaddy, I thought that my life was over, but I had his babies to raise so I had to go on. I dedicated my life to them and built this town as a monument to his memory. I dared anything or anyone to get in my way. I never gave love a second chance. There was only one love in my life, and I was determined to keep it alive until I joined the man responsible for it." She opened her eyes and looked at Bev. "I've often wondered what might have been if I had given love the opportunity to enter my life just one more time. Instead, I put a dead man as a barrier between me and that opportunity." Her eyes shifted to the ring that Bev was fingering and then back to her granddaughter's face. "I've played the grieving widow longer than you have been alive. It's been a very lonely existence, and, until the day I die, I'll regret that I closed the door to the joy of being loved by another good man."

The bell on the entrance gate to Ray's Tiburon house rang at 8:00 Sunday morning. He was in the kitchen fixing his breakfast. Through the intercom the messenger informed him that the package that Ray was expecting had finally arrived. Retrieving it, Ray returned to the kitchen and placed it on the island counter.

For the next hour he cooked around it, ate around it, and washed dishes around it. He cleaned the house, worked on his computer, and literally ignored the inevitable until lunchtime. It was noon exactly when he finally sat down and faced the decision that he had to make. Should he open the package or not? If he did, what would be gained by knowing more about Colton Cameron? If he didn't, what would he lose?

When he weighed the last two questions, only one came out a winner. Picking the package up he walked into his living room, where he had built a fire in the fireplace earlier that morning. Unceremoniously, he placed the manila envelope into the flames. They roared to life. He watched it burn until there was nothing but ashes.

"I guess that takes care of that," he said aloud.

Dousing the blackened embers, Ray picked up his car keys and left the house. He had destroyed the past in order to build a future. It remained to be seen if Bev was willing to do the same.

Thirty minutes later Ray was sitting in Sausalito on the same bench in the Downtown Plaza where he and Bev had bumped into each other months before. That day had been pivotal in their relationship, and he found comfort relaxing, partaking of the view, and enjoying the coming and going of the visiting tourists.

He hadn't spoken to Bev since she called to tell him that she had arrived safely in Stillwaters. That meant that one whole day had passed without his hearing her voice. He had hoped that she would call him, but since she hadn't, he would call her. Ray didn't want her to think that he was pressuring her, but he was in this relationship for better or for worse, and he didn't want to be in it alone. All he could hope was that she would make the decision that he wouldn't be.

Taking out his cell phone he called her. He would love to see her, but the sound of her voice would be good enough for now. Her cell phone rang incessantly until it finally went to voice mail. He was disappointed but he left her a message.

"Call me."

Pocketing his phone, Ray returned his attention to the ferry boat that was skirting across the Bay getting closer to shore. Growing bored as he waited for its arrival he turned his attention to the newspaper that he had bought to help pass the time. Unfolding it, he had started reading the front page when his cell phone rang. It was Bev.

"Hey, you," he said, his voice a smile. "How's it going?"

"Pretty good, how about you?"

Bev's voice was warm and inviting, compared to the confusion and uncertainty he had heard the last time they had spoken. But there was a combination of noises in the background that made it difficult to hear her.

"I'm doing fine, but what is all of that noise? Where are you?"

"Look up and you'll see."

Ray did as directed. The ferry boat had docked and on its deck stood Bev, dressed in a blaze of red and waving like the queen that she was. Standing, Ray waved back. The grin on his face threatened to become permanent. Who else but Bev would make an entrance like this? What a woman!

He spoke into the phone. "You're looking mighty good to me."

"And so do you." As she walked down the gangplank onto shore, Bev continued to talk on her cell phone, and Ray did, too.

"Why did you take the boat here instead of going to Tiburon?" With glowing eyes he watched as she sauntered toward him.

"I planned on walking around a bit, then checking into a hotel that holds wonderful memories." Bev stopped in front of Ray and kept talking on the phone. "Then I had planned on calling the man that I love and asking him to join me there for old time's sake. What do you think you would have said?" She switched the phone off and stood looking into his eyes.

Ray followed suit. "First I would have said, 'hello you.'" He wrapped his arm around her waist. "Then I would have said, 'Hell yeah!'"

He drew her to him and kissed her passionately. Bev responded. She didn't care that they were on display in a public area. This was a repeat performance. Anybody who didn't like it could keep on steppin'. She loved this man. They broke the kiss, breathing heavily. Ray stepped back to look at her.

The dress that Bev was wearing was long and sleeveless. Fancy red sandals complemented the look, as did her painted toes. She was carrying a large red and white stripped shoulder bag slung across her shoulder. As usual her makeup and hair were flawless and so was she. He also noticed that she wasn't wearing any jewelry around her neck.

"Where's your luggage?"

Bev gave him a sly smile. "I'm wearing everything that I'll need. I've got a toothbrush and a change of underwear in my purse."

Ray hardened instantly.

Bev gave a rakish chuckle and whispered in his ear, "We'd better get you to the hotel while you can still walk."

He whispered back, "You're so bad."

"Let's see if I can get worse." Hooking her arm through his arm, they started walking. "Why are you here, hon, sitting in the Plaza?"

Ray looked at her with surprise, pleased by the endearment. It was the first one that he could remember directed at him. "I was relaxing and remembering the last time that we were here together."

"It was a good memory, wasn't it?"

"The best."

They strolled in silence for a moment as Bev thought about how she would word what she was about to say.

The talk with Grandy had been her motivation to come to Ray. It hadn't been difficult to convince Uncle Gerald to fly her to San Francisco, and she had spent the night in Darnell's condo. It was a journey that she shared with Ray, as well as some conclusions that she had reached.

"When I was in San Francisco, I took some time to myself before I came to you. I needed that time alone, with no one giving me their opinion or taking this side over the other about what I should do. I wanted to be able to think clearly because the decision that I had to make was really hard for me."

Ray listened closely and remained silent. He could hear a resolution in her tone that he hadn't heard before. His heart raced in anticipation.

"I took Colton's ring, wrapped it up, packaged it, and sent it to Darnell. I called her and told her that it was coming. The ring belongs to her now. It's time for me to let Colton go." She squeezed Ray's hand. "I'm so sorry if I made you feel secondary, but you were never secondary in my life. I love you, and I haven't said those words to a man in a long, long time. I'm so glad that I get to say them again, and especially to you."

Ray's eyes misted. "It's a new beginning for us both."

Bev nodded in agreement. Her eyes were also glazed with unshed tears. It seemed that they each had waited a lifetime for this moment.

"The package came from the investigator today." Ray knew that he didn't have to clarify what he meant. She knew. "When I got it I . . ."

"Destroyed it," Bev interrupted. "And you didn't open it or read its contents." She finished the statement for him.

Ray was startled. "How did you know?"

Bev stopped and looked into his eyes. "I know the type of man that you are." They resumed walking.

"I'm glad that you think so highly of me, but, believe me, I've had my own demons to face."

Arriving at the hotel, they paused under the colorful awning. Ray drew her to him.

"It looks as if we've made it." Ray motioned toward the ornate hotel doors.

Bev caressed his cheek and gave him a soft kiss. "It looks as if we really have."

EPILOGUE

Eighteen Months Later

Darnell Cameron Stewart disconnected her cell phone, turned over in bed, and shook her husband out of a sound sleep.

"Thad! Thad! Wake up! We've got an emergency."

A disoriented Thad Stewart sat straight up. "What? Is something wrong with the baby? Is the house on fire?"

He started to scramble out of bed. Darnell was already on her feet, putting on her robe as she headed for the closet.

"No, the baby is fine and so is the house, but Mama and Ray are back from their honeymoon and the woman has lost her mind!"

Behind a yawn, Thad looked at his wife in confusion. "What's happened?"

"Ray bought Mama a houseboat for a wedding gift," she bellowed from the confines of her closet. "They're in Sausalito moving into it as we speak. They're going to live there!"

Clothes in hand, Darnell hurried back into the bedroom and started rushing around like a woman possessed. Crawling back in bed, Thad pulled the covers over his head. Darnell came to a dead stop.

"What are you doing? We've got to get to Sausalito and stop this madness. My mother can't live on a houseboat."

Thad peered at her over the folds of the plump goosedown comforter. "Get back in bed, baby. It's too early for this nonsense."

"Nonsense?" Darnell's hand went to her hip as she tried to hold her temper. She spoke slowly and distinctly so that her husband could understand each word. "Obviously you don't understand the extent of the problem. My *mother* is living like some *pirate* on a *boat* floating on the water."

"Like a *pirate*?" The word struck Thad as humorous, and he began to laugh.

Darnell watched him with growing irritation. "I don't see what's funny. This is serious!" Her protest went unheeded as he laughed louder and harder, rolling across the bed and pounding the mattress. "Like a pirate!"

His fit of laughter threatened to become addictive, and Darnell fought the urge to join him in laughter. As his howls of glee grew more pronounced, she stomped to the bed with the intention of telling him off, but before she knew it she had joined him in his antics and she was laughing, too.

In Sausalito on a bright yellow houseboat trimmed in blue, Bev and Ray Wilson pulled in the wooden plank that allowed visitors aboard.

"I give Darnell until noon to drive here and try to get into our business," Bev told Ray, grinning in triumph as they placed the plank on board.

"I'm putting my money on Thad to stop her." Ray followed Bev to the door of the houseboat, enjoying the sway of her hips.

"I'm hoping." She had to give her son-in-law credit. He did know how to handle her daughter. "But just in case."

Reaching inside the door she withdrew a laminated sign adorned with a yellow ribbon for hanging. She showed it to Ray.

"Perfect." He gave Bev a quick kiss and then picked her up unexpectedly. She squealed in delight.

As her husband carried her across the threshold of their new home, she placed the sign on a hook in the center of the front door and locked the door behind them.

The sign swaying in the breeze was plain and simple. It read DO NOT DISTURB.

THE END

ABOUT THE AUTHOR

Crystal V. Rhodes is an author and an award winning playwright. Her first novel, *Sin*, received critical acclaim. Her second novel, *Sweet Sacrifice*, was nominated for the Romance Suspense Book of the Year. Her third novel, *Grandmothers, Incorporated*, co-written with L. Barnett Evans, was selected as Best Book of the Year by two websites. Her fourth novel, *Sinful Intentions*, received the BlackRefer.com Annual Reviewers Choice Award as Best Romance Novel. Her novel *Singing a Song* . . . was selected by the publisher to promote the first Genesis Press Writing Contest in 2009. Still Waters . . . is her fifth Genesis Press release.

The Written Word Magazine has named Rhodes as one of its Ten Up and Coming Authors in the Midwest. As a playwright, she has been the recipient of numerous nominations and awards for her stage plays. She has a Master's Degree in Sociology and has written for newspapers, magazines, radio, and television. Visit her website at *www.crystalrhodes.com.*

2011 Mass Market Titles

January

From This Moment
Sean Young
ISBN: 978-1-58571-383-7
$6.99

Nihon Nights
Trisha Haddad and Monica Haddad
ISBN: 978-1-58571-382-0
$6.99

February

The Davis Years
Nicole Green
ISBN: 978-1-58571-390-5
$6.99

Allegro
Patricia Knight
ISBN: 978-158571-391-2
$6.99

March

Lies in Disguise
Bernice Layton
ISBN: 978-1-58571-392-9
$6.99

Steady
Ruthie Robinson
ISBN: 978-1-58571-393-6
$6.99

April

The Right Maneuver
LaShell Stratton-Childers
ISBN: 978-1-58571-394-3
$6.99

Riding the Corporate Ladder
Keith Walker
ISBN: 978-1-58571-395-0
$6.99

May

Separate Dreams
Joan Early
ISBN: 978-1-58571-434-6
$6.99

I Take This Woman
Chamein Canton
ISBN: 978-1-58571-435-3
$6.99

June

Doesn't Really Matter
Keisha Mennefee
ISBN: 978-1-58571-434-0
$6.99

Inside Out
Grayson Cole
ISBN: 978-1-58571-437-7
$6.99

2011 Mass Market Titles (continued)

July

Rehoboth Road
Anita Ballard-Jones
ISBN: 978-1-58571-438-4
$6.99

Holding Her Breath
Nicole Green
ISBN: 978-1-58571-439-1
$6.99

August

The Sea of Aaron
Kymberly Hunt
ISBN: 978-1-58571-440-7
$6.99d

The Finley Sisters' Oath of Romance
Keith Thomas Walker
ISBN: 978-1-58571-441-4
$6.99

September

October

November

December

Other Genesis Press, Inc. Titles

2 Good	Celya Bowers	$6.99
A Dangerous Deception	J.M. Jeffries	$8.95
A Dangerous Love	J.M. Jeffries	$8.95
A Dangerous Obsession	J.M. Jeffries	$8.95
A Drummer's Beat to Mend	Kei Swanson	$9.95
A Good Dude	Keith Walker	$6.99
A Happy Life	Charlotte Harris	$9.95
A Heart's Awakening	Veronica Parker	$9.95
A Lark on the Wing	Phyliss Hamilton	$9.95
A Love of Her Own	Cheris F. Hodges	$9.95
A Love to Cherish	Beverly Clark	$8.95
A Place Like Home	Alicia Wiggins	$6.99
A Risk of Rain	Dar Tomlinson	$8.95
A Taste of Temptation	Reneé Alexis	$9.95
A Twist of Fate	Beverly Clark	$8.95
A Voice Behind Thunder	Carrie Elizabeth Greene	$6.99
A Will to Love	Angie Daniels	$9.95
Acquisitions	Kimberley White	$8.95
Across	Carol Payne	$12.95
After the Vows (Summer Anthology)	Leslie Esdaile T.T. Henderson Jacqueline Thomas	$10.95
Again, My Love	Kayla Perrin	$10.95
Against the Wind	Gwynne Forster	$8.95
All I Ask	Barbara Keaton	$8.95
All I'll Ever Need	Mildred Riley	$6.99
Always You	Crystal Hubbard	$6.99
Ambrosia	T.T. Henderson	$8.95
An Unfinished Love Affair	Barbara Keaton	$8.95
And Then Came You	Dorothy Elizabeth Love	$8.95
Angel's Paradise	Janice Angelique	$9.95
Another Memory	Pamela Ridley	$6.99
Anything But Love	Celya Bowers	$6.99
At Last	Lisa G. Riley	$8.95
Best Foot Forward	Michele Sudler	$6.99
Best of Friends	Natalie Dunbar	$8.95
Best of Luck Elsewhere	Trisha Haddad	$6.99
Beyond the Rapture	Beverly Clark	$9.95
Blame It on Paradise	Crystal Hubbard	$6.99
Blaze	Barbara Keaton	$9.95

Other Genesis Press, Inc. Titles (continued)

Blindsided	Tammy Williams	$6.99
Bliss, Inc.	Chamein Canton	$6.99
Blood Lust	J.M. Jeffries	$9.95
Blood Seduction	J.M. Jeffries	$9.95
Blue Interlude	Keisha Mennefee	$6.99
Bodyguard	Andrea Jackson	$9.95
Boss of Me	Diana Nyad	$8.95
Bound by Love	Beverly Clark	$8.95
Breeze	Robin Hampton Allen	$10.95
Broken	Dar Tomlinson	$24.95
Burn	Crystal Hubbard	$6.99
By Design	Barbara Keaton	$8.95
Cajun Heat	Charlene Berry	$8.95
Careless Whispers	Rochelle Alers	$8.95
Cats & Other Tales	Marilyn Wagner	$8.95
Caught in a Trap	Andre Michelle	$8.95
Caught Up in the Rapture	Lisa G. Riley	$9.95
Cautious Heart	Cheris F. Hodges	$8.95
Chances	Pamela Leigh Starr	$8.95
Checks and Balances	Elaine Sims	$6.99
Cherish the Flame	Beverly Clark	$8.95
Choices	Tammy Williams	$6.99
Class Reunion	Irma Jenkins/ John Brown	$12.95
Code Name: Diva	J.M. Jeffries	$9.95
Conquering Dr. Wexler's Heart	Kimberley White	$9.95
Corporate Seduction	A.C. Arthur	$9.95
Crossing Paths, Tempting Memories	Dorothy Elizabeth Love	$9.95
Crossing the Line	Bernice Layton	$6.99
Crush	Crystal Hubbard	$9.95
Cypress Whisperings	Phyllis Hamilton	$8.95
Dark Embrace	Crystal Wilson Harris	$8.95
Dark Storm Rising	Chinelu Moore	$10.95
Daughter of the Wind	Joan Xian	$8.95
Dawn's Harbor	Kymberly Hunt	$6.99
Deadly Sacrifice	Jack Kean	$22.95
Designer Passion	Dar Tomlinson Diana Richeaux	$8.95

Other Genesis Press, Inc. Titles (continued)

Do Over	Celya Bowers	$9.95
Dream Keeper	Gail McFarland	$6.99
Dream Runner	Gail McFarland	$6.99
Dreamtective	Liz Swados	$5.95
Ebony Angel	Deatri King-Bey	$9.95
Ebony Butterfly II	Delilah Dawson	$14.95
Echoes of Yesterday	Beverly Clark	$9.95
Eden's Garden	Elizabeth Rose	$8.95
Eve's Prescription	Edwina Martin Arnold	$8.95
Everlastin' Love	Gay G. Gunn	$8.95
Everlasting Moments	Dorothy Elizabeth Love	$8.95
Everything and More	Sinclair Lebeau	$8.95
Everything but Love	Natalie Dunbar	$8.95
Falling	Natalie Dunbar	$9.95
Fate	Pamela Leigh Starr	$8.95
Finding Isabella	A.J. Garrotto	$8.95
Fireflies	Joan Early	$6.99
Fixin' Tyrone	Keith Walker	$6.99
Forbidden Quest	Dar Tomlinson	$10.95
Forever Love	Wanda Y. Thomas	$8.95
Friends in Need	Joan Early	$6.99
From the Ashes	Kathleen Suzanne Jeanne Sumerix	$8.95
Frost on My Window	Angela Weaver	$6.99
Gentle Yearning	Rochelle Alers	$10.95
Glory of Love	Sinclair LeBeau	$10.95
Go Gentle Into That Good Night	Malcom Boyd	$12.95
Goldengroove	Mary Beth Craft	$16.95
Groove, Bang, and Jive	Steve Cannon	$8.99
Hand in Glove	Andrea Jackson	$9.95
Hard to Love	Kimberley White	$9.95
Hart & Soul	Angie Daniels	$8.95
Heart of the Phoenix	A.C. Arthur	$9.95
Heartbeat	Stephanie Bedwell-Grime	$8.95
Hearts Remember	M. Loui Quezada	$8.95
Hidden Memories	Robin Allen	$10.95
Higher Ground	Leah Latimer	$19.95
Hitler, the War, and the Pope	Ronald Rychiak	$26.95
How to Kill Your Husband	Keith Walker	$6.99

Other Genesis Press, Inc. Titles (continued)

How to Write a Romance	Kathryn Falk	$18.95
I Married a Reclining Chair	Lisa M. Fuhs	$8.95
I'll Be Your Shelter	Giselle Carmichael	$8.95
I'll Paint a Sun	A.J. Garrotto	$9.95
Icie	Pamela Leigh Starr	$8.95
If I Were Your Woman	LaConnie Taylor-Jones	$6.99
Illusions	Pamela Leigh Starr	$8.95
Indigo After Dark Vol. I	Nia Dixon/Angelique	$10.95
Indigo After Dark Vol. II	Dolores Bundy/ Cole Riley	$10.95
Indigo After Dark Vol. III	Montana Blue/ Coco Morena	$10.95
Indigo After Dark Vol. IV	Cassandra Colt/	$14.95
Indigo After Dark Vol. V	Delilah Dawson	$14.95
Indiscretions	Donna Hill	$8.95
Intentional Mistakes	Michele Sudler	$9.95
Interlude	Donna Hill	$8.95
Intimate Intentions	Angie Daniels	$8.95
It's in the Rhythm	Sammie Ward	$6.99
It's Not Over Yet	J.J. Michael	$9.95
Jolie's Surrender	Edwina Martin-Arnold	$8.95
Kiss or Keep	Debra Phillips	$8.95
Lace	Giselle Carmichael	$9.95
Lady Preacher	K.T. Richey	$6.99
Last Train to Memphis	Elsa Cook	$12.95
Lasting Valor	Ken Olsen	$24.95
Let Us Prey	Hunter Lundy	$25.95
Let's Get It On	Dyanne Davis	$6.99
Lies Too Long	Pamela Ridley	$13.95
Life Is Never As It Seems	J.J. Michael	$12.95
Lighter Shade of Brown	Vicki Andrews	$8.95
Look Both Ways	Joan Early	$6.99
Looking for Lily	Africa Fine	$6.99
Love Always	Mildred E. Riley	$10.95
Love Doesn't Come Easy	Charlyne Dickerson	$8.95
Love Out of Order	Nicole Green	$6.99
Love Unveiled	Gloria Greene	$10.95
Love's Deception	Charlene Berry	$10.95
Love's Destiny	M. Loui Quezada	$8.95
Love's Secrets	Yolanda McVey	$6.99

Other Genesis Press, Inc. Titles (continued)

Mae's Promise	Melody Walcott	$8.95
Magnolia Sunset	Giselle Carmichael	$8.95
Many Shades of Gray	Dyanne Davis	$6.99
Matters of Life and Death	Lesego Malepe, Ph.D.	$15.95
Meant to Be	Jeanne Sumerix	$8.95
Midnight Clear (Anthology)	Leslie Esdaile Gwynne Forster Carmen Green Monica Jackson	$10.95
Midnight Magic	Gwynne Forster	$8.95
Midnight Peril	Vicki Andrews	$10.95
Misconceptions	Pamela Leigh Starr	$9.95
Mixed Reality	Chamein Canton	$6.99
Moments of Clarity	Michele Cameron	$6.99
Montgomery's Children	Richard Perry	$14.95
Mr. Fix-It	Crystal Hubbard	$6.99
My Buffalo Soldier	Barbara B.K. Reeves	$8.95
Naked Soul	Gwynne Forster	$8.95
Never Say Never	Michele Cameron	$6.99
Next to Last Chance	Louisa Dixon	$24.95
No Apologies	Seressia Glass	$8.95
No Commitment Required	Seressia Glass	$8.95
No Regrets	Mildred E. Riley	$8.95
Not His Type	Chamein Canton	$6.99
Not Quite Right	Tammy Williams	$6.99
Nowhere to Run	Gay G. Gunn	$10.95
O Bed! O Breakfast!	Rob Kuehnle	$14.95
Oak Bluffs	Joan Early	$6.99
Object of His Desire	A.C. Arthur	$8.95
Office Policy	A.C. Arthur	$9.95
Once in a Blue Moon	Dorianne Cole	$9.95
One Day at a Time	Bella McFarland	$8.95
One of These Days	Michele Sudler	$9.95
Outside Chance	Louisa Dixon	$24.95
Passion	T.T. Henderson	$10.95
Passion's Blood	Cherif Fortin	$22.95
Passion's Furies	AlTonya Washington	$6.99
Passion's Journey	Wanda Y. Thomas	$8.95
Past Promises	Jahmel West	$8.95
Path of Fire	T.T. Henderson	$8.95

Other Genesis Press, Inc. Titles (continued)

Path of Thorns	Annetta P. Lee	$9.95
Peace Be Still	Colette Haywood	$12.95
Picture Perfect	Reon Carter	$8.95
Playing for Keeps	Stephanie Salinas	$8.95
Pride & Joi	Gay G. Gunn	$8.95
Promises Made	Bernice Layton	$6.99
Promises of Forever	Celya Bowers	$6.99
Promises to Keep	Alicia Wiggins	$8.95
Quiet Storm	Donna Hill	$10.95
Reckless Surrender	Rochelle Alers	$6.95
Red Polka Dot in a World Full of Plaid	Varian Johnson	$12.95
Red Sky	Renee Alexis	$6.99
Reluctant Captive	Joyce Jackson	$8.95
Rendezvous With Fate	Jeanne Sumerix	$8.95
Revelations	Cheris F. Hodges	$8.95
Reye's Gold	Ruthie Robinson	$6.99
Rivers of the Soul	Leslie Esdaile	$8.95
Rocky Mountain Romance	Kathleen Suzanne	$8.95
Rooms of the Heart	Donna Hill	$8.95
Rough on Rats and Tough on Cats	Chris Parker	$12.95
Save Me	Africa Fine	$6.99
Secret Library Vol. 1	Nina Sheridan	$18.95
Secret Library Vol. 2	Cassandra Colt	$8.95
Secret Thunder	Annetta P. Lee	$9.95
Shades of Brown	Denise Becker	$8.95
Shades of Desire	Monica White	$8.95
Shadows in the Moonlight	Jeanne Sumerix	$8.95
Show Me the Sun	Miriam Shumba	$6.99
Sin	Crystal Rhodes	$8.95
Singing a Song...	Crystal Rhodes	$6.99
Six O'Clock	Katrina Spencer	$6.99
Small Sensations	Crystal V. Rhodes	$6.99
Small Whispers	Annetta P. Lee	$6.99
So Amazing	Sinclair LeBeau	$8.95
Somebody's Someone	Sinclair LeBeau	$8.95
Someone to Love	Alicia Wiggins	$8.95
Song in the Park	Martin Brant	$15.95
Soul Eyes	Wayne L. Wilson	$12.95

Other Genesis Press, Inc. Titles (continued)

Soul to Soul	Donna Hill	$8.95
Southern Comfort	J.M. Jeffries	$8.95
Southern Fried Standards	S.R. Maddox	$6.99
Still the Storm	Sharon Robinson	$8.95
Still Waters Run Deep	Leslie Esdaile	$8.95
Still Waters...	Crystal V. Rhodes	$6.99
Stolen Jewels	Michele Sudler	$6.99
Stolen Memories	Michele Sudler	$6.99
Stories to Excite You	Anna Forrest/Divine	$14.95
Storm	Pamela Leigh Starr	$6.99
Subtle Secrets	Wanda Y. Thomas	$8.95
Suddenly You	Crystal Hubbard	$9.95
Swan	Africa Fine	$6.99
Sweet Repercussions	Kimberley White	$9.95
Sweet Sensations	Gwyneth Bolton	$9.95
Sweet Tomorrows	Kimberly White	$8.95
Taken by You	Dorothy Elizabeth Love	$9.95
Tattooed Tears	T. T. Henderson	$8.95
Tempting Faith	Crystal Hubbard	$6.99
That Which Has Horns	Miriam Shumba	$6.99
The Business of Love	Cheris F. Hodges	$6.99
The Color Line	Lizzette Grayson Carter	$9.95
The Color of Trouble	Dyanne Davis	$8.95
The Disappearance of Allison Jones	Kayla Perrin	$5.95
The Doctor's Wife	Mildred Riley	$6.99
The Fires Within	Beverly Clark	$9.95
The Foursome	Celya Bowers	$6.99
The Honey Dipper's Legacy	Myra Pannell-Allen	$14.95
The Joker's Love Tune	Sidney Rickman	$15.95
The Little Pretender	Barbara Cartland	$10.95
The Love We Had	Natalie Dunbar	$8.95
The Man Who Could Fly	Bob & Milana Beamon	$18.95
The Missing Link	Charlyne Dickerson	$8.95
The Mission	Pamela Leigh Starr	$6.99
The More Things Change	Chamein Canton	$6.99
The Perfect Frame	Beverly Clark	$9.95
The Price of Love	Sinclair LeBeau	$8.95
The Smoking Life	Ilene Barth	$29.95
The Words of the Pitcher	Kei Swanson	$8.95

Other Genesis Press, Inc. Titles (continued)

Things Forbidden	Maryam Diaab	$6.99
This Life Isn't Perfect Holla	Sandra Foy	$6.99
Three Doors Down	Michele Sudler	$6.99
Three Wishes	Seressia Glass	$8.95
Ties That Bind	Kathleen Suzanne	$8.95
Tiger Woods	Libby Hughes	$5.95
Time Is of the Essence	Angie Daniels	$9.95
Timeless Devotion	Bella McFarland	$9.95
Tomorrow's Promise	Leslie Esdaile	$8.95
Truly Inseparable	Wanda Y. Thomas	$8.95
Two Sides to Every Story	Dyanne Davis	$9.95
Unbeweavable	Katrina Spencer	$6.99
Unbreak My Heart	Dar Tomlinson	$8.95
Unclear and Present Danger	Michele Cameron	$6.99
Uncommon Prayer	Kenneth Swanson	$9.95
Unconditional	A.C. Arthur	$9.95
Unconditional Love	Alicia Wiggins	$8.95
Undying Love	Renee Alexis	$6.99
Until Death Do Us Part	Susan Paul	$8.95
Vows of Passion	Bella McFarland	$9.95
Waiting for Mr. Darcy	Chamein Canton	$6.99
Waiting in the Shadows	Michele Sudler	$6.99
Wayward Dreams	Gail McFarland	$6.99
Wedding Gown	Dyanne Davis	$8.95
What's Under Benjamin's Bed	Sandra Schaffer	$8.95
When a Man Loves a Woman	LaConnie Taylor-Jones	$6.99
When Dreams Float	Dorothy Elizabeth Love	$8.95
When I'm With You	LaConnie Taylor-Jones	$6.99
When Lightning Strikes	Michele Cameron	$6.99
Where I Want to Be	Maryam Diaab	$6.99
Whispers in the Night	Dorothy Elizabeth Love	$8.95
Whispers in the Sand	LaFlorya Gauthier	$10.95
Who's That Lady?	Andrea Jackson	$9.95
Wild Ravens	AlTonya Washington	$9.95
Yesterday Is Gone	Beverly Clark	$10.95
Yesterday's Dreams, Tomorrow's Promises	Reon Laudat	$8.95
Your Precious Love	Sinclair LeBeau	$8.95

Order Form

Mail to: Genesis Press, Inc.
P.O. Box 101
Columbus, MS 39703

Name ______________________________
Address ______________________________
City/State ____________________ Zip ____________
Telephone ____________________

Ship to (if different from above)
Name ______________________________
Address ______________________________
City/State ____________________ Zip ____________
Telephone ____________________

Credit Card Information
Credit Card # ____________________ ☐ Visa ☐ Mastercard
Expiration Date (mm/yy) ____________ ☐ AmEx ☐ Discover

Qty.	Author	Title	Price	Total

Use this order form, or call 1-888-INDIGO-1

Total for books ____________
Shipping and handling:
$5 first two books,
$1 each additional book ____________
Total S & H ____________
Total amount enclosed ____________

Mississippi residents add 7% sales tax